As the Children Slept

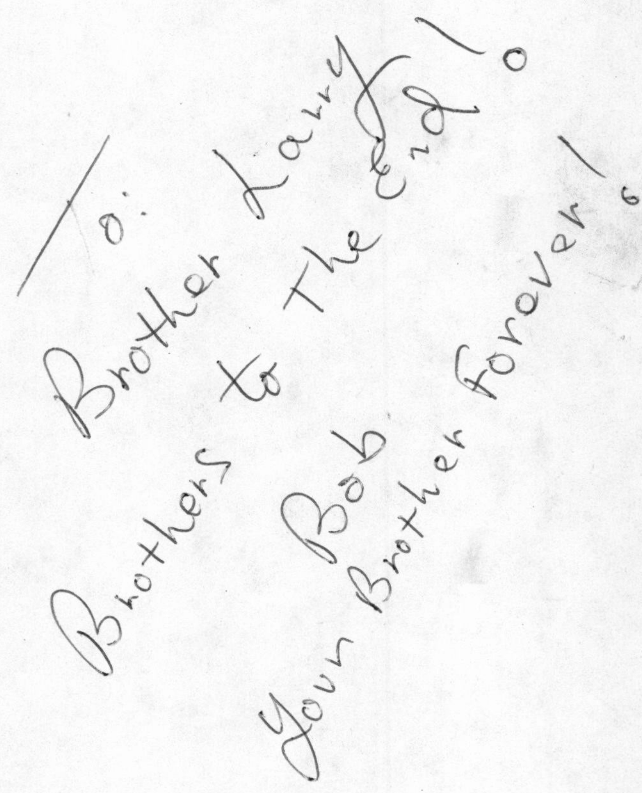

As the Children Slept

A Novel by R.E. Willis

Tate Publishing & Enterprises

As The Children Slept

Published by Tate Publishing & Enterprises, LLC
127 E. Trade Center Terrace | Mustang, Oklahoma 73064 USA
1.888.361.9473 | www.tatepublishing.com

Tate Publishing is committed to excellence in the publishing industry. The company reflects the philosophy established by the founders, based on Psalm 68:11,
"The Lord gave the word and great was the company of those who published it."

Cover design by Lynly Taylor
Interior design by Kandi Evans

Published in the United States of America

ISBN: 978-1-60696-504-7

1. Fiction: War & Military
09.11.04

Prelude

The year is 2010. The war on terror has gone well for the U.S. The terrorists are on the run. They have limited geographic areas to hide in. They know that their time is nearing an end. Our strategies had been effective in keeping them contained. Change in the Middle East is inevitable. Iraq and Afghanistan's fledgling democracies are taking hold; Israel and the Palestinians are close to forming an independent Palestinian state. However, ominous dark clouds are forming on the Middle East's political horizon.

The changing political landscape has taken Iran deeper into its Theocracy. The Mojahedin of the Islamic Revolution and Radical Clerics have taken a brutal grip on their nation's youth. There was a massive pro-democracy demonstration in Tehran by the nations' youth. The Islamic Revolutionary Guard used brutal force to put down the demonstration—made China's Tiananmen Square look like a Sunday social. Iran has withdrawn deeper into her own paranoia. Feeling her very existence is being threatened, she has become dangerous in her thoughts and actions.

The European Union is indifferent to Iran's posture. Their only concern is to keep their oil supply flowing. The U.S. keeps a watchful eye on Iran's every move. Yet, world opinion concerning the U.S. is at an all-time low. The EU and other nations feel that we are forcing our values on people and nations that do not want them. The U.S. does its best to conform to U.N. policies; however, these policies are ineffective. The U.S. warns the world about Iran's true intent to dominate the Middle East, spread their Theocracy, and drive out democracy. The U.S. has no alternative but to apply its own pressure and sanctions on Iran. The U.S. has no choice but to maintain a noticeable presence in the Persian Gulf.

How it all began

The date is May 20, 2010. Three speeding vehicles rumble, bouncing and jouncing, through the southwestern desert of Iran. They are several hundred miles northwest of Bandar Abbas. Given the desert landscape, one could easily conclude that these vehicles are in a hurry to get to "nowhere." If you didn't know better you'd think the drivers were lost, or better yet, in some sort of Baja desert race. The dust from their speeding vehicles is only rivaled by a desert dust storm. This, however, is not the case. The lead vehicle is on a GPS heading to an exact location. The passenger in the lead vehicle is acting as the navigator for this convoy. He anxiously watches for known "way points" and keeps in close radio contact with the vehicles following.

As the vehicles progress through the desert the navigator alerts the convoy that they are about to arrive at their destination. Within minutes a small blockhouse comes into view. It appears to be some sort of remote relay pumping station. In all likelihood it is probably used for an alternate oil pipeline to the gulf. Or so it appears.

The three vehicles pull up and stop abruptly—it appears the drivers learned to drive either full speed or dead stop. As quickly as the vehicles stop twelve of the meanest looking hombres jump out of the lead and third vehicles. These boys are the poster children for nasty and mean. The smallest one in the group is six feet tall the others appear around six inches taller. These men are focused, disciplined, determined and above all, armed to the hilt. They immediately form a perimeter around the blockhouse. They pause for just a moment, then the lead guard motions to the occupants of the second vehicle to disembark from their vehicle. Four individuals emerge from the vehicle carrying metal brief cases. They appear nervous and guarded in their demeanor. They head to the blockhouse door. The leader of the four cleans the dust off a keypad and a small porthole at around eye level. He then proceeds to punch in an alpha-numeric code and looks into the small porthole—a retina scanner. Instantly the door opens. The four individuals enter the blockhouse. They step up to a second set of doors and repeat the whole process again. The doors open, but this time it is an elevator. They step in to the elevator and select to descend. The ride down is not a long one; they descend only a few hundred feet.

When the four individuals arrive at the bottom of the elevator shaft they step out into a small chamber. There inside this chamber are several technicians working on what appears to be a warhead—nuclear warhead. When the technicians see the four individuals they become extremely nervous—they scurry about like the three blind mice—nervously following the commands of the four individuals.

The four individuals open their metal brief cases. There inside are what appear to be components—circuit boards and what appears to be a foot-long lead-lined case. Out of it comes a tube of a liquid that appears to be mercury. It isn't. It is experimental liquid plutonium. This new liquefied plutonium is twice as lethal as its solid cousin. It takes a fraction of the amount to create nuclear fission.

The technicians cautiously and nervously begin to assemble the parts into the warhead. The four senior individuals are giving constant commands, only compounding the fears of the technicians. At the point of introducing the liquid plutonium into the warhead, the senior of the four barks a commanding order "Careful, you fool! You'll kill us all!"

The technician reacts as any normal person would—with total fright. Everyone gasps as he juggles the vial of liquid. This infuriates the four individuals to the point where after the technician put it back in its case the leader of the group grabs the technician and throws him to the floor screaming, "You incompetent fool, I will have you shot!" The other technicians are terrified. It is all they can do to keep from running away. They keep one eye on the warhead and one on the escape route—the elevator.

Once again the leader of the group barks his command, "Assemble this thing—it must be operational today!"

While the four senior members impatiently watch the technicians nervously assemble their components, one of the lead members responds, "It is done! The revolution lives! We will now remove the imperialist's boot from our throat! Never again will the world dictate policy to us. We now have a seat at the world table."

"Not so fast," responds one of the other members. "We must ensure that the warhead is viable."

The lead member responds, "Ha, a mere technicality." He turns to the technicians and barks out a command in a loud voice. "You, run the diagnostics on the warhead now!"

The lead technician tries to interject a thought, "But, sir—"

When he begins to speak four sets of eyes turn on him and

stare. The technician can feel their eyes burn holes right through him. The technicians connect several computer leads to the warhead as the four members stand by and smugly watch. The lead technician signals for the others to begin the diagnostics.

NAASC: North American Aero Space Command - Colorado USA.

May 20, 2010, at 0515 hours—1445 hours Iranian time—the U.S. spy satellite SCRAM-1 is passing over the Persian Gulf, just entering space over Iran. SCRAM-1 (Strategic Cryptic Reconnaissance All Terrain Monitoring System) is a newly deployed spy satellite system with high-resolution digital cameras that can take real-time video—see the smile on your face—from a classified altitude. The SCRAM-1 system is also highly maneuverable in and out of various orbits and can loiter over an area for extended periods. Air Force Staff Sergeant William "Mase" Mason is the non-commissioned officer in charge of the duty watch. It's a night just like every other night. As SCRAM-1 is coming into the Gulf region. Airman First Class Reynold "Renny" Billings calls to Staff Sergeant Mason, "Hey, Mase! SCRAM's in the Gulf! Do you want me to patch you into the video feed?"

"Ya, Renny, send it to my terminal. Let's check on the neighborhood—see if any of the 'Iranian refugees' are looking to relocate into Iraq."

Both men laugh knowing well that anyone crossing the Iran/Iraq border is an Iranian agent looking to destabilize the democratic government in Iraq.

At 0530 hours—approximately 1500 hours Iranian time—while casually observing the video feed coming in, all appears to be normal. No unusual traffic near the border.

"What the heck was that!"

The control room comes alive. Alert screens light up, telemetry starts pouring in. SCRAM-1 seems to blink in and out as if it were blinking after it had its picture taken with a bright flash bulb. Mase begins to yell commands to his crew. He begins to follow the written Air Force protocols. He calls the officer of the day.

"Major Jensen, sir, we have a NU-DET, I repeat, we have a NU-DET," he gives the GPS co-ordinances.

Mason informs his duty officer that there has been a nuclear detonation in southwestern Iran—telemetry estimates that the blast was in the range of a 50 mega-ton blast. Major Jensen initiates Air Force Defcon protocols. He calls the joint chiefs as well as the president on his dedicated line. The president knows that when this phone rings it's the real deal.

The End

The year is 2060. Much has happened in my lifetime. As I stand musing over my life I hear a faint voice calling to me that seems to grow in its intensity. It reminds me of a truck coming at me in the distance in how it gets louder as it approaches. "General…General, sir, I hate to interrupt your thoughts, but, well, it's nearing 'D' hour sir. We are ready."

I turned and smiled. "Thank you, Sergeant."

I have a few moments so I briefly turn back to my thoughts. I look out at the sky. Man, is it blue today! I just never saw the sky like this. It reminds me of my wife's eyes. Looking at the sky pulls me back to my daydreaming. As I drift off into my memories I find myself in my youth fishing on the Rainy River back in northern Minnesota.

—

It was the 20th of May 2010, my 25th birthday. I was home on leave from the Air Force. I made this trip every year since I left home. My family lived on the Rainy River on the Minnesota/ Canadian border. Known by many, this was a fisherman's paradise. It wasn't uncommon to find professional anglers trying their best to land a record-sized walleye pike.

It was around 6:30 a.m. My dad and I were trying to catch the morning feed cycle. All of sudden the two-way radio crackled and broke the morning silence. It was my mom. "Sam, do you copy?"

My dad answered, "What's up?"

"Listen, guys, you'd better get back in here. Something big is happening in the news."

My dad winced. "Oh, give me a break! We just got settled in! Can't this wait?"

Mom was quick to respond. "No! Get in here now!"

My dad looked at me with raised eyebrows, "Damn, she's serious! Up anchor, Son. We have to get this rig moving."

I immediately hauled up the anchor. Dad quickly started the motor and we were making a beeline back to the dock. We got to the dock within minutes. As we docked the boat Dad said, "Get up the hill. I'll stow the gear and be right behind you."

When I got into the house I could hear the newscaster speaking with all seriousness. "Again, at this hour our details are sketchy. However, the White House has confirmed that at 0530 Mountain Time this morning NAASC reports that satellites and ground monitoring stations confirmed that there was a nuclear detonation in the southwestern desert of Iran. The president has recalled all military personnel…"

The Plane Trip

I knew I had to get back to my team pronto. My mind kept racing as I mulled over what had just happened. Whose bomb was it? Was it ours? Did some pilot finally come unglued and go rouge? How will we react? Will we be deployed? What's next? I just kept running scenarios through my mind. All I knew was that I had to get back to Hunter Air Field to my team.

As I gathered my things I glanced out the front dining room window. I chuckled to myself when I saw Dad sitting in his pickup truck with the engine running. It reminded me of our F22 pilots during an alert—sitting on the tarmac focused and determined, just waiting for the green light to proceed. I believe if someone gave the signal the old man would have probably tried to launch that truck. I could see he was totally engrossed in what the radio was reporting. The guy could get intense. When watching a martial arts match the man couldn't sit still—he was right in the match as if he were one of the opponents.

It took just a few moments to get my things together. During my packing my mom shadowed my every move. She had such a way of reassuring that everything was going to be fine. Her level-headed, practical approach to life taught me a lot about managing my team. "Keep your wits about you, don't jump to any conclusions until you have your facts straight, treat people with respect, and above all don't ask your team to do what you wouldn't do yourself." My dad complemented my development by adding a few extra values: "Treat all people with dignity and respect, lead by setting the example, maintain your physical, mental, and spiritual well being at peak levels, and most of all, remember the five Tang Soo Do codes: Honor your country, honor your family, be loyal in friendship, never retreat in battle, and when in battle, kill with a sense of honor." This was the warrior's code. How could I ever forget these values—my family practiced them with honor and distinction.

As I approached the door my mom's eyes said it all. She was stressed. She looked at me and said tearfully, "I know you will, but I have to say this for me—take care of yourself."

I smiled and replied, "Don't worry, Mom, I'll be just fine."

After I said this she grabbed and hugged me. It was this same hug that helped me grow to become a man—it spoke volumes to quieting my spirit and generated a sense of assurance that all would be well. After we hugged, she reached over to the counter top and grabbed a brown paper bag. I grinned. "What's this?" I asked in a knowing voice.

"Well," she replied, "I know it's a long trip back to Georgia so I thought I'd pack a few munchies for you to help keep the edge off things on the way back. Anyway, you know your dad needs an excuse to pig out on munchies. I thought you guys could eat and B.S. on the way to I-Falls."

International Falls Airport was a one-gate terminal located in the infamous "Ice Box of the lower forty-eight states," known for its extreme subzero temperatures in the winter months.

As I approached my dad's truck I could hear the newscaster describing the incident.

"It's unclear at this time who is claiming responsibility for the blast. We are unsure of the casualties. The fallout from the blast is being monitored. It appears to be moving in a northwesterly direction…"

As we drove to the airport my dad made some small talk about fishing. I could see that he was trying to cover up his concern. My dad served in Gulf War I. He knew what it was all about. After a few minutes of his small talk I turned to him and said, "Dad, any advice on this mess?"

"Ya…ya, I do trust your instincts and your training, Son. Remember, having a well-executed plan is important, but you must stay flexible in how you get the job done. Remember, Son, be flexible in your planning. Adapt and improvise."

"Thanks, Dad. I'll do my best."

"There's no doubt that you will, Son. I'm proud of you."

As we pulled into the airport parking lot the reality of the situation started to set in. I knew that this could be the last time I saw my family. Like an athlete about to hit the playing field, my anticipation of the possible events caused my pulse rate to go up. I found myself becoming keenly focused—extremely aware of my surroundings. I was getting into what my team called "the zone." I grabbed my gear and headed to the airport entrance. When we got inside the terminal I turned. "Don't worry, Dad. I'll be okay." We shook hands and hugged. I smiled at him and said, "I love you, man."

"I love you too, Son. I am proud to be your dad."

As he turned to leave I felt the little boy in me tear up.

As I approached the ticketing agent she looked down at my gear and commented, "Been fishing?"

I smiled and replied, "Yes, I'm home on leave, thought I'd fish the Rainy."

Her smile changed when she heard I was home on leave. She immediately commented, "You're military?"

I handed her my ID card for verification. She proceeded to check me in for my flight; however, she spent some time in reviewing the seating arrangements.

After a moment she responded, "Well, Captain, you're in luck. It appears that you've been bumped up to first class on your trip to Georgia."

Surprised at what she said, I smiled and asked, "Are you sure?"

With a wide grin on her face and very soft eyes she replied, "Oh yes, it shows right here that you are in the first cabin from Minneapolis to Hartsfield, Georgia."

I was sure the look of bewilderment on my face said it all. I couldn't think of anything else to say but "Thank you." As she handed me my boarding passes she winked and wished me luck.

The Journey Begins

The commuter flight to Minneapolis took about an hour and a half. As we gained altitude the engines seemed to generate a rhythmic hum throughout the cabin. As we leveled off in altitude I looked out to the horizon—sunny with some clouds. I lost myself to my memories.

I drifted back to my childhood. I was recalling my days of growing up in a martial arts studio—a Do Jang (Korean for marital arts school). My parents were both instructors. I recalled the many days that I would cry when my parents would lead me in by the hand for my training. I was just three years old when they started my training, and I hated it.

One day as Dad was wiping my tears he said, "Son, this is a tradition that Grandpa Sam taught me. Some day you will understand why it is important that you learn this tradition and pass it on to your family." He was right.

I remembered my first-degree black belt test. I was eight years old. In a flash I could recall the hours of grueling practice, the lectures of the history and the science behind each technique that I was taught. What stuck in my mind was the way my parents taught—when they asked the class to do fifty pushups on their knuckles, they would do seventy-five first. Not one of us students ever complained that they were asking too much of us.

Like the big white clouds passing by my window, my

thoughts kept floating by my mind's eye. In a flash I recalled my second, third, and master-level black belt tests. The years of martial arts training took me on a never-ending journey of self-development—body, mind, and spirit. Over the years I was trained in every aspect of what Tang Soo Do was about, including weaponless defense, hands and feet, disarming an attacker, Hap Ki Do, as well as the use of knives, swords, staffs and short sticks. We practiced close quarter disarming an assailant with a gun; however, they had to be right on top of you to make your technique work. What an education! The old man was right! What a character builder.

At the end of every class we recited the five Tang Soo Do codes. I must have recited those codes a million times, but it wasn't until joining my special operations team that I came to realize the true depth and value of what those codes meant.

As I stared out my window musing I heard a voice call me back to reality.

"Sir, excuse me, sir, would you like a beverage?"

I responded with a smile and a "No thank you." I was in a hurry to get back to my thoughts. A moment later a voice came over the speaker announcing that we were fifteen minutes away from landing.

My layover in Minneapolis was relatively short, but I was intent on getting back to my team. As they say, "Time stands still when you are in a hurry." After boarding the jet we were airborne in good time. I got settled in post haste and slipped back into my thoughts. I recalled how my team was formed. What a crew.

The Team

It seems like yesterday when I met my first team member, Paul Venegas. As I remember it was July 27th 2008. I was conducting training at Fort Bragg. After a tough day of training I thought I'd head out to the local watering hole. There were several to choose from and plenty happening in any one of them.

When I walked into the club I could feel the energy in the air. All it would take was one wrong move and the place would erupt. We couldn't put that many hard core GIs in one place without a little excitement. I found my way to the bar. The bartender walked over to me, "What'll it be?"

I paused for a second, "How about a draft?"

"Come'n at ya."

I would have to take my drinking slow and easy. In this environment I didn't want to lose my edge.

It was around 2100 hours, and all seemed to be going well. I did, however, enjoy watching the table directly in front of me. There sat five GIs and three women. From the sounds of it this was a lively bunch. All of a sudden one of the women jumped up and yelled, "You bastard!" She then proceeded to throw her drink into the face of the GI whose lap she was sitting on. It appeared he had gotten a bit too friendly. The first thought that passed through my mind was, "You are in for it now, sister!" Sure enough, he jumped up out of his chair and proceeded to slap her to the floor. Seeing this triggered all kinds of alarms in my head. The first thought I had was, "Damn, I'm going to get involved," even if only to get her out of the area. The five roared with laughter and settled back into their drinking. The big GI turned away from the girl as if nothing had happened.

I walked over and offered the girl my hand to help her up. She accepted.

"Are you alright?"

"Yes, it's my dignity that's injured." She smiled. "It's good to see that real men still exist." As we turned to walk away she turned back as to pick up something she left behind. I didn't give it a second thought. All I wanted to do is get her out of the area. I thought she was picking up her purse, when all of a sudden she swung her arm with the ferocity of a home run hitter…Smash! Glass flew like shrapnel in every direction. It was obvious she was going to get the last lick in. She had picked up a beer mug, planted it right upside the big GI's head, then scurried off. All hell broke loose. The remaining four jumped up and turned towards me. Obviously, I'd become their object of affection.

In any event I was ready for the battle. As they started for me I immediately began to size up who had to go first. Then all of a sudden out of nowhere came a stranger flying in with a picture-perfect split kick. With a deep sounding "thump" I watched two of them take a foot to the chest and drop like a sack of potatoes. The stranger landed on his feet, turned to me, and said, "That should even the odds."

After seeing what had just happened to their two buddies, the other two GIs put their hands up. "Look, we don't want any trouble."

I turned to my newfound friend, "Wow! Thanks, man. I owe you big time."

He responded, "Hey, no problem, man. I hate that macho B.S. Those clowns were looking for it all night long. They shouldn't have treated that girl like that."

I smiled and agreed with my new friend. As he started to walk away I called to him, "Yo, can I buy you a beer?"

He turned and smiled. "Cool, let's drink."

We made our way back to the bar. I smiled and extended my hand for a shake, "I'm Sam D'Angelo."

He grasped my hand and shook firmly, "Dude, I'm Paul Venegas."

"What brings you to Bragg, Paul?"

"I'm here for advance tactical training (also known as ATT)."

"No way! So am I!"

Our conversation just flowed. You could not have found two people from such different backgrounds, yet we both seemed to believe in the same values and codes for living. Paul grew up in the streets of Boston, while I grew up in the Northwood's of Minnesota. This was weird for the both of us. It just didn't figure. What the hell was the bond? We didn't know each other from Adam, yet from the moment we met we knew that we could trust each other with our lives.

The night was getting old. It was time to pack it in. I had an 0800 meeting in the morning with the brass to discuss the ATT.

I gulped down the last of my beer and smiled. "Well, Paul, it's time to pack it in. I've got an 0800 meeting with the brass. I can't tell you how much it means to me to know that I have a brother like you out there in the world. Let's meet for another round of beers tomorrow night, say 2000 hours?"

"It's cool. I've got a meeting with my new team leader in the morning. I hear the dude is an Air Force stud. I got to make sure I impress the man. You're on for the beer tomorrow night."

The next morning at 0745 I was off to my training briefing. I knew that I would be meeting with the top Special Forces brass. They had become very interested in my proposal for continued martial arts training for all Special Forces Members. As I approached the post's fitness and training area I could see many of the trainees preparing themselves for the day's events. As I walked into the meeting area I was greeted by two full bird colonels. The room was full of people.

"Good morning, Captain D'Angelo. I'm Colonel Beckworth and this is Colonel Martinez we are here to observe and evaluate your proposed program. Also, we would like to introduce you to several other instructors who will be assisting you. Your training team." Colonel Beckworth turned around and called to the others. "Gentlemen, shall we begin?"

I looked over at the group approaching me and smiled.

Beckworth noticed. "Someone you know, D'Angelo?"

"Yes, sir."

There standing before me were Paul and three others.

As the team approached me, Colonel Martinez started the introductions. "Captain D'Angelo, this is Sergeant Paul Venegas, U.S. Army Rangers, Master Instructor in the art of Sho Do Kan."

Smiling I answered, "We've met, sir."

The colonel grinned. "Yes, I see." He continued, "This

is Sergeant Dennis Clark, U.S. Air Force, Master Instructor Go Ju Ryu." The colonel continued the introductions. "This is Sergeant Kym Cato, U.S. Army Rangers, Master Instructor Nin-Jitsu, and finally, this is Sergeant Neal Thomas, U.S. Army Rangers, Master Instructor Aikido."

Colonel Martinez continued his discussion, reminding the team that this was a crucial turning point in the continued development of the U.S. Special Forces tactics. Someone in the pentagon felt that we were getting so technical we could become too reliant on technological warfare. He didn't want his forces to lose the "warrior's" edge.

From the moment the team met we were brothers forever. We did so well together that the pentagon left us as a team. We became the poster boys for U.S. Special Operations. They studied our team's chemistry and did their best to figure out what made us tick. They never really got it. We were true warrior brothers. They wanted to fashion other Special Operations teams after our model.

We came from diverse backgrounds and geographical regions. I was a "mutt" from a U.S/Canadian border town, Baudette, Minnesota. Paul was from Boston, Massachusetts, where he grew up in the Spanish ghettos. Kym was Am-Asian from Dallas, Texas. Dennis was an African-American. He hailed from Minneapolis, Minnesota. The enigma of the group was Neal Thomas. Neal was from a costal town in Southern California. To look at Neal one would try to guess if he was a Viking warlord or a body building surfer.

Man, the fun we had. Dennis had a sense of humor that wouldn't quit. His laugh made the team laugh. The man could find something funny in any situation. Neal on the other hand was just the opposite. The best we could get out of him was a smirk. What was truly unique about this team was how we functioned together. Just like a pack of hunting raptors. Each member instinctively knew what the other member's actions would be in any situation. We constantly would be there to cover our brother's back. For us it was "covering your brother's six."

The Landing

As the flight crew was preparing for our landing in Atlanta I slowly drifted back to reality. I couldn't believe the two-hour flight was over. My intensity started to return. As I headed for the main entrance to the terminal I called Paul on my cell phone. "Dude, where you at?"

"We're across from the main exit, hurry up, boss."

"I'm on the way."

As I approached the vehicle I could see the team was in the zone. These guys knew when to play and when to work.

Paul yelled, "Come on, boss, we have a chopper waiting for us up at Dobbins Air Base. They'll get us down to Hunter."

Twenty minutes later we were on a chopper heading down to Savannah, Hunter Air Field…

The Trip to Hunter Field

The flight to Hunter took forty-five minutes. My team was wired. We all knew that this was the real deal; we were going to be deployed. As we flew to Hunter the team settled into their thing. Everyone had their own way of settling in. That is, centering their thoughts, or as we called it, getting into the zone. Paul liked to read western novels. He had a romance with the western frontier and tough sheriffs. Dennis was a strategist. His thing was playing chess against his handheld PDA at the advanced level. He couldn't get enough of it. Kym's thing was playing Spanish word games on his PDA. As for Neal and I, well, we were the heady types. Whenever we got the chance we would get into our own heads and drift away in our thoughts and memories. No doubt Neal took himself to a beach somewhere in California.

It didn't take me long to lose myself in the sounds of the chopper. The thumping sounds of the rotors cutting through the evening air, city lights beginning to glow below us, and the sun sitting low on the horizon was all I needed to drift away. As I looked around the chopper at my team I began recalling our training in the Nevada desert…

—

It was April 13, 2009 when we arrived in Nevada. As we made

our approach for landing I searched the area for familiar landmarks. I just couldn't find any. I had never seen this area before. My travels had taken me to nearly every airbase in the west, but this one was new to me. As the jet approached the base operations area I could see the ground crew, several officers, and what appeared to be civilians, patiently waiting for us. The ground crew scurried about preparing the Gulf Stream for passenger disembarking. I just loved these small jets. You were on the ground and doors opened in short order. You were at your destination without the typical airport hassles.

As I emerged from the jet I looked down from the top step. I recognized one of the officers. It was Colonel Martinez. As our eyes caught each other's I saluted, and the colonel returned my salute. As I descended down the aircraft stairway Colonel Martinez approached me. "How was your trip, captain?"

"Very good, sir," I replied. With a smile on my face I remarked, "Excuse me, sir, but where in the hell are we?"

"Son, welcome to Area 51." The colonel turned to the others and says, "Gentlemen, we will go through the formal introductions tomorrow morning. Right now Captain D'Angelo and his team should get settled in. We have a great deal to cover over the next six weeks."

He turned and signaled for the waiting vehicles to come forward, and in a flash several staff cars rolled up onto the tarmac. We saluted the colonel, stowed our gear in the vehicles, and were brought to a nearby barracks. When we pulled up to the entrance of the billeting area Dennis remarked, "Whoa, dude! The place looks like a throwback to WWII."

It was an older styled wooden building. A typical yesteryear military barracks.

Neal, of all people, piped up, "Let's see, sleeping in a bed eating three squares a day versus sleeping on the ground eating whenever we can, an occasional MRE, or better yet, bugs, snakes, oh yeah, and for dessert we could eat some green leaves and bark off our favorite tree. Thank you, but I'll forego the nature trip for a cot and a cooked meal any day."

Hearing this, the team broke out into their trademark hearty laugh. When we entered the barracks two airmen greeted us. "Good evening, captain." They nodded as to acknowledge my team. "Gentlemen, this way to your quarters." What was to follow defied logical thinking.

The accommodations were great. The rooms, the chow, and recreation areas were great. The fitness center was like one I had never seen. The only thing was the entire installation was underground! The barracks was a facade. We were in an entire city complex underground. We traveled using a tramway, and it was no short ride. Along the way we passed through several quadrants—Base Operations, Engineering, Research and Development, and something called "Combat Simulation Training."

When we arrived at the living quarters section of the base we were greeted by a staff of caretakers. They were all Air Force personnel. It seemed we were getting the red carpet treatment, but I wasn't sure why.

The caretakers led us to our rooms. I couldn't believe my eyes. Outside a phenomenal living and sleeping area, it had a view. What stopped me dead in my tracks was I was looking out a large picture window at the Rainy River.

"Do you like it, sir?" asked a young sergeant.

"How did you guys do this?"

The sergeant responded, "They'll brief you on this tomorrow, sir." At that she smiled and said, "If you need anything, please dial '51' on your phone. We'll bring it to you."

As I stood there in mild shock, my senses started to pick up on different sites, sounds, and smells. I kept thinking this was impossible. I'm 1200 miles from home, yet I could hear the wind blowing through the pines, smell my mother's flower garden. I could hear each fish's splash. I could see all types of birds fly by—bald eagles, waterfowl, and songbirds of all types. It was so real to me I knew that if I stepped through the window I'd be back in Minnesota, yet reality was that I was underground in the Nevada desert.

Combat Simulation Training (CST)

The next morning at 0600 I headed to the chow hall to meet my team for chow, or so I thought. As I approached the entrance to the chow hall I was greeted by an airman in full formal Air Force uniform.

"Good morning, Captain. Breakfast for one?"

This took me by surprise. I chuckled to myself. Yeah, right, breakfast. How about chow, pal? I quickly composed my thoughts and responded, "Oh, ah, no, Sergeant, I'm meeting with my team. There'll be five of us. Thank you."

"Very well, sir. Please follow me."

What a rush when we walked into the so called chow hall area. I didn't expect a five star restaurant atmosphere, but I was standing in the midst of one. As we walked towards my table I noticed four groups of GIs sitting around a cluster of tables. There were twenty troops in total. As I crossed the room they all looked up at me at the same time.

Instantly, I smiled and said to my escort. "Hold it a minute, sergeant, I know these guys. I trained them at Fort Bragg." Not only did I train these guys, they were the cream of the crop. I walked over to the tables, smiled, and said, "Good morning, gentlemen. You're a long way from Bragg, aren't you?"

"Good morning, sir!"

I smiled. "Enjoy your meal, gentlemen. I understand we've got a tough schedule ahead."

I no sooner sat down and my team was being escorted to my table. From the bounce in their step I could see that they were energized. When they got to the table there smiles said it all. Paul's said, "Good morning, boss. Sleep well?"

Dennis looked over at the other tables and said, "Isn't that the Gomez, Swenson, Brodrick, and Templeton teams?"

Kym chimed in, "That's them. Must be a Bragg reunion!"

Dennis jumped right in again with his commentary. "Ya know, boss, something is definitely up. Think about it, we're getting the royal treatment, those guys were the best of our trainees…I'm sure the brass has got something big planned for us."

I looked at the team and said, "Whatever it is, I'm sure we're gonna enjoy this trip."

The Training Begins

At 0645 we caught the tram and headed for the CST unit. We had no idea what to expect. As the tram was slowing to a stop I could see Colonel Martinez at the entryway speaking with a four-star general. As we all looked out of the tram's windows, Neal responded first. "Do you see who's standing there with Martinez?"

Standing there with Colonel Martinez, large as life, was General Theo Cornelius, the Chairman of the Joint Chiefs of Staff. This man was the most decorated soldier in the modern armed forces—he even had the Congressional Medal of Honor. It was a well know fact that General Cornelius was a Special Operations team leader earlier in his career. It was he who insisted on having me and my team set up our ATT at Bragg.

As the tram came to a stop Cornelius and Martinez turned and walked inside the CST area. We were not far behind them. As we stepped inside the CST entrance several airmen directed us into an auditorium. As we walked in, there on the stage was General Cornelius, Colonel Martinez, and several civilians. I noticed that there was a large group of civilians sitting in the first two rows.

As my team got through the door and scoped the audience I could see that they were becoming uncomfortable about the apparent situation.

Paul responded with disgust. "Oh, man! Civilians! These guys have to be CIA."

Hearing this Dennis and Kym added their nickels' worth. "Another catch and snatch operation."

Neal sighed and made a deep hmmmm sound, then said, "Great…All this training and we get used like this."

In short order all the teams had arrived and were seated in the auditorium. General Cornelius started his approach to the podium. To look at the man was awesome. He was African American, six feet four inches tall, and had a build that most professional athletes could only wish for. In Special Forces language, or anyone's language for that matter, this man was a "stud." As he approached the podium Colonel Martinez called the room to attention. "Ten Hut!"

We jumped to our feet and stood at attention. As the general reached the podium he paused and looked out over the crowd. In a commanding voice he began to speak. "At ease, please be seated. Shall we get started? Today we will be entering into the 22nd century. As you will see, how wars are fought and won by the United States Military will not resemble anything that you have been taught and trained for. How troops are deployed will change. Weaponry that fires a solid projectile will become obsolete. We are now entering a new era of stealth technology. Today we enter into the era of holographic warfare and pulse weaponry. With us today are distinguished members of a research team who are the architects of this extraordinary achievement. Over the next six weeks you will be trained and qualified in the art of stealth unlike anything you can imagine—pulse weapon use and maintenance as well as holographic warfare. You are the first of many who will be trained in the use and application of this new technology. Train hard and train well. Happy hunting, gentlemen."

As the general turned to walk off the stage, Colonel Martinez called the room to attention. "Ten Hut." Again we immediately jumped to our feet. As the general left the room the colonel called the room back to a rest position. "At ease, troops. As you were. Let's begin with an overview of the events for the next six weeks."

The colonel went through a laundry list of events for the six week period. He received a resounding "Ooh Rah!" when he spoke to the issue of a happy hour and dinner that evening. It was a social event to get to know our instructors and to meet the project's architects.

We spent our first few days in lectures discussing theory, tactics, and the laws of physics. We knew that it was necessary, but it was tough staying awake. We knew that our instructors were preparing us for the hands-on portion of our training.

Our first lecture was on stealth technology and theory. What a lecture! Leave it to Dennis to liven things up. Our instructor was PhD Franz Detrich, a German physicist. Dr. Detrich recapped the history and applications of stealth in battle, comparing contrasting how nature itself used stealth. He explained that all types of living creatures adapted their colors to their environments, using light spectrum to their advantage. However, when he got into the discussion of camouflaged uniforms all hell broke loose. Dennis just couldn't leave it alone.

As I recall, the conversation went something like this:

Dr. Detrich, "Ya, Ya, und now ve have new composite fiber clove-us for all personnel."

Dennis hearing this chuckled and replied, “Ya, ya heir Detrich und vhat in the hell mis da clove-us!?”

Detrich’s eyes open wide with surprise and responds, “Ya, ya Sergeant Clark, und da clove-us you vear.”

Dennis laughed, as only Dennis can do. He responded, “Nine, nine, heir Detrich, in the clove-us is where I make love to my woman!”

At that the room erupted into a roar of laughter. Dr. Detrich was himself amused at Dennis’s depiction of the situation. However, we realized Dr. Detrich’s lecture was preparing us for our future. Painted faces and camouflage had become passé. We were about to step into the future of stealth warfare.

The Dinner

We broke for the day at 1800 hours. We sat through a full day of presentations and took in a lot of information. It was worth it, though. Our social hour was to begin at 1900 hours with dinner to follow. Knowing my crew they'd be prompt for the social hour. I figured it would be a nice evening meeting and "glad handing" our instructors and their staffs.

It was around 1910 hours when I arrived at the dining area. It appeared that quite a crowd had already arrived. As I approached the entrance I was greeted by the sergeant who escorted me to my room the night before.

"Hello, Captain D'Angelo. Enjoying your stay?"

I smiled, "Yes, Sergeant, the view is great!" At that I proceeded to walk inside to the dining area.

As I entered the room I scanned the crowd for familiar faces. Sure enough, my team was perched at the bar with Gomez, Swenson, Brodrick, and Templeton. I could see my guys and the others were having a great time. They didn't see me coming. I walked up to them, put my left hand on Paul's shoulder and the other on Gomez's, leaned in and said, "Hey! Who's buying the next round?!"

Paul responded, "Hey, boss! Drinks are on the house!"

At that we got into the moment and enjoyed each other's company. We shared a bond that was hard to describe. We looked beyond each other's human flaws. We were brothers in spirit.

At 1920 hours Colonel Martinez and General Cornelius entered the room. What was it about the general? His very presence commanded respect. Call it charisma or pizzazz, he definitely had it. As the general slowly made his way around the room greeting his guests we stood there like school boys waiting to get their favorite athlete's autograph. Our boyish antics were so obvious that Dennis remarked, "Who's gonna jump up and down first and scream 'It's Him, It's Him?'" At that we all seemed to slip back into adulthood.

As the general approached one group of civilians Dennis started to laugh, "Hey, boss! This is gonna be interesting. The old man is over at Detrich's group–"Ya, ya da clove-us!" Dennis could barely contain himself. "Ha, ha, ha!"

Like naughty boys huddled up, laughing and looking over their shoulders to see if the teacher was looking, we carried on for a few moments. Paul, Kym, and Neal were watching Detrich's group when they all commented at once, "Whoa, who the hell is that!"

Dennis and I turned and looked. "Ya heir Detrich, you old fox you," said Dennis.

Standing there with Detrich and crew was the most drop dead gorgeous woman I had ever seen. The first opinion came from Paul, "That's got to be his daughter. That old duffer couldn't possibly land a prime fox like that."

Then Dennis, "No way! That's his secretary—she's his eye candy."

Kym and Neal took the conservative approach, "Na, she's got to be his student. You know, an understudy—protégé."

I smiled and said, "No matter who she is, every GI in the room is gonna be chasing her tonight."

We all laughed and agreed that none of us had what she wanted. She was in a league well beyond us.

A few moments later the general approached our group. As he approached he smiled and extended his hand. “Captain D’Angelo, what a pleasure it is to meet you and your team. Gentlemen, let’s see if I can get my facts straight. Let’s see, you’re Sergeant Paul Venegas from Boston, Massachusetts. You attended Boston College. You played some football for the Eagles’ right?”

“Ah…yes, sir, I did.”

“And you are Sergeant Dennis Clark from Minneapolis, Minnesota, home of the Golden Gophers. You majored in computer engineering correct?”

“Yes, sir…that’s correct.”

“Oh yes, you are Sergeant Kym Cato, a Texas Longhorn. You are a linguist, is that correct?”

“Yes, sir, I am.”

“Well then, you must be Sergeant Neal Thomas, Southern Cal right?”

“Yes, sir.”

“I believe you are working on a PhD in the field of human anatomy and physiology, correct?”

“Yes, sir.”

“Oh, by the way, D’Angelo, you have a pretty impressive record at the academy.”

“Thank you, sir.”

“Gentleman, please join me at my table this evening. We have a great deal to discuss.”

At that he turned and headed for Gomez’s team. It was

apparent the general was going to individually meet with every team.

At around 2030 hours dinner got started. The general got right to his point. "Men, thank you for joining me this evening. I want you to know that I have been watching you from the pentagon. I am impressed with the way you conduct yourselves—with code and with honor. Yes it's true that your brothers and sisters are to be admired for their service; I can't tell you how proud and honored I am to have you and them under my command. It's just that there's something different about the five of you. As I've watched you throughout your careers I have found that you possess something special—an indomitable spirit. You are true warriors, brothers of the spear."

This was powerful stuff. We were riveted with the general's discussion. "Let me explain this brotherhood. The spear represents the ultimate battle. Warriors meet face to face for the ultimate test—life or death. This ultimate battle is not just a test of skill and strength but of spirit. When these warriors met their opponents on the battlefield they came eye to eye. They looked beyond their opponents' eyes into their soul. Only those who were strong in spirit survived the battle.

"Throughout history the brotherhood of the spear has been evident. Throughout the ages of warfare you will find individuals and groups who stood out from the rest. In ancient Asia there were many conquerors and dynasties—China, Korea and Japan. Yet history shows that within these cultures great warriors existed. Think about the code that these warriors lived and died by, think about the Greeks, Spartans and Trojans, the Romans, the list goes on to modern-day warriors. What is it that they all had in common? They all lived by a code, a code that I call 'the code of the spear.' They were brothers in this code with indomitable spirits that would not be vanquished by their opponents. They were selfless warriors who would sacrifice themselves for a greater good. They put their country's and people's needs before their own needs. This I submit to you is the true brotherhood of the spear. You are a unique group. I believe that you are together to fulfill some great purpose. Be true to your code. Seek through the God of your choice divine guidance and wisdom to live your lives and to fulfill your calling in life."

We were totally blown away by the general's discussion. I felt overwhelmed by all that he said. Yet, it seemed to fit with the same codes that I learned as a young martial artist. As the dinner was coming to a close the background music seemed to liven up a bit. It was obvious that dancing was next on the agenda.

General Cornelius and Colonel Martinez smiled at the team. The general said, "Gentlemen, if you'd excuse us. Colonel, care to join me for a night cap? Enjoy the rest of the evening gentlemen."

We all stood up as the two officers left our table. As we sat down we all looked at each other. Neal turned to me and said, "Boss, did he just pass the baton off to us?"

Kym beat me to the punch, "Ya damn straight he did!"

"Oh man! I'm not sure I can live up to his expectations," said Dennis.

"Hold it, guys!" I responded. "I don't think he was unloading some heavy mission on us. I think he was asking us to keep the warrior spirit alive. You know, ensure it survived into the future."

Paul lifted his drink and saluted, "Bothers to the end!"

We all lifted our glasses and followed the toast, "Brothers to the end!"

The music was getting louder and the dance floor was getting full. I retreated to the bar. I positioned myself so I could see what was going on. It took no time at all for the "bees" to start buzzing around Dr. Detrich's table, and these boys had one flower in mind. I watched in amazement as this young woman with charm, poise, and grace accepted every ones request for a dance—my team included. Her smile seemed to light up the area she was in. The way she moved, her genuine interest in the conversations that she was having was amazing. She treated every suitor that came to her table as if he were one of the "knights of the round table."

After Dennis danced with her he came to the bar where I was standing. "Yo, boss, you've got to meet this lady—you know she's a PhD. This lady is on her game."

I smiled at Dennis, "I don't know, she's pretty busy. Besides, it's getting late and I've got to hit the rack early tonight—we've got a tough day ahead of us tomorrow."

"Ya right, boss! Dude, have you met your match?"

I sheepishly grinned, "No…I ah…ya…ya, I have, she's way out of my league. Besides, I'd make a fool of myself trying to make conversation with her. She's drop dead gorgeous and smart. I wouldn't even know how to start a conversation let alone get her interested in me."

Dennis laughed, "Damn, who'd ever imagine that the boss would throw in the towel before the match began."

Hearing Dennis's words I winced as if I were in pain. "Oh, man, it's not like that, it's just that a guy has got to know his limits. She's got me out classed and out gunned. No contest."

Dennis turned and left to rejoin the party. As for me, well, I just stood there admiring the view. I just could not take my eyes off of her. As I watched her I noticed every so often her eyes caught mine. Each time they did she'd smile and give me a slight nod. When she did I felt like running away. I wanted so much to meet her but my speech center shut down and my feet felt as if they were glued to the floor.

As I looked at my watch I could see that it was nearing 0000 hours. I gulped down the last of my beer and figured I'd call it a night. As I was heading for the door a voice called to me, "Good night, captain."

I turned in the direction of the voice and it hit me. "Oh God! It's her!" I thought to myself. I nervously smiled, "Ah…Goodnight, ma'am," and started on my way.

She responded, "Alex."

I stopped and turned quickly. "Excuse me?"

She smiled and responded, "My name…Alex is my name."

I smiled, "Oh…Good night, Alex."

Well, like a school boy I headed to my room muttering her name to myself and kept going over the "I should have, could have" scenarios in my mind.

At 0800 sharp we reported to the CST unit for hands on stealth training. Dr. Detrich began his discussion of Einstein's theory of how a gravitational field could bend space. Therefore, one could argue that light should be capable of being bent or curved. As he spoke, Alex entered the room. She smiled at the team, and Detrich continued explaining his theory of how light could be curved or bent. As he spoke I could not take my eyes off of Alex, and my thoughts started to run wild. I jus wished we could have a do over from last night. I'd never waste an opportunity to meet her again. As I spiraled away in my thoughts Detrich's words started to meld into a blah, blah, blah sound. That smile, those blue eyes, I couldn't think straight.

As I faded back in from my thoughts of Alex, Dr. Detrich's voice became loud and clear.

"Ya. Und enough of da theory. Now ve prove it can be done. Ya, und Dr. King vill demonstrate how it is done."

We chuckled as we looked at each other as if to say, "Who the hell is Dr. King?" It took a fraction of a second for the little voice in my head to say, "Duh! There is only one other PhD in the room—Alex."

Alex smiled at Dr. Detrich. "Thank you, Franz. Gentlemen, today you will learn the application of how to bend light around your position thus causing a bubble of invisibility."

Dennis responded first, "No freaking way! Invisible!"

Alex smiles and says, "Yes freaking way—invisible."

"Okay, Dr. King, how is this done?"

She smiled at me and said, "Alex. Please, call me Alex."

She took me right out of my game. Here I thought I had composed myself. Wrong! Like a school boy infatuated with his grade school teacher, I blushed, smiled, and embarrassedly respond, "Oh…Okay, Alex, how is this done?"

Alex's grin told me that she knew she had me on the ropes. "Okay," she responded. "I am an Astro-physicist working out of NASA. Do you recall in 2005 the space probe that we sent to impact a comet?"

The team nodded yes.

"Well, that was a diversion to keep the world looking in the wrong direction. We secretly launched two other probes—Prospector 1 and Prospector 2—on a mission towards the asteroid belt. It was our intention to land in two specific areas, grab several hundred pounds of a particular chunk of rock we were interested in, and return it home. Well, gentlemen, we did it! The samples we brought back are so rare that we're not sure if much more of the stuff exists in the universe. What we found was a magnetic crystalline form of Iridium. This crystal is so complex that it will take us years to map its structure.

"Unfortunately, we learned the hard way as to its extraordinary properties. We lost several good people studying the stuff. After we recovered the Prospectors' payloads we rushed them off to Los Alamos for testing. We were excited about our find. We thought we were on the brink of solving our future energy source. Our first test was to try to get a better picture of the crystal's structure. You know, harmlessly poke at the thing and get a feel for what it was made of. A small team of researchers set up a lab experiment to get a better look at the crystal's structure. They took a salt-grain-sized fragment of the crystal and bombarded it with an isotope. Well, from what we can gather the fragment released a pulse of energy that wiped out the lab equipment and killed the researchers. We were devastated. Instead of finding a new source of energy we believed we had opened Pandora's Box. Think about it. If a salt-grain-sized fragment could do this kind of damage, just think what a pound of the stuff could do!

"I can't tell you how hot the debate was for keeping the stuff on the planet or launching it back into space. We were faced with a conundrum. Keeping it on the planet did not seem like a viable option. Getting it off the planet scared the hell out of us. What if the rocket failed on the way up? If we shot it into the sun to dispose of it what would be the reaction? Blow up the sun? If we shot it in a straight line away from us would it someday cross our path? There were too many unknowns. Now that we had the stuff we didn't know how to get rid of it."

At that moment Dr. Detrich chimed in, "Ya, ya, und it vas Dr. King who discovered the vay to control da crystal's true potential."

Hearing this, with admiration, we all looked over at Alex. What's this! I thought to myself. She's blushing!

Detrich's comment seemed to embarrass Alex. She looked down as if she were inspecting her shoes.

As we were all remarking as to how incredible of an achievement she had accomplished, Alex stood there hands behind her back, slightly swaying side to side, head tilted slightly down, looking up at us with those beautiful blue eyes and an innocent, girlish smile on her face.

Seeing this made my heart melt. I did all that I could do to restrain myself. I wanted to grab her and just hold her. It was at that moment I saw into the depths of her spirit—a gracious, gentle, humble, and kind spirit. At that moment I knew in my heart of hearts that I wanted to be with her for the rest of my life.

As the clamoring settled down and we all regained our composure, Alex continued her discussion.

"First, thank you, gentlemen, but you must realize that it was a team of us who made the discovery. With Dr. Detrich's leadership and encouragement we made our discoveries."

"What happened, Alex? I mean, how did you unlock this mystery?" Paul asked.

"Well, Paul, as we were putting the accident's pieces together I was studying lab surveillance video to get a better understanding of the energy released. At the point when the energy was releasing I noticed, as I can best describe, a wobbling or hesitation in the video footage, then it went blank. At first I thought nothing of it. It just seemed to be an interruption in the video due to the pulse of energy. You know, the same as electromagnetic pulse interruption during a nuclear blast, obviously on a micro scale.

"Well, something caught my eye. I could accept the EMP theory of why the video seemed to wobble, but what didn't add up was for a split second the stand that the crystal fragment was on seemed to disappear. I just couldn't let this go. As a researcher my curiosity was piqued. I took the video footage to my team at NASA. It was there that we dissected the video footage down to the microsecond. Voila! A nanosecond before the energy pulse, the light around the stand was curved! The stand and everything on it disappeared from view. The wobble that we saw in the video was actually a bubble of light that formed around the immediate area of the fragment. The bubble causes the light around the source, in this case the fragment, to come in from all angles, thus covering the immediate area with the images of the surrounding area. Thus, what occupies the immediate space disappears from view…invisibility.

"The dark side of what we learned is that when the bubble of light bursts it gives off a hyper intense pulse of magnetic energy. An energy burst so powerful that it, within the burst's radius that is, will render all electrical impulses, living organisms or machine, permanently inoperative. Needless to say, gentlemen, our discovery is what led to General Cornelius's 'we are entering into the 22nd century' speech."

As Neal, Dennis, and Alex got into a sidebar discussion on how the energy burst disrupted the electrical impulses in living organisms and machines, I drifted off in my thoughts as to the limitless applications for this new technology. General Cornelius was right! We would never fight wars in a conventional way again.

As the group seemed to get back at the task at hand, Dennis asked, "Alex, just how does this work? I mean, how the hell did you harness this beast?"

Alex paused, looked down, and then lifted her head, pursed her lips, wrinkled her nose, and said, "You know, Sergeant, I'd be happy to explain it to you, but are you sure you want to go down that theoretical path?"

Dennis got the drift of Alex's message. She was about to take us on a journey through the land of dissertation. The land of a PhD's theoretical dissertation.

He responded, "Ah…no, ma'am. I'll take your word for it."

At that we entered into our second phase of training…stealth applications.

Dr. Detrich smiled and said to me and the team, "Ya, und now ve enter into phase two of da training—stealth applications. Und you vill be assigned to da stealth simulation unit where you vill train in da practical applications of da stealth technology."

Hearing this I turned to my team, "Okay, boys, saddle up! It's time to move on." With puppy dog eyes and a woeful sound to my voice, I asked, "Excuse me, Dr. Detrich, who will be instructing us?"

I no sooner got the words out of my mouth and Alex responded.

"Why, we will, of course! Someone has to keep an eye on General Cornelius's prize team!"

Once again the little boy in me took over. Instead of smiling and thanking Alex and just treating it as a nonevent, I jumped to my feet and shouted gleefully, "Oh, hey, that's great!"

Stealth Training

Alex and Dr. Detrich led us into a football-field-sized training simulation area. As I walked into the training area and scoped it out, I turned to Alex and said, "This place is great! We've never trained in desert areas like this." The landscape was so realistic: the rock outcrops and the dunes.

She smiled and said, "Gentlemen, do you remember how to play hide-n-go-seek?"

We all nodded affirmatively.

"Well, our mission today is to teach you to hide so you'll never be found. Shall we begin?"

Dr. Detrich motioned to a staff member at the door. Instantly, six technicians came marching in carrying what appeared to be heavy-duty backpacks. At the sight of the packs the entire team groaned, remembering the weight of the gear that we trained with and carried.

Alex smiled, "Easy, guys. Looks are deceiving."

As the six bulky packs sat on the ground Alex walked over and lifted one up and slipped it on. She pulled the cinch straps tight, ran to one of the rock outcrops, and scurried to the top. She was a good thirty feet off the ground. She settled in at the summit, smiled, and yelled, "Come on, you sissies, get moving."

Dr. Detrich added, "Ha, und vich of you sissies vil be da last to da top?"

A mad scramble ensued. All that was needed was some slapstick comedy music and we would have been on target. We were laughing and yelling so hard that we were running into each other and tripping over our own feet.

Paul got the drop on all of us. He had his pack in hand and was starting to put it on before the rest of us. To Neal's surprise, the muscle-bound beach boy misjudged the weight of his pack. He grabbed it and threw it up to his shoulder as if it weighed the same as our field packs. Out of his hands it flew, only to hit Kym, knocking him over. Dennis, not to be out done by Paul, loosened a main cinch on Paul's pack. Paul and he spent time undoing each other's cinches. I quietly picked up my pack, casually walked away from the team, slipped on my pack, and climbed to the summit.

When I got to the summit Alex smiled, "Still worried about the weight of the packs?"

"Wow! These things are light. Are they full of gear?"

Alex nodded.

In a flash, the team made it to the top.

Alex smiled and said, "Okay, gentlemen. Let's deploy these toys." Down the rock face we came.

As we gathered at the bottom of the rock outcrop Alex asked us to remove the packs for unloading. With our packs in front of us, Alex led us through the unloading process. First items to be unloaded were our BDUs (battle dress uniforms).

Alex smiled and said, "Remember the composite fiber 'clove-us' that Dr. Detrich spoke of?"

We all laughed, especially Dennis.

"Well, these are them. Gentlemen, although these uniforms appear to be the same as your current field uniforms, they are not. These new uniforms are made of what we call 'smart fibers.' In the desert sun they will regulate your body temperature to keep you cool. In the cool desert nights they will regulate your body temperature to keep you warm."

Alex then asked us to remove the helmets from our packs. They resembled pilot helmets, only they were much sleeker and really lightweight. She then asked us to put the helmets on with visors up. So we did. She then asked us to form a wide circle around her and to turn our backs to her. So we did. She then asked us to put down the visors. Instantly information started coming across the visors—just like an aircraft heads-up display. The visors were adjusting focus to our eyesight. The earpieces adjusted volume to the sounds we were hearing.

"Gentlemen, look to the left corner of your visor and then the right corner."

We all started to laugh. When we looked to either corner of our visors we could see behind us without turning around.

"Okay, team, we're going to drop the lighting in the area."

As the technicians lowered the lighting in the training area, our ability to see never changed. We were in what Alex called the "ever-light" mode. The team agreed that this technology was great.

"Ha, goodbye, night-vision goggles!" Kym exclaimed.

Alex went on to show us many more functions on the helmet: enhanced long-range vision, amplified listening techniques, as well as infrared scanning. As Alex explained the helmets features Dennis decided to dig into his ruck-sack a little deeper.

"Hey, what's this?" he asked, holding what appeared to be another backpack and a rifle shaped weapon.

Alex smiled. "Well, Sergeant, you are holding the replicas of the weapons systems you will be training with in four weeks. For now we will concentrate on your stealth training."

Dennis laughed, "Ha…plastic guns! Instead of bullets we can yell bang, bang, you're dead."

"Gentlemen, shall we continue?"

Alex directed us to take out a smaller satchel from our packs. It had a little bulk to it. Alex smiled and said, "Gentlemen, I would like to introduce you to the 'Magnetic Amplifier Generator System.' This is your stealth unit. Shall we take a tour?"

She instructed us to open our satchels. Inside was a box about the size of two notebook computers stacked on top of each other. On the top of the unit was a flattened mesh type of antenna that could be erected into a cone-shaped dish several inches above the cover. She instructed us to open the cover to the panel and screen inside. Next she had us place a finger, or toe, of our choosing onto the bio-scan port to the side of the unit. As soon as we did the unit activated. Once this was done Alex said, "Shall we practice?"

The team nodded with high anticipation.

We spent the next several hours briefing on the use and deployment of the "Magnetic Amplifier Generator System." Saying the name was too cumbersome so the team quickly adapted the name. They nicknamed the system MAGS.

Alex was enthused as to how quickly we came up on the learning curve. She commented, "Well, gentlemen, you've got this unit down cold. Let's take MAGS out for a spin. Let's see if you can hide yourselves."

The fun was about to begin. Alex looked at the team.

"Okay, guys, this is how it's going to work. I will leave the area and give you twenty minutes to deploy and hide. After that I'll come and find you. Simple enough?"

Dennis laughed and said, "Oh, a challenge! Wanna bet? You'll never find me."

Alex smiled and replied, "Tell you what, you can deploy as a team, individuals, or pair up. It doesn't matter, I'll find you."

The team started to laugh.

"So what's the bet going to be?" asked Dennis.

Alex paused for a moment, then smiled. "Tell you what, Dr. Detrich has asked me to invite you all for a round of beers tonight. So, let's go for a round of beer per capture. Every one I find they buy a round. I will buy a round for everyone I don't find. Fair enough?"

The team agreed.

"Who's first?" Alex asked.

Neal stepped forward. "That'll be me, ma'am!"

"Great! The rest of you can come with me. You will watch from our observation area. Neal, I'll be back in twenty minutes."

Neal hustled off deep into the simulation area, did a quick study of the area, and proceeded to set up his MAGS.

Like clock work Alex entered the simulation area. She methodically scanned the area. She moved slowly as she studied the ground and the surroundings. For no apparent reason she climbed up onto a low outcrop of rocks, sat, watched, and just waited. Several minutes later she jumped down and walked over to a huge boulder. She looked up at the boulder and said in a teasing way, "Peek-a-boo, I see you, Neal."

Seeing this, Dennis started laughing and yelled, "Yes! One round for us, she blew it!"

All of a sudden at the top of the boulder appeared Neal.

Paul and Kym turned to me with a surprised look on their face. "Wow, boss! She is good!"

"Looks like we took a sucker's bet. She's gonna kick our butts at this game." I replied.

As Neal and Alex walked into the observation area Neal was shaking his head in bewilderment.

Alex smiled and said, "Next please!"

Kym stepped forward. "You're on!"

"See you in twenty minutes," Alex replied.

At that, the game began again. Alex entered the simulation area with the same methodical, deliberate pace that she used in her first search. As we watched we could see that a grouping of low-lying boulders caught her eye. Alex slowly approached the boulders and said, "Now whose cute butt is this!" Then she gave a light kick forward—in the order of a love tap.

No sooner she did that, up jumped Kym. "Dude!" Kym yelled.

Paul and Dennis groaned.

Dennis looked at me and said, "Oh man, two to zip."

I kept wondering to myself, "What's the trick? What are we doing wrong?"

Once again a dejected soul, Kym, walked through the observation area's entrance.

Alex smiled at me and said, "Captain, would you like to give it a try?"

Before I could answer Paul and Dennis chimed in. "We'd

like to give it a go. Our team will equal two rounds, fair enough?"

"You're on! I'll see you shortly."

Paul and Dennis took off for the simulation area laughing.

Right on schedule, Alex entered the simulation area. She maneuvered throughout the area in the same fashion she had done twice before—slowly and methodically. I could see from this search she was not having an easy go of it. What's this? I thought to myself, did these guys finally figure it out? I watched in amazement as Alex searched and pondered as to where Dennis and Paul had hidden.

Several minutes into the search, when it appeared that she was going to give up, I watched her stand in one spot looking left and right as she studied the ground. All of a sudden a look of "aha" came over her. She turned and walked toward the entrance of the simulator a few yards from the entrance, stopped, smiled, and said, "Gotcha!"

Dennis and Paul step forward. "No way! How did you do that?"

Alex smiled and said, "You two nearly had me on this one. I'll explain everything in my debriefing."

After saying this she looked up at the observation window and signaled for me to come down. When I entered the simulation area, she smiled and said. "Looks like you're the team's last hope, Captain. Want to go double or nothing?"

I chuckled, "No, that's okay. Something tells me you're a shark at doing this."

Alex smiled and said, "I'll see you in twenty minutes."

I had the advantage of watching Alex find the others but just couldn't figure out how she did it. I knew my best bet was to do something the others didn't do. With a sense of excitement I dashed up into the rocks. I knew I had to move quickly. I found an area that had a straight rock face from the ground up about thirty feet. I climbed down and began the sequence of setting up my MAGS when Alex entered the simulation area.

This was utterly weird. I was looking at her as if I were standing in the open. Yet, she didn't see me. As she approached my position I stood with my back tight to the rock wall. Several times as she approached my position she looked right at me. I thought for sure she could see me. As she got closer and kept looking right at my position I almost laughed. This process was difficult to get used to. All my instincts and training told me to get under cover and hide. Yet here I was standing out in the open and apparently well hidden…it defied logic.

Alex slowly passed by my position. I got her! She's missed me! I thought. And so it appeared. She continued her search deeper into the simulation area. I watched as she turned around and headed back. She appeared to be perplexed. She kept searching and pondering my whereabouts. I had all to do to keep myself from breaking into a laugh. I believed I had beaten her.

As Alex got to my position I could see she was deep in thought. She slowed her pace and for no apparent reason decided to stop and gather her thoughts. She turned and stepped up to put her back to the rock face. As she leaned back to put her back to the wall she balanced herself on her left foot with her right foot for support on the wall. She was so close to me that I became conscious of my breathing. I thought for sure she could hear me. While she looked over her left shoulder back to the simulation area entrance, she reached down with her right hand, grabbed my left, and said, "Come here often?"

I broke into a laugh, "How in the hell did you do that?"

She just grinned and said, "Let's go."

Dumbfounded and muttering to myself, I shut down my MAGS, picked up and stowed my gear, and headed for the debriefing room.

When we got to the debriefing room Dr. Detrich was there to greet us.

"Ya, gentlemen, und how did it go today?"

Dennis started to laugh. "Well, heir Doctor, your assistant will be killing a great deal of her brain cells this evening."

Dr. Detrich smiled. "Ya, vhas is dis about brain cell killing?"

Paul jumped right in, "Well, Doctor, we bet Alex a round of beer that she couldn't find us when we deployed our MAGS. We lost."

"A round of beer for each of you! Ya ya, maybe you are right about da brain cell killing, ha, ha, ha."

Alex moved to the front of the debriefing room. She smiled at the team and began her discussion. "Well, gentlemen, I think you did a great job today. With a couple of weeks of practice you'll be masters at this."

Everyone on the team groaned.

"Okay, Alex, how did you do it?" I asked.

"Okay, let's begin," she replied. "First, there was nothing wrong with how you chose your positions. I found Neal, Kym, and Captain D'Angelo because of a simple mistake in deploying your MAGS; you were too conservative in powering them up." She continued, "Neal."

"Yes ma'am?" he replied.

"Where did you place your MAGS for deployment?"

"At the base of the rock that I was crouching on, ma'am."

"Did you adjust the MAGS output to take into account that you were going to be several feet off the ground and in all likelihood would stand up?"

"No, ma'am," Neal replied.

Alex smiled and said, "I saw the top of your head popping in an out of your cover. Alex went on. "Kym, where was your MAGS deployed?"

"In front of me," he replied.

"When you deployed the MAGS, why did you crouch down?"

Kym replied, "When you were approaching I felt like I was standing out in the open. I did it out of instinct to get under cover, I guess."

"When you did that you backed right out of your cover—your 'six' was hanging out," Alex replied,

"That explains the kick in the pants," said Kym.

Alex went on, "As for you, Captain D'Angelo, you had a near perfect setup. What gave you away was your left hand had pierced your veil of cover. Had it not been for that I'd have never found you." She continued her discussion, "As for you two," as she pointed at Paul and Dennis, "I give you an A+. Your set up was both daring and quite ingenious."

"Ya, so ingenious. You found us…how?" said Dennis.

"I grew up in a small farming community in Wisconsin, Chetek, ever hear of it?" said Alex.

Both men shook their heads no.

"Since I was a little girl my dad took me deer hunting. He

taught me how to track and hunt. He taught me how crafty a deer could be. You see, some deer are so smart that they'll back up in their own tracks to get off a trail, and that's exactly what you two did."

It was a long day of training. However, I could see that the team was learning a great deal—and loving it, too.

Dr. Detrich began his closing remarks and spoke of our remaining time in training. "Ya, tank you, Alex. Und I am sure vhit dis training da team has learned a great deal." The team began to applaud her for her efforts. "Und now ve must plan our most important training. Ya, und now ve vill train in da fine art of drinking beer!"

At that the team saluted Dr. Detrich with a resounding "Ooh Rah!"

The Social Hour

As we parted from our training we agreed to meet at the bar at 1900 hours. When I arrived at the bar it was obvious that my team and Dr. Detrich had gotten a head start with a round of beers. They were laughing and joking, apparently having a great time. It appeared that heir Detrich was an entertainer. The music was just right; the crowd was into partying and having a good time. Time for me to dive in and have some fun!

I headed straight for my team and Dr. Detrcrich; however, halfway across the room a lively bunch of people called out, "Hey, Cap! Come on over!"

It was the Gomez, Swenson, Brodrick, and Templeton teams. What a crew. These boys wasted no time getting into the party mode, meeting and corralling the entire female population of the base. As I approached the group, Bronson Templeton stood up and motioned for me to sit with his team. As I got to his table, I smiled and said, "One beer, guys. I have to get over to my team."

I knew that I had to make my visit brief. At any moment Alex was going to show up and although these were great guys, I didn't want to waste one minute not being around her. Bronson began introducing me to his guests. As I sipped my beer I asked Bronson, "How's training going?"

"Great!" He responded.

The young woman to my right smiled at me and introduced herself.

"Hi, I'm Angie."

I smiled and offered my hand for a shake. "It's a pleasure to meet you, Angie. I'm Sam."

Angie smiled with a girlish grin and with a sassy tone to her voice she replied, "Yes, you're Sam D'Angelo. Alex spoke of you."

"Oh she did, did she?" I responded in an inquisitive tone hoping that Angie would tell me that Alex was head over heels for me.

She just smiled and responded with, "Mmhmm."

That's it! No Mr. Wonderful? No juicy stuff? Hearing Angie's comments I knew I had to get back to my team and try to figure this thing out.

A few minutes later Alex entered the room. Dennis spotted her first. He stood up and yelled, "Hey, Alex! Over here!" Dennis gave me a slight poke in the arm "Boss, check this out!"

Alex smiled as she crossed the room. I couldn't take my eyes off her. As she approached I could see that she had on a great-fitting pair of jeans, cowboy boots, and an Air Force Academy T-shirt. My pulse rate went up.

As Alex approached the table we all stood up. Alex blushed and said in an embarrassed tone, "Aw, come on, guys! I thought we were a team!"

At that we all laughed and sat down. Alex had such a presence about her. No matter who you were she'd make you feel respected.

With the crew at my table Alex didn't stand a chance. As the beer flowed so did the dancing. The boys just wouldn't leave the girl alone. She never turned down one dance. She was what every man dreams of in a woman—charming, witty, personable, and, aw hell, the list is too long to mention. She already had my heart in her hip pocket, but it seemed she was collecting a few extras.

As the music settled down to a slower pace we all seemed to settle in to our conversations. At the start of one song Alex smiled at me and asked, "Sam, would you like to dance?"

"Sure!"

As I stood up it hit me; she called me Sam! All the time I'd been around her she'd called me captain. As we headed for the floor I recalled Angie's girlish "I know something you don't know" antics, which made me think, Ah ha! Now we get down to some serious business!

When we got to the dance floor we turned toward each other. Believing the most appropriate way to waltz was to have an appropriate space between us, I offered my left had as the lead and appropriately placed my right hand on her side. Wrong! Alex smiled, stepped right into my space, snuggled up to me, turned her cheek and put it on my chest and off we went. I wanted to scream out loud, "Yes!"

For the brief duration of the song we were lost in the moment. Neither of us spoke. Alex's firm, gentle hold on me never changed. I made sure that I held her firm, but I also made sure that I didn't overpower her. As the music ended Alex looked up at me and smiled. Her eyes just ripped into my soul.

I smiled back and asked if she'd like to take a walk out in the atrium area. She nodded and off we went.

The atrium was beautiful. The lighting, the fountains and

water falls, pools with fish in them, all types of foliage, you couldn't ask for a better spot. The conversation just flowed between us. You'd swear we knew each other for years. There were so many things we had in common and so many differences. I learned so much about her. Alex grew up on a dairy farm in Wisconsin. She said her dad owned some property and a managed a dairy herd and all sorts of animals. In school, Alex was in the gifted child's program. She was expedited through the school system. She graduated top in her class in her early teens and attended the University of Wisconsin where she excelled in math and science. From there she was accepted into the PhD program at MIT. Her dissertation was in Astro Mining Concepts and Feasibility for Mining Minerals In Near Space. She had a dog she called "Woobie Dog."

We could have talked all night. I looked at my watch and smiled at Alex. "It's 0030 hours. We should probably call it an evening."

Alex smiled at me and nodded.

"Can I walk you to your room?" I asked.

Alex smiled and replied, "Ya, I'd like that."

I didn't want the night to end. I had so much I wanted to ask her and to tell her. I knew it was a short distance to her room. I had to collect my thoughts to make sure we ended this night on a high note. As the door to her room came in sight I fought with myself. Do I kiss her? What if she doesn't want me to? Do I just say good night? Quick Sam, think!

As we drew near, Alex stopped and looked up at me, and in a soft and tender voice she asked, "Sam, is there someone special waiting for you at home?"

I smiled and answered, "Oh, no. I just haven't found the

right girl yet. Besides, being in Special Operations doesn't leave you much time for a private life with training and all…How about you?"

Alex's eyes lit up as she smiled and said, "Yes. His name is Tucker."

Hearing this made my heart drop. I moaned in my spirit. I wanted to die on the spot. It was all I could do to keep from running away.

"Oh wow! I'm happy for you, Alex," I responded. "Tell me about him." This was the last thing I wanted to hear.

Alex's face lit up. "I know it's getting late. Do you mind?"

"No. Not at all." My heart ached. I knew I had to be respectful and listen. After all, Alex didn't mislead me into believing I had a chance with her. I did it myself.

"Well, where do I start," she said.

"What does he look like?"

Alex responded, "Oh, well, he's tall. He has chestnut-colored hair. I just love his coloring. He has such gorgeous features. I'd say he's 6 feet 4 inches to the top of his head. He is a super listener. We love to go for rides. I talk with him for hours on end. He's got great muscle tone and he is quite athletic. He won a few championships in his day."

Damn it! Tall, dark, ladies' man, handsome, athletic. I hate this guy!

To be polite I asked, "So when did you meet Tucker?"

Alex smiled, "Oh, I met Tuck when he was nine years old. He lived on a farm not too far from my parents' farm. It was love at first sight."

To add insult to injury Alex looked at me with those beautiful eyes, smiled, and said, "If you're ever in the neighborhood I'd love to introduce you to Tucker. Maybe you'd like to go for a ride with us."

Thinking fast on my feet I responded, "Oh, Ah…I'd like that. But, well you know, I'd feel like I was interfering with your private time together."

"Nonsense!" she replied. "I'm sure you two would get along famously."

"Great. It's a date," I said.

At that she stood on her toes, kissed me on the cheek, and said in a soft tone, "Goodnight, Sam."

As I walked away dejected and confused I reach up and touched my face. Her kiss felt so warm. Her lips so smooth and soft, yet I was second fiddle.

Landing At Hunter Air Field

As I drifted in and out of my thoughts I heard a voice that sounded like someone talking in a tin can while someone was beating on their chest. I soon realized it was the chopper pilot.

"Captain D'Angelo, we are five minutes out from Hunter, sir."

As I gazed out of the chopper I knew that this time it wasn't another drill. We were going to be deployed. World events were unfolding so fast it brought the true meaning of "The Fog of War" to light.

As we descended to land on the chopper pad I could see Colonels Martinez and Beckworth waiting for us.

I turned to my team. "Saddle up, boys…We ride!"

"Ooh Rah, boss! Brothers till the end!"

What an enigma my team was. To see them at play you'd never believe that they were highly trained, razor sharp, and disciplined warriors. It's as if someone hits a switch and out pops disciplined, intense, focused, and determined warriors. Their faces changed to rock hard determination. I swear they could kill with their eyes.

The chopper was about four feet off the landing pad when I yelled, "Let's go!"

The team and I hit the deck before the chopper did. To stay under the rotor blast, we ran toward the colonels in a crouched position. As I came out from under the blast I stood erect and saluted the waiting officers.

"Let's go, son," said Colonel Martinez. "You and your team need to report to command operations immediately for a debriefing."

"Yes, sir! We're on the way."

I motioned for the team to follow me. It was as if they could read my mind. Without speaking a word they could anticipate my and each others' moves. Our communications were more body language and hand motions than anything else.

As we entered the operations briefing area I noticed that they had the briefing room set up for a video conference. The large video screen had a blue hue to it. We seated ourselves in the front of the room. There were several other Special Operations teams and officers already seated. When both colonels entered the room, the room was called to attention. From the back of the room a voice called out, "Ten Hut!"

Immediately we stood at attention.

Colonel Beckworth responded, "As you were, men."

He continued, "Men, as you are aware, at 0530 mountain time today, NAASC detected a nuclear detonation in the southwest desert of Iran. We are unsure whose warhead it was, but one thing is for certain: a world of hurt is about to happen! We have Intel that the Iranians are massing troops on their east and west borders. They have surface-to-air and surface-to-surface missiles in several strategic locations. They have the Gulf bottled up. No one is going to get in or out of the Gulf without them letting them do so. The Whitehouse has been in constant contact with the Iranian government. We are sending in hazmat teams, food, and aid. The Reagan and carrier battle group is in the Gulf so we have a good presence there.

"The problem is the Iranians have been making rumbles that they believe it may have been one of our bombers armed with a nuke that crashed in their desert. To complicate things, in the not-so-distant past we have deployed high altitude reconnaissance missions over the area in question. Intel coming out of Iran gave us reason to believe that the nuclear research facilities they have been building were a ruse. We kept our surveillance in the southwestern desert just northwest of Bandar Abbas. Our Intel kept tracking high-level officials and guests going to an obscure site. Hell, from the air, and from the ground, it appeared to be an oil pipeline relay station to the Gulf.

"Our Intel has kept a close watch over the comings and goings of several North Korean and Chinese weapons merchants. It appears that all of the noise about the Iranians building a bomb was just that…noise. Their true intent was to make an oil-for-nuke deal with the North Koreans and Chinese. Obviously, they made the deal. Our Intel was looking for the Iranians to engineer a nuke outright. We never expected that the Iranians would piecemeal one together.

"Needless to say, gentlemen, this situation is extremely fluid. Any wrong moves by any nation could lead us to the threshold of Armageddon. Communications between the U.S., Iran, EU, and United Nations are wide open. The president is keeping us on high alert; however, he has asked that we stand ready until he and the Department of Defense get a handle on what happened. All military installations are in alert status—locked down. All personnel are to report for duty—no communications in or out of installations. We will issue the standard postcards for mailing to your homes and loved ones. In just a few moments we will be video conferencing with several other sites including the Pentagon to receive a briefing by the Joint Chiefs. Gentlemen…may God be with us all."

Hearing this, the meeting room began buzzing like a beehive. Technicians were making final preparations for the video conference, team leaders huddled up with their teams to discuss their speculations, and all we knew was that we were on the brink of something very big.

As the technicians were completing their conferencing setup, the lead technician spoke into his headset microphone, "Ah, roger that. This is Hunter, we are ready. We read your audio five by five. Visual in five, four, three, two…"

At that a familiar face appeared on the screen. It was General Cornelius. In his commanding way he began to speak, "Good evening to you all. I know that you all have questions as to what has happened and what will happen next. The president will be addressing the nation shortly after this briefing. Let me assure you that the president is firm in his resolve to move forward through this disaster through peaceful means, through dialogue and diplomacy. It is his hope and desire that as a nation we come together with charitable hearts to show compassion for those who were affected by this horrific tragedy."

The general continued his briefing, "The president has asked congress to release emergency aid funds. As I speak aid is being dispatched to the affected area. In addition to food and medical supplies, the president has dispatched teams of medical, hazmat specialists, and logisticians to assist in the search and recovery efforts in Iran. It is important to stress that the president has issued a directive to all field commanders in the Gulf Theater that they are in no way to make any moves that could be interpreted as a hostile gesture. In the president's words, 'This is a time that calls for restraint, prudence, clear judgment, and understanding.' We will keep you updated as events unfold."

As the video conference came to a close Colonel Martinez came to the front of the room to address the group. He paused as if to gather his thoughts. "Gentlemen, I am hopeful and confident that our government officials will successfully find solutions to the tough problems that lie ahead. However, this is not a time in which we can idly stand by and watch. This is a time for us to ensure 'our swords are razor sharp.' Therefore, at 0600 tomorrow, we will begin training intensely for the possibility of war. I will not have any of my troops perish because he or she was inadequately trained. You will drill morning, noon, and night."

He glanced over to me and my team and said, "HALO jumpers!"

Dennis cringed and whispered to me, "Aw crap, boss, here it comes."

The colonel continued, "My high-altitude low-oxygen jumpers…Well, let's just say that you will jump from heights so high that you should be able to see Saint Peter's sandals from your vantage point."

At the conclusion of his speech the colonel smiled and thanked everyone for their hard work and dedication.

As the colonel turned to exit, the room was called to attention. "Ten Hut!"

We waited for him to exit the area and then began to

mill around to meet with the other teams. It was our way of comparing notes and getting a perspective on things.

As the teams began to disperse to their quarters my team and I took our time leaving the room. I could sense that each of us had concerns about the situation.

Paul spoke up first. “I’ve got a bad feeling about this one, boss.”

The others nodded in agreement.

“Why’s that, Paul?” I responded.

“It just doesn’t add up. I believe the Iranians are setting us up for a sucker punch. You know, act all friendly to draw you in close and then when your guard is down drop the hammer on you. I mean think about it, they hate us and what we stand for, we’ve helped two democratic governments form on either side of their nation, they’ve misled the entire world concerning their goal for building a nuke program. When the crap hit the fan what did they do? Blame the U.S. They light up their own desert and then claim it’s our nuke! Now they are opening their arms to embrace us for our aid. I don’t know, it’s just too weird for me.”

Growing up in the streets of Boston had taught Paul a great deal about reading situations. He learned to read peoples’ words and actions—see the bigger picture. From a very young age he was able to avoid trouble. He always trusted his gut feelings…survival instincts.

“Good instincts, and I agree with your assessment of this mess. I guess all we can do now is watch and wait.”

The other members of the team nodded in agreement.

It had been a long day for us all. “Tell you what, guys, we’ve got one hell of a day in store for us tomorrow. I suggest we head back to our barracks, hit the rack, and write, or should I say sign, some postcards and call it a day."

At around 0245 hours the most horrendous sound came blaring from alert speakers outside my room. In a flash I could hear the thundering of personnel grabbing and running with their gear. As I headed to the staging area I could hear several of the troops grumbling, "Dude, couldn't the old man let us catch a few more z's before jerking our chains?"

With our gear in tow, my team and I headed for our staging area. We were ready to rock and roll. As I stood watching the staging activities I commented to the team, "Wow! What a sight. The old man can be proud of these guys. They are on their game." Everyone knew their part in this exercise and executed it to perfection. Things were happening fast. Transport planes were moving into position. Personnel, trucks, equipment, and supplies were being staged to be loaded onto the planes. I thought for sure we would be given the order to stand down—alert over. However, we proceeded to board and load the waiting aircraft.

Dennis commented, "Looks like the old man is getting his money's worth today."

As we boarded the troop transport, Colonel Beckworth, in full battle dress, was on board waiting for us. He yelled to me, "Let's move em, Captain D'Angelo. I'll brief you and your team on the mission when we are airborne. Right now, saddle up! We ride!"

My team and I boarded the transport first. Several other teams were approaching the aircraft when Colonel Beckworth signaled to them to hold back. The colonel then signaled the crew chief to close the hatch. He then turned to the pilots.

"Okay, gentlemen, let's go. We've got to make our next pick up."

The pilots wasted no time getting tower clearance for take off. As the aircraft gained altitude, Colonel Beckworth came to the aircraft's rear area where we were seated. I could see from the expression on his face that the news was not going to be good.

"Men, at 0245 hours this morning the Iranians shot down three transport planes carrying technicians, food, and medical supplies. All three hundred passengers are lost and presumed dead. It appears their radar units saw these aircraft as a threat. The Aircraft Carrier Reagan and its battle group were in the area so they dispatched search and rescue planes for survivors. Well…the Iranians saw the jets leaving the Reagan's flight deck so they fired 'Silkworm' surface-to-surface missiles at the Reagan and several battle group tenders. They sunk two tenders and punched a pretty good hole in the Reagan. The Reagan got a squadron of fighters off before becoming inoperative. Let's just say that when the fighters did their thing, they rearranged some of Iran's shoreline. They managed to take out the missile batteries that fired on them and several others. Men, we are heading up to Dobbins Air Base to pick up a few more teams—teams who you are well acquainted with. I'll brief you on our destination and mission when we are in route."

I must admit that in hearing what the colonel had to say a sick feeling came over me. I was scared, yet excited. I felt a rush of adrenalin. My senses seemed to become acute. This is it, I thought to myself. All the training and preparations now come into play. I paused for a moment and recalled the advice my dad gave me. "Trust your instincts and your training." At that I settled into my thoughts.

—

The flight up to Dobbins Air Base was a short hop. As we approached the runway we could see personnel and equipment staged in various areas. Man, this was going to be a huge mobilization. As we taxied into the base operations area the team seemed to perk up. Dennis smiled and said, "Ah, hell…I need to go back to Hunter."

Paul laughed and said, "Don't we all."

Dennis paused for a moment, looked at the team with a grin and an impish spark in his eyes…a kind of look that said, "Go ahead, ask me why."

"Okay, dude, why," said Kym.

"I left my wallet in my other pants."

"The question is, where did you leave your pants?" said Kym. We all smiled.

As the aircraft came to a halt the crew chief lowered the tail section loading ramp. Several groups approached the ramp and began boarding. Like us, they were loaded down with gear. The first troop coming up the ramp looked up and smiled.

It was dark and difficult to make out the image. However, a familiar voice called to me. "Hey, Cap! Can we join this party?"

I knew that voice…it was Bronson Templeton. I stood up and laughed. We had become friends when we were in Nevada training. As we shook hands I said to Bronson, "Who's with you?"

"The crew, dude."

It was a reunion. Up the ramp came the rest of Templeton's team with the Gomez, Brodrick and Swenson teams behind them. What a sight. We made our pick up and were airborne in a flash. We wasted no time in settling in. We knew that we were in for a long flight in this "flying box car." We knew we had to make the best of it.

The Pentagon

On the morning of May 21, 2010, as U.S. forces were being mobilized, the Secretary of Defense and the Joint Chiefs were meeting and debating strategies, options and battle plans. The president made it clear that he wanted options that very day. As the debate raged on between the Secretary of Defense and the Joint Chiefs, General Cornelius watched and listened intently. He was taking in and considering all view points. Then as if he were an arbitrator listening to two litigants arguing their case he interjected his opinion.

"Gentlemen, we have made our thoughts and concerns known to each other, and the time has come to make a decision. What we decide this day will alter the course of history and have long lasting effects not only on our nation but the world as a whole. Let's review the facts as we know them today.

"Fact number 1: The Iranians have nuclear capabilities. We know of at least one nuclear warhead. However, they have 'Plausible Deniability' concerning this fact. For several years the U.N. Nuclear Inspectors have all but turned their backs on their nuclear programs. Fact number 2: Our intelligence has shown that since the mid 1990's the Iranians have invested heavily in mid to long-range defensive and offensive missile system technology. Both are formidable and accurate systems. Fact number 3: Since the mid to late 1990's the Iranians have built fortified defensive positions strategically located throughout their country, especially along the Gulf, in particular the Straits of Hormuz and along their borders with Iraq and Afghanistan. They have methodically and insidiously built up their army's size and defensive capabilities. They watched and learned from our two wars with Iraq. Their defenses are designed to withstand the punishment we threw at the Iraqi defenses.

"Fact: 4: The war on terror has depleted our armed forces. Our forces have been dramatically reduced and replaced by advanced technology. Fact 5: Our nation's temperament and will to fight a sustained war has drastically changed since the war on terror first started. Fact 6: World opinion has dramatically shifted away from supporting the U.S. in armed conflict. The U.N, the EU in particular has become vociferous concerning our activities in the Middle East. They strongly feel that we are imposing our values and will on the Middle East. Anti U.S. sentiment is at an historic high. There have been many anti U.S. protests throughout the world. Fact 7: The Iranians have waged an aggressive and effective propaganda campaign over the past ten years concerning their desire to live in peace and their continued fear of aggression by the U.S. Fact 8: Iran sits on an ocean of oil. The EU, China, North Korea, Pacific Rim nations, Russia and the Balkan States are dependant on Iranian oil. Any disruption of their oil flow could lead to extreme and dire consequences."

In hearing this, the Secretary of Defense stood to his feet, paused as to gather his thoughts, and said, "Gentlemen, I thank you for your thoughts and counsel. A grave responsibility has been laid at our feet. So many lives are at stake. However, we did not ask for this war. It was thrust upon us. Let history view our actions as noble and just. Let our actions be swift, with impunity and decisiveness. Let our victory be sure and swift. May God guide our hand in the battles to come."

He continued, "General Cornelius, over the past year you have been actively planning for and training special teams in the use of advanced and unheard of technology. Well, it is time to unleash it. I would like you to reveal your plan for 'Operation Mirage.'"

The general smiled and thanked the Secretary of Defense. "Thank you, Mr. Secretary. Gentlemen, let us adjourn to the war room to discuss Operation Mirage…"

The Battle Plan

The room that the group entered was a technologically advanced theater designed for 360-degree viewing. Given the holographic nature of the presentations, viewers found themselves sitting in the midst of the presentation. The group sat at a horseshoe-shaped table arrangement with General Cornelius at the podium in front of the group. Each seat was a plush rap-around swivel leather captain's chair. The computer system was built into the table tops. Instead of computer screens, all data was projected in a 3-D image in front of each person at the table. As for keyboards and a mouse, well those were things of the past. All computer commands were activated by touch, eye activated and or voice activated.

As the group settled into their seats the lights in the room were dimmed. A soft light shined on General Cornelius as he began his discussion.

"Gentlemen, let us begin our discussion with the principles of a well defined and successful battle plan. That is, the battle's objective, the enemies assumptions about our actions, how we will exploit their reactions to our plans, our methods for fighting this war, and of course, how we intend to prosecute this war with the lowest number of casualties possible.

"First is our objective. Considering the facts and circumstances as we know them, it is imperative that this operation does not take the form of any war we have engaged in. What we unleash in this conflict will be 100 years more advanced than any known tactics and weaponry. It is our plan to prosecute this war with 22nd century tactics and weaponry. Think about it, gentlemen, the Iranians have seen our tactics in play. They are an intelligent, adaptable and formidable opponent. As a result of what they have learned about our tactics they have strategically located their defenses throughout their country and have hardened them to withstand our attacks. Our intelligence shows that they have purchased and built advanced radar and missile systems. They have invested heavily in state-of-the-art radar systems capable of instantly recalibrating itself when jammed. They have a sophisticated network of defenses located in the Zargos Mountain Range that are buried deep in the mountains and well fortified.

"However, we have pinpoint accurate intelligence on all of their fortified positions along the Gulf and Straits of Hormuz. Our SEAL teams have been in and out of country for several years observing the construction of their defenses as well as have GPS data on each site's location. Our SCRAM-1 system has kept accurate account of the positioning of their ground forces as well as the movement of their mobile armaments. We know their rotation methods and cycles—how, when and where they move their troops and equipment. We even have pinpoint data on their supply caches.

"Second, the Iranians' assumptions about how we will prosecute this war are of course a major issue. However, it is apparent from how the Iranians have set up their defenses and equipped and mobilized their forces that they are prepared to defend themselves from sustained air bombardment followed by fast-moving ground attacks…Gulf Wars I and II respectively.

As I will demonstrate in our holographic battle plan simulation, our plan calls for the appearance of a massive mobilization of forces. We will give the Iranians a convincing appearance that we intend to do as they expect.

"Third is our plan to exploit the Iranians reaction to what they believe our battle plans to be. As my holographic simulation will demonstrate, our plan will lead to the Iranian forces to become totally disoriented and confused. As the plan unfolds, the Iranians will be responsible for inflicting massive casualties on themselves.

"Fourth, we will deploy a technology that has no known defenses against it: holographic and magnetic pulse weapons."

The general paused for a moment, then turned and with a slight gesture with his hand signaled his aids. The lights went out and in an instant the entire room became a three-dimensional holographic representation of the map of Iran. "Gentlemen, would you please join me for a virtual tour through our battle plan."

The general, with the help of his aids, began to recite GPS coordinates for the computer system to follow. As they did the hologram instantly changed. The group found themselves standing in the Zargos Mountains at a well fortified radar and missile site. They continued their virtual tour throughout Iran, covering the entire map in the matter of one hour. They toured air defenses, air fields, troop placements and heavy armored mobile unit placements… tanks, mobile troop carriers, mobile and stationary missile launchers and gun placements. They virtually walked amongst the Iranian defenses.

As the tour progressed, the Secretary of Defense commented to General Cornelius, "General, I've known of this technology but never fully understood its potential and application. This has been both encouraging and insightful. Your people have done an outstanding job!"

"Thank you, Mr. Secretary, we have built our entire battle plan around this technology."

"Great! Now let's get down to business. How are you going to prosecute this war?"

The general smiled and paused as to collect his thoughts and replied. "Sir, we will win this war with fewer troops than we deployed in Afghanistan."

The secretary responded quickly, "You intend to do what! General, need I remind you that you will be engaging one of the largest and best-equipped armies in the Middle East? Let alone that they have demonstrated that they have nuclear capabilities. Dear God, man, they will be fighting to defend their own homeland! I am sure that they will in no way fight this war half-heartedly. General Cornelius, I understand that we have new age weaponry, but no war was won by half-hearted measures. No war was successfully prosecuted without boots on the ground. Hell, we proved that in Gulf's I and II. Now we are in a fight for our very existence. This is not a skirmish where we punish some bad actions to teach a lesson. We need to bring the Iranian government to their senses…Live and let live."

The general listened intently to the secretary's views. When the secretary finished his statement the general smiled and responded, "Mr. Secretary, never before in the history of warfare has an army had the advantage of total invisibility and weaponry that is indefensible. As you will see in our battle simulation, the plan that we have chosen will lead to the permanent shut down of the Iranians' nuclear program, their advanced warning and weapon systems will be rendered useless, their communications systems—radio, microwave, TV and phone systems—will be rendered permanently inoperative. They will spend years rebuilding their communications infrastructure. They'll be so busy with rebuilding they won't have enough time to meddle in Middle East affairs, specifically with their neighbors' new democratic systems. Most importantly, the majority of Iranian casualties will be from them firing on themselves. "

As the secretary listened to General Cornelius' assessment he smiled, placed his hand on his chin, pursed his lips, nodded his head and paused for a moment to contemplate all that he had heard. He then turned to the joint chiefs and said, "Gentlemen, this is a bold plan. It's important that we see both sides of this plan. My question to you is what is the down side? What happens if the Iranians don't take the holographic bait?"

The group turned to General Cornelius for the answer. "Well, sir, a worst-case scenario predicts that of the 500 special operations team members that are deployed we stand to lose 60% of them. Our worst-case simulation does not predict them as killed in action. Rather, these operatives will be lost because they will be stranded in country with no possible means of extraction from country.

"We calculate that those closest to the Gulf areas will be extracted. However, those deep in country will have little to no chance of reaching an extraction point. We have no problem deploying them; it's just that after we've tipped our hand they will be hunted by the Iranians. If they are not summarily executed when they are captured they will be held as negotiation pawns.

"As for our ground forces, well, our losses will come from our taking the Straits of Hormuz. We calculate light casualties for our diversionary forces landing along the Gulf; however, what concerns us is that if the Iranians do not capitulate early in the battle a wholesale slaughter of their forces will ensue. This presents us with an immense public relations problem at home and on the world stage. It gives the appearance that the U.S. is a bully beating on a defenseless and peace-loving Iran. But we must stay focused on the potential this plan brings to light. Think about it, gentlemen, we will usher in a new era of warfare. One that will demonstrate to the world that the age of 'attriting' an opponent's army is secondary to destroying their ability to wage war…To strip them of the weapons and means to wage war. We will in effect put all potential foes on notice that if they choose to engage us in armed conflict they will have to do so using primitive weapons. The world will be put on notice that any aggression toward us and we can move on any opponent at will and with impunity."

"General, let's see what this holographic simulator can do. I understand that your computer runs its programs as a 'super adaptive artificial intelligence system.'"

"Yes, sir, that's correct. The program is designed to study and learn from its opponent's moves, evaluate the level of threat of the said moves, and then counter the moves it perceives that pose the greatest threat."

The general turned to his aids and signaled them to begin the simulation. Instantly another three-dimensional holographic presentation began. The room became the battle field. The first event was the instantaneous deployment of the advanced Special Operations teams all equipped with the new state-of-the-art weapon systems. As the group studied the deployment of the Special Operations personnel, digital readouts of the troops' location and equipment appeared above each troop.

Seeing the data and deployment scheme one of the joint chiefs, Marine General Jeswald "Jes" Milford, called for the computer to freeze program. It instantaneously did. He walked up to one of the holographic troop images pointed at the troop's equipment and said "General Cornelius, these are the troops that will deploy the holographic technology correct?"

General Cornelius nodded his head.

"What would happen if we removed this troop from the program?"

"The short of it is we have redundancies built into our plan. It's our intention to deploy for optimal effectiveness."

General Cornelius continued. "As you may recall our original stealth technology was based on the shape of a diamond. It was found that the diamond presented optimal reflective angles. As such, we will use a similar strategy in deploying our teams. Gentlemen, look at it this way, we will create a maze of magnetic fields in which our SCRAM-1 system will project life-size three-dimensional images on. In effect we will create a 'hall of mirrors effect.' No matter where you are positioned you see the projected imagery. The teams will deploy at the precise angles and elevations from each other, therefore creating the optimal delivery of our holographic imagery. What is unique about this deployment is that if any part of our holographic grid is rendered inoperative the other grid segments will pick up the mission. No matter what happens each portion of the grid will deliver a significant portion of the planned holographic weapon. You must keep in mind that our back-ups have back-ups."

General Milford replied, "Okay, General, that seems plausible, but let's look at the rest of the system. We understand that this technology is supported by our SCRAM-1 satellite system."

"Yes that's correct. SCRAM-1 plays an intricate role in the holographic projections."

General Milford listened and nodded as General Cornelius concluded his thoughts.

"This sounds almost too good to be true. As in all military actions we know that even the best-made plans face serious challenges. If anything can go wrong it generally will. With this in mind, just as a hypothetical situation let's say that SCRAM-1 fails just before the war begins, what then?"

General Cornelius smiled and responded, "Overlord will take over and complete the mission."

Hearing this, the group reacted by looking at each other with puzzled looks. "Overlord…what exactly is Overlord?" asked the secretary.

"Gentlemen, when SCRAM-1 was first conceived," said General Cornelius," it was decided that a redundant system would be put into place. This is a sleeper system that will remain dormant until SCRAM-1 goes off line. It is designed to remain in a classified high altitude orbit out of sight until a time SCRAM-1 is rendered inoperative by an attack or if a catastrophic failure occurs. You must remember SCRAM-1 is a constellation of satellites. The likelihood of a one hundred percent failure is highly remote at best."

Hearing this, the secretary and the joint chiefs agreed that in theory this segment of the battle plan appeared viable.

General Milford spoke up. "Gentlemen, it's my boys who are going to hit the beaches, let's take a look at how we are going to deal with the fortified positions. After that, what do you say we take this simulation out for a spin? I'll drive if you don't mind General Cornelius."

General Cornelius laughed. "Be my guest. Throw your best curve ball at the system. Let's see what happens."

General Milford moved back to his seat and began giving verbal commands to the computer system. Instantly the holographic battle resumes.

The secretary and the joint chiefs watched intently as Special Forces were deployed throughout Iran. General Milford did his best to frustrate their deployment; however, as he made his counter moves the computer system adjusted the deployment. The computer scored a ninety five percent deployment rate.

Next in the program was the simulation of the stealth platforms—F117 Night Hawks, F22 Raptors and B2 Bombers deployment. The group marveled at the tactics and weaponry. Each platform was equipped with magnetic pulse cannons. Again General Milford did his best to frustrate the simulation, yet the computer adjusted for an optimal plan and scored a ninety percent kill rate on all advanced warning and missile systems, airfields and mobile systems. What astounded the group were the computers' projections of one hundred percent shutdown of all communications systems and nuclear facilities.

The final segment of the simulation was the ground war.

General Milford was anxious to see how this would unfold. The group understood that the ground war was to be the linking pin in winning this war. If we failed to capture the Straits of Hormuz we would in all likelihood cut off our flow of oil from the Gulf. The group watched in amazement as the simulation projected the capture of the straits.

After the simulation was completed the Defense Secretary looked around the table at the Joint Chiefs and said, "Gentlemen, are there any questions concerning Operation Mirage? Are we in agreement that this operation should go forward?"

All present nodded their head.

The secretary then said, "Gentlemen, let us brief the president." He then voice activated his computer terminal by giving the command, "Whitehouse." Instantly, a video conference with the president began. The holographic image made it appear that the president was sitting there with the joint chiefs. The secretary greeted the president, "Mr. President we have a plan…"

The Trip to the Gulf

With the teams and gear loaded and aircraft at altitude Colonel Beckworth addressed the teams. "Men we are on our way to a staging area in the Iraqi desert, Camp Omega. We will join a group of one hundred Special Operations teams. Our primary objective will be to strategically deploy the MAGS holographic devices throughout Iran. We will be briefed on the specifics of our deployment when we are in country. For now let's just kick back and enjoy the ride."

After the colonel's speech we all slipped back into our private worlds and thoughts. As I gazed out of the aircraft window I watched the dawn darkness give way to an orange glow. As the sun moved up on the horizon I drifted back to my days of training in Nevada—at Area 51.

As I drifted back to 2009 I recalled the last four weeks of our training. They were intense. We spent twelve hours a day in lectures and in practical applications training. As if our days weren't long enough, we had a few hours of technical reading to go through in preparation for our next day's training. This left us little time for socializing. However, we managed to party when we could and when we did it was in true team fashion…all out.

Every one of us took our training seriously. We knew that we were the first of many who would be trained to master this new magnetic technology. We had grown up with some great science fiction books and movies that portrayed beam weapons and "cloaking" abilities, invisible warriors and vessels that could be hidden. Just the thought of it being a reality was mind bending. We drove ourselves to achieving operational perfection. Our training was in all aspects of this new technology. We were required to learn how to optimally deploy it, program and maintain it.

Holographics Training

Weeks three and four were the application, deployment tactics, and maintenance training of the MAGS holographic projectors. Our first day of training in MAGS holographic projections, as in any other day of training, started off with a lecture by Doctor Detrich. We just enjoyed listening to the man.

"Ya und today ve begin training in da exploitation of ze human mind. Ve call dis ze Eldridge Effect. Vhat is most important is dat ze imagery created und seen vill be as close to reality as one can conceive. As an example, please, all of you form a circle around me. I vill stand in ze center of da room."

Doctor Detrich quickly positioned himself in the center of the room and continued, "Ya und now I vould like you all to form a circle about me. Ya vun here at my front, und vun at my rear, und on the side und udder side und so on."

We quickly got into position around Doctor Detrich. I got in front of the doctor with Paul directly behind him. Neal was at his left, Dennis at his right while Kym was in between Dennis and Paul at the doctor's five.

"Captain Sam, vhat do you see?"

I paused for a moment to study the doctor closely to make sure I didn't miss any details. "Well…obviously I can see the front of you, your metal gray frames on your glasses, your gray hair and gray beard, your face, your lab coat, front pockets with pens in them and insignia on the left jacket pocket. I notice that you are wearing your favorite sneakers today. You have on a pair of black pants and from the looks of it you're wearing a blue polo shirt. Oh ya, your hands are in your lab coat's pockets. How did I do?"

The doctor smiled and said, "Good observations. Und now I ask you, Sergeant Paul, vhat do you see?"

Paul laughed. "Well, doc, all I can see is the back of you—your head, back, legs, feet, arms, you know your cute backside."

Doctor Detrich laughed. "Ah, so you cannot see vhat Captain Sam sees und Captain Sam cannot see vhat you see. Das is good. How about da others, is it da same for you?"

Neal, Kym and Dennis all agreed. "Ya, doc, we can't see each others' perspectives."

"Alex, please provide our team members vith their special tools."

I knew right away that something was up. "Okay, Doctor," she replied.

Alex went around the room and handed each person a face shield and apron. She then handed each person a paint ball pistol loaded with a variety of colored pellets.

Doctor Detrich continued his discussion. "Is it not correct zhat you are perfect marksmen?"

Paul answered first, "For all the hours we've put in qualifying on our weapons training I should hope so."

The doctor replied. "Ah…das is good. I am sure then you vill hit vhat you aim at…ya."

The team laughed.

Dennis jumped right in, "Okay, doc, were do you want us to put our shots?"

Doctor Detrich smiled and responded, "Ya, I vould like da four of you to make sure you are directly across from da person on your opposite side. Sergeant Kym please position yourself exactly between the two you are standing between. Please, all of you take aim at my body only. I do not vish to be shot in da head…no, das is not good."

At that we all took aim at Doctor Detrich's body. The entire team began to chuckle.

Dennis whispered to Kym, "Dude, this is gonna be a massacre."

Doctor Detrich continued, "Ya, und now are you ready?"

"Yes! Are you sure you want to do this?" I asked.

"Vell, vith such good shots I am not sure I vill survive. But, ve must prove da theory of holographic warfare. So, on my count of three you vill shoot me vit your paint pellets. Und ready! Vun, two…three!"

At that we fired at the doctor. The sounds of paint balls splattering filled the room. Kym hit the wall across from the doctor, Paul and I shot each other as did Neal and Dennis. We were dumbfounded. Alex was laughing, safely out of our range.

"Oh…vhat is da matter? Maybe you should take vun step closer and try again. I am sure you vill be successful dis time."

So like good soldiers we took one step closer, raised our pistols, and took aim and waited for the signal to fire.

Doctor Detrich began his count, "Und vun, two…three!"

Once again the sounds of paint balls splattering filled the room. Not one of us hit the doctor. The man was standing right in front of us and we were missing him by a mile.

"Damn crappy sights on these things," Neal mumbled.

"The paint balls are being deflected around you…I mean obviously something is redirecting the shots.…right?" I asked.

Doctor Detrich smiled, put his hand to his chin, slowly stroked his well-groomed beard, and said, "Ah…so your thesis is dat da MAGS can be deployed to deflect projectiles, und you based your analysis on vhat you observed vith your eyes…no?"

I paused and then answered. "Ya…that's about it…I guess."

The doctor turned to the rest of the team, "Und do you all support zis thesis?"

The team chimed in. "Ya, doc, we do."

Doctor Detrich smiled at the team and said, "Ya und you present good logical argument on observable actions and known results. However, your conclusions are not correct. Und da reason for my conclusion is dat you did not shoot at me."

"If it wasn't you I tried to cap, then whose butt did I shoot at…your evil twin's?" asked Dennis.

"Ya, vun could argue that you shot at my evil twin. However, da truth is you shot at my image. I am not in da room with you."

Paul was incredulous. "Whoa…doc you're jerking our chains, right? I mean you're standing large as life right here. You're casting a shadow, we can smell your cologne, hell, we can see the lint and wrinkles on your clothing."

In a blink of the eye Doctor Detrich disappeared. The team stood there speechless. A moment later the door opened and in walked Doctor Detrich. "Shall ve get down to business, gentlemen?"

—

For the next two weeks we poured ourselves into our training. Doctor Detrich and Alex had a unique way of taking us through the training. Their playful yet highly professional styles made things seem down to earth, logical, and easy to apply. Our training was demanding, yet it was still a great deal of fun. We were drilled to perfection on every aspect of holographic warfare, the theory, application and maintenance of the MAGS Holographic devices. At the end of the two weeks we could set up, operate, program and maintain the MAGS blindfolded.

As our last day of holographic training was nearing an end Doctor Detrich could hardly contain himself. He was extremely pleased at the progress we had made. Like a proud parent, he stood before us smiling and nodding his head. We could tell from the gleam in his eyes that he was about to make one of his profound speeches.

"Ya…I vould say zhat, as usual, you all graduate dis portion of your training vith high honors. Ya…you make me proud. Und now ve must discuss some serious business…Ya, ve must discuss taking a beer together tonight…" He smiled and laughed. "Und second thought, maybe we take several beers! Let us meet for da celebration at 1930 hours tonight."

"Ooh Rah, Doc!"

As I was heading for the door Alex called to me. "Hey, Sam! Wait up. We can walk together."

So off to the tram we headed. As we headed back to our rooms Alex said, "This must have been a tough two weeks for you guys. All work and no play."

I smiled, "You're not kidding. It was all the technical

reading that got to me. It was hard to keep my eyes open at night…great bed-time reading."

As we exited the tram Alex paused, reached and softly touched my arm. "Hey, Sam, what do you say we go out for dinner before meeting the guys for a beer? We haven't spoken much over the last two weeks. We've got some catching up to do, wouldn't you say?"

If I were a poker player I'd lose my shirt. I started chattering like a magpie. "Yeah, definitely…I'd like that. Do you want me to come by your room to meet you or do you want to meet at the club?"

I could see from Alex's grin she was having fun watching me make a fool of myself. "Pick me up at my room at let's say…1800," she replied.

At 1800 sharp I arrived at Alex's door. I knocked once. Immediately the door opened. There she stood. I felt weak in the knees. That smile, those eyes, the way she was dressed—a sleek fitting sweater, mini-skirt. I was speechless at the sight of her.

Alex smiled and broke the silence. "Ready to go?" she asked.

Hearing her voice snapped me back to reality. "Ah…ya. Wow! You look great, Alex! I mean…ah…"

I just stammered as I tried to recover from my self-induced coma. She had me cold. I did my best to turn my mindless dribbling into a compliment and intelligent conversation.

Her eyes shined as she smiled. "Oh! Thank you, Sam. I hoped you'd like my outfit."

As we walked to the club I noticed that Alex kept cadence with my step, and she seemed to playfully bump her leg into my leg. A couple of steps I thought for sure we were going to get tangled up, but we both just laughed when it happened. I knew better than to read too much into it. I just found it attractive that she was that comfortable and uninhibited with me. Maybe this friendship was going to be a special one.

As we entered the club the host greeting guests smiled and said, “Such a handsome couple. I have a special table for you.”

He led us to a cozy corner out of the way from the main crowd. The lighting was just right. It seemed to accent every one of Alex’s beautiful features. The lines and sculpture of her face, her big beautiful blue eyes, her curly auburn hair. I could sense the crowd watching her every move as we headed toward our table. She carried herself with such poise. Being with Alex made a deep sense of obligation come over me.

Right then and there I made up my mind that I had to be the best friend that I could be with Alex. Although my heart of hearts wanted to be with her for a lifetime, I was in no way going to confuse the issue for her. She was in love with Tucker and out of respect for her and him I made up my mind to stand down. Alex King wasn’t for the taking. My pursuit for Alex’s heart ended at that point. It was strictly friendship here on. This realization helped me relax.

Alex wasted no time getting right inside my head. “Well, Sam, there is so much I’d like to learn about you…were do we start?”

I smiled, “Anywhere you’d like.”

Alex grinned. “Okay, but we will save religion and politics for last.”

“It’s a deal.”

As the dinner progressed we walked down our respective

memory lanes recalling all our childhood and young adult memories. We had a lot in common. Her family owned a modest dairy operation in Wisconsin while my family owned and operated a few fitness centers in Minnesota. Our families were about the same size and make up. Our upbringing seemed to be mirror images of each other. Our cultures and values seemed to complement each others. We had strong parents who taught us traditional family values. They taught us to honor and respect our elders, to act with dignity, honesty, and high integrity, and to live a moral and disciplined lifestyle…to develop our body, mind, and spirit.

Even our dinner seemed to create fun. As Alex was stabbing a carrot on her plate it shot right across to my side of the table. I speared it with my fork and held it up. "It's mine now!" And I proceeded to eat it. She laughed. As I got into my salad I spilled some on the table.

"Maybe we should get deep bowls for our meal to keep our dinners corralled," said Alex.

None of our antics seemed to faze us. We just kept our conversation going. One would think that having dinner for the first time together you'd be self-conscious as to proper etiquette Not us! We were comfortable in our own skin. We had nothing to prove nor were we embarrassed to be ourselves.

Alex looked at her watch. "Wow! It's 2030, where did the time go? Do you want to head over to the bar and meet the team or stay for awhile and visit?"

For me, the answer to that question was easy. "Waiter! Please, two more red wines."

Alex laughed, "That's what I like about you, Sam. You're not afraid to make a decision."

Our conversation continued, however, what I found extremely puzzling was that in our brief moments of silence we seemed to gaze into each other's eyes. Maybe it was my wishful thinking or one too many glasses of red wine, but I could swear that the tone of Alex's voice and her soft eyes were sending a message that she was looking at me with serious interest. I must be delusional, I thought. So I quickly put those thoughts right out of my head.

Our conversation seemed to shift from a light-hearted discourse to a more sober and focused discussion.

Alex smiled, looked right into my eyes, and said, "Do you believe in God?"

Hearing this I did not hesitate to answer, "Ya, ya, I do, though I know that in today's world of political correctness it is not accepted to be so open about it. Here's how I see it. Think about how complex our world and the universe are. I mean think about how complex 'life' or any living thing is. It is the epitome of arrogance to think that it just happened because of a chain of cosmic events. I believe that all of the wonders of the world and universe got a helping hand from something much greater than ourselves. As for those of us who choose to worship God, I believe that all true believers are following their own path in life, a very private and personal path. A path on which they alone work out their salvation with their God. Who are we to deny that, or any person their right to believe in something greater than themselves?"

"You speak with such conviction."

I continued. "Sorry. The truth is that I believe that some day organized religion is going to get it right…they are going to quit bickering amongst themselves and realize that the path to God can take many different routes. I believe that they are going to get focused on the true message of love, forgiveness, tolerance and charity." Having voiced my thoughts, I wasted no time in my rebuttal question to Alex. "Enough of what I believe, what about you? Do you believe in God?"

Alex smiled. "Yes I do. I agree with your views. However, expressing my beliefs has been difficult. The scientific community has a difficult time accepting anything outside the realm of science. If they can't see it or measure it, it isn't provable and therefore it isn't real. I've had some great debates with colleagues about this, especially when we get to issues that science can't explain. They always seem to retreat to 'it's a phenomenon' when they can't rationally explain what has taken place. They just can't credit it to the possibility that God is involved. I love spinning their wheels when I ask about the 'big bang' theory. They just hate it that they can't pinpoint what caused the great explosion that created the universe. I tell them that the answer is easy, 'God lit the fuse.' This always sends them right up the wall. I agree with you, Sam. I mean what harm can come from believing in something greater than yourself? Living a life in which you humbly respect the rights and views of others, do good instead of bad and act compassionately toward others in need."

As we sipped our wine I proposed a toast.

"The martial art that I practice has five codes of conduct. One of them is be loyal in friendship. Tonight I would like to propose a toast to a lifelong friendship between us."

Alex blushed, lifted her glass and said, "To a lifelong friendship. No matter where life takes us may we never forget this moment."

We sipped our wine and smiled at each other. Alex seemed to slip off into a moment of thought. I could see she was pulling it all together, kind of analyzing the evening.

I broke the silence. “Shall we join the gang at the bar?”

Alex agreed. So off we went to finish a great evening.

As we entered the bar the place was alive with music and lively people. Paul saw us enter first. He stood up and motioned us over to the table where Doctor Detrich, the team, and their guests were seated. These guys were primed. Paul made room for two more chairs and motioned for us to sit by him and his guest. As we drew nearer I could see he was sitting with Angie, the technician I met a few weeks prior.

As we sat down the team chimed in, “Why, Cap, where have you two been?”

To my surprise Alex jumped right in to play their game. “That’s for us to know and for you to find out!” She then cuddled into me looking back at the team with that sassy look of hers.

The team erupted into a “Whoooa… Ooh Rah!”

As the night was drawing to a close we all started heading back to our rooms. I didn’t ask, I just started walking Alex back to her room. Once again Alex got into cadence with my step and playfully bumped into my leg. As we approached her door things got quiet. I could see that she was deep in thought. She broke the silence with a question.

“Sam, can I ask you a real personal question?”

“Why of course you can. You’re my new best pal, aren’t you?”

Alex smiled. “With all the failed marriages today do you think you’ll get married some day?”

"I hope to have a family. How about you, Alex? Are you going to get married some day?"

"Yes…I plan on it. I hope to have a family, too. But aren't you afraid that the marriage will fail? I mean the odds are against people marrying for life. It's like they start off with good intentions but at the first sign of problems they seem to give up on making the marriage work, or even worse they lose interest in their partner and run off with someone else. Don't you think that they should change the part of the wedding vows that say 'I Do' to something like, 'Maybe I will'?"

I could sense that this was an important subject for Alex. I needed her to know my thoughts, "Seriously, Alex, when I marry it will be for life. I know that it will be difficult at times. But watching my parents work through their problems gives me hope that love will conquer any problem. I want my wife to be my equal partner and companion in life's endeavors. Come what may, it's my intention to grow deeper in love as the years pass. I believe that if two people start their partnership in love, stay focused on trusting, respecting, caring, and nurturing each other they can't fail."

Alex's eyes seemed to become teary. With a slight crack in her voice and a bit of a forced smile she said, "I envy the girl who wins your heart, Sam D'Angelo."

At that she stepped into me, firmly hugged me, rose up on her toes, kissed my cheek, and quickly went into her room. Once again I went walking to my room muttering to myself. I just couldn't figure this woman out.

MAG Pulse Weapons Training

Our last two weeks of training had finally arrived. Not only were we were going to get the first crack at this new technology, we were going to go on ten days of leave at the conclusion of the training.

Obviously, we had no clue as to what we were in for. All we knew was that when it came to weapons we were on our game. As usual, Doctor Detrich started his first day with a lecture and practical application. As he stood before us preparing for his lecture, Dennis got up, walked to the front of the room, and pinched the doctor's cheek.

"Vhat is da meaning of dis?"

"Just checking, doc."

"Ya…Und you vere checking vhat—if I am available for a date? Sergeant Dennis, you think I'm hot, no?"

"You are a stud! I was making sure you were you and not another Kodak moment!" replied Dennis as he got back to his seat.

The doctor began his lecture. "Ya…Und now ve enter da veapons training phase of your training. Da veapons you vill be introduced to are da most advanced veapons da vorld has known. Vith such awesome power comes an awesome responsibility. Let us engage in dis training vith all seriousness as ve venture into da theory, application and maintenance of such awesome veapons.

"First, if you please, a short story. As you know my country had a dark period in its history. My family like many German families vere naively led down a path by a mad man who, for a brief moment, created a vision for my country that appeared to raise national pride…a vision of strength und pride. Dis mad man explored developing advanced veapons. He explored da development of da atomic bomb, rockets, und so on. At first his argument for such veapons made sense…ve needed such veapons to appear strong to da vorld and to protect ourselves from aggressors. History demonstrates dat his intent vas to dominate da vorld. You see, as da children of the nation ve vere asleep. Ve vere so busy admiring ourselves and our accomplishments ve lost sight of vere this mad man vas taking us. Ve lost sight of da balance between being strong as a nation und projecting our strength at da vorld.

"The important lesson to be learned is as my papa vould teach us as children. He vould say, 'It is a man's responsibility to create a safe environment in his home. He must live at peace vith his neighbors yet be strong in defending his castle. Derefore, remember mine children, to keep your family safe da master of da house must be strong, prepared and diligently stand vatch as da children sleep.'"

It was obvious that this new technology was going to catapult the U.S. into a hyper-super world power…a position of world leadership never achieved by any nation or people. Once this technology was unleashed no foe would withstand our defense. We would be capable of interdicting any foe with impunity. We as a people were now faced with a grave responsibility. We could never lose sight of the fact that we have to live peacefully within the world community. Yet, at the same time our peaceful existence would not preclude us from having and maintaining a strong defense. As the martial arts adage went, "You must keep a razor sharp edge on your sword at all times."

In his usual fashion Doctor Detrich's lecture had a practical side to it. At the front of the lecture hall was a pedestal that stood about three and one half feet tall. Its surface was about one square foot. It had two metal terminals protruding up from the surface about six inches and about six inches apart. The device looked harmless enough; we were sure we were in for a surprise. Doctor Detrich began his lecture.

"Today ve explore the basics of magnetism. I vould like a volunteer…Ah…Ya, Sergeant Neal, you are a strong man. Please assist me."

Neal cautiously approached the front of the room. "Okay, doc, this isn't one of your surprises is it?" Neal commented.

Doctor Detrich laughed. "No, no all ve vill do is test your ability to place dis metal rod evenly between dese two posts. However, you must not touch either post in placing da rod."

At that he handed Neal a one foot long metal rod.

"Ya, Und now ve conduct our experiment. Please, Sergeant, take off your vatch. I vould hate to see such a beautiful vatch get damaged. Und all you have to do is ven I tell you pass da metal bar down between da two posts and touch da dividing line between da terminals."

Neal smiled and said, "Okay, doc, let's do it."

Doctor Detrich reached down and turned on the device. Neal took a firm grip on the rod and began to pass it between the protruding rods. Instantly, the rod that Neal was holding was pulled to one of the protruding terminals. Neal pulled with all his might but could not remove the rod.

Doctor Detrich said, “Slide da rod off da terminal.”

Neal gave the rod a hard pull, then nearly fell backward when the rod released from the terminal. Neal laughed, “Whoa, doc…one hell of a magnet you got there.”

Doctor Detrich laughed, “Ya, und vhat happened?”

Neal smiled and said, “Easy enough I guess. The magnetic force between the two terminals attracted the rod. The force was strong enough to stop me from getting the rod to the bottom.”

“Ya…das is good. Vhat you are saying is dat you could not overcome da gauss strength of da magnet, no?”

Neal smiled and responded, “Ya, that’s about it.”

Doctor Detrich continued. “Basically, vhat took place is da magnetic field affected da molecular alignment in da metal rod derefore creating a force dat attracted da rod to da terminal. Und now vun more demonstration. Please, Sergeant Kym, come forward und assist me.”

Kym jumped to his feet, looked at the team, and winked. Oh brother, here we go, I thought to myself. Knowing Kym’s flare for the dramatic I was sure we were in for a show. As Kym approached the pedestal he acted cautious and apprehensive. One would think he was approaching an alien device.

He asked, “Hey, doc, is this thing on?”

Doctor Detrich smiled and responded, “Ya, und it is harmless…go ahead touch it…see for yourself.”

Kym slowly reached out to touch one of the terminals. As he made contact he began to shake, yell, and convulse as if he were being electrocuted.

Everyone laughed.

When Kym finished his antics, Doctor Detrich handed him a small digital desk clock. "Ya…Und now another simple experiment. Please Sergeant Kym, slowly move da clock toward da center of the terminals. Tell us vhat happens as you approach the terminals." Kym slowly reached forward with the clock.

He got to about one foot away and said, "It quit working, doc."

Doctor Detrich smiled and said, "Ya…Und da clock is kaput, no?"

Kym laughed. "Ya, ya heir doctor, und da clock is kaput!"

Doctor Detrich smiled. "I have so much fun vith dis team. As ve have demonstrated an invisible field of magnetic energy extended beyond da terminals…da magnetic field. Vith da metal rod it affected the rod's molecular alignment und attracted it. Ya, und vith da clock da magnetic field disrupted its electrical function. Ya, und vun can conclude dat such an invisible force can be devastating. Und now ve must prepare for your training."

Doctor Detrich looked at the team and in a serious tone said, "Und vhat you have played vith here today is but a child's toy. Und now ve vill begin training vith magnetic power dat is infinitely times stronger and more concentrated dan any natural magnetic force known to man."

So off to the simulator we went. As we entered the simulation area we saw those familiar ruck-sacks from several weeks prior. There ahead of us was Alex. She was dressed in the battle dress regalia that we were about to dress in. The woman looked good in any type of clothes. She'd probably look good dressed in a potato sack. As we approached we could see that she was busy making last-minute preparations for our live-fire exercise.

When she saw us enter she smiled and said, “Okay, boys, here’s your toys!”

“Oh, say, can Alex come out and play?” said Dennis.

“Why of course she can. Someone has to teach the boys to shoot straight.”

“Whooa…Ooh Rah!”

The team was quick to get dressed in their battle dress uniforms. This stuff was really cool. The sleek fit of the helmets and the uniforms made you feel energized. We looked great in this stuff if I have to say so myself. Talk about futuristic! As we approached the firing line we moved to our stations. There on the platform was a sleek backpack and rifle-shaped weapon. The backpack was made of a composite fiber, very lightweight, about five inches thick and was contoured to fit comfortably on your back. The weapon was connected to the backpack by a composite fiber mesh cable.

The weapon itself had a fold in stock and pistol grip so that it could be holstered to your hip. The barrel was hexagonal in shape with what looked like a slightly flared shot gun choke on the end of it. The trigger mechanism was biometrically activated. A smart chip was imbedded in the weapon system with every armed forces member’s biometric signature on it. The biometric function was designed to achieve either of two functions, weapon activation or weapon detonation. What was unique about the trigger mechanism was that it was not your traditional trigger that you would pull with your finger. It was activated by lightly squeezing the pistol grip. Another unique feature of the trigger mechanism was that how you squeezed the pistol grip would determine whether you would be in semi or automatic firing mode. A continuous squeeze put you in fully automatic firing mode.

As we donned our gear we buddy checked each other to ensure we were ready to go. As we approached the firing line we could see that Alex was focused and concentrated. This was the first time we witnessed the extra serious side of Alex. We had seen some tough instructors in our day. The look about Alex would definitely put her on that list.

"Gentlemen, today you will begin your qualifying round in the use of the Magnetic Pulse 100 series Weapon AKA, the MPW 100. It is an anti-personnel weapon with the capacity to take out small vehicles and electronic devices and disrupt communication systems, field radios, satellite and cell phones and the like. Over the next two weeks we will drill on targeting and firing this weapon in all conceivable conditions. For now, I will demonstrate targeting and firing at life sized targets from two hundred yards."

Alex stepped up to the firing line, dropped her helmet visor down over her eyes, un-holstered her weapon, quickly locked the pistol grip and rifle stock into position, raised it up just above her hip and fired.

We were expecting some sort of a loud weapon discharge with some sort of explosion at the target. All we heard was hiss reminiscent of someone disconnecting an air hose from filling a tire…Fhssst…and for the explosion, well; all we saw was an electrical discharge at the target, like static electricity you would see in the dark when removing a wool sweater. Alex raised her helmet visor and turned to the team.

"I thought we would get some sort of zap sound with a bang at the end. Wow, Alex, what gives?" asked Dennis.

Alex smiled. "Well, simply put, these smaller handheld weapons do not create the same plasma discharge as the larger weapons. You see, the larger the energy discharge, the more the air around the energy discharge is heated, thus giving you the loud noise. It's the same as a lightning discharge. The immense electrical discharge superheats the air around it thus giving off a loud noise, a thunder clap. Now let me ask you, what did you see?"

I stepped up and answered, "Well, I noticed that the energy from the discharge seemed to splatter on the target, like the paint balls that we shot at Doctor Detrich, only the energy seemed to distort the air, kind of like how the air is distorted when heat rises off a hot surface…I guess you could say it shimmers."

Paul chimed in, "Ya…you could see the trail of energy all the way to the target…I mean the air had a distorted look to it."

Alex smiled. "You're right. What you saw was the energy's disruption of the air molecules as it traveled at the speed of light to the target. Now, it's your turn. Let's get up to the firing line. We've got a lot of work to do."

Our first go at the MPW 100 was target acquisition and one energy pulse. Kind of a let's get acquainted with the weapon drill.

Like a drill sergeant Alex walked the firing line behind us giving commands. "Okay, gentlemen, on my mark. Drop your visors. Do not, I repeat do not un-holster your weapons." She said in a commanding voice. "First, you must visually select 'weapons system on.' Next, look at your target."

Alex paused for a few seconds. As we looked down range at our targets information streamed across our visors. The visor's binocular function brought the center of the target into close view. A faint iridescent blue spot appeared dead center on the target.

"Have you acquired your targets?" asked Alex.

"Ma'am, yes, ma'am!"

"Okay, gentlemen, keeping your target acquisition, unholster your weapons, raise them to a comfortable position to your sides, and squeeze off one energy pulse."

Instantly a hissing sound filled the air. Five direct hits on target.

"Stand down, gentlemen! Holster your weapons!"

"Ooh Rah, ma'am!"

We were abuzz with excitement. This was the most awesome weapon we had ever trained with. Alex could see we were primed and ready to go. She wasted no time meeting us at our energy level. She commenced to teach us targeting and firing techniques.

When our training got to the automatic firing aspect of the MPW 100's things got interesting. Alex put on a quick draw and fire presentation that would have scared any old west gunslinger. Alex challenged any one of the team to a timed quick draw and shoot contest. The goal was to see who could hit the five targets the fastest. Well, given his love for the old west, Paul couldn't resist the challenge.

"Okay, Alex, let's dance."

Paul stepped up to the firing line in a shoulder-wide stance.

He held his hands down by his hips shaking them to loosen his wrists. He moved his head in a circular motion to loosening the muscles in his neck, dropped his helmet's visor, and turned to Alex. "Howdy, ma'am. Say when."

"Okay, cowboy. Ready, draw!"

In an instant Paul had his weapon in position firing in a fanning motion. The technician timing him read the score. "Five hits in seven tenths of a second."

"Ooh Rah!"

Alex stepped up to where Paul was standing smiled at him. "Excuse me, partner," she said with a Texas drawl.

Alex dropped her visor. Took a shoulder-wide stance and looked back at Paul. "Okay, partner, say when."

"Ready…draw."

In an instant Alex's weapon was up and the targets were hit. The technician called out the score. "Two tenths of a second, five hits on target."

"She waxed you, man!" said Kym.

The team broke into a cheer. "Whooa, Ooh Rah, Alex!"

"You moved so fast I couldn't see you fan your shots at the targets," said Paul.

"I didn't need to fan my weapon," said Alex. "I let the targeting function do all the work."

As the team settled down Alex said, "Okay, gentlemen, back to your positions. I will teach you the multiple targeting technique that I used." Alex's teaching was superb. She didn't just talk the stuff she could walk the talk.

The days past fast. The next phase of our training introduced us to Gelatin Man. Gelatin Man was a manikin made up of gelatin substance. His purpose was to emulate the fleshy and watery consistency of the human body. Within this manikin was an electrical pulse system that was on the same equivalence of the human body's electrical impulses. Alex taught us that no matter where you hit Gelatin Man, the shot was always fatal. A total electrical system shut down. Even a slight graze would cause an instant shut down.

Our last week of training was when we got to fire larger wattage weapons. We fired vehicle-mounted weapons that would take out an aircraft, helicopter, armored personnel vehicles, large and small transports and tanks. Now we got into the weapons that made some noise. These weapons were so awesome that it was hard to believe that they were real.

As we trained we spent hours in the simulator. We practiced every conceivable firing situation and solution imaginable. The firing solution that really got us was when Alex demonstrated the rearview targeting technique. In a holographic scenario Alex walked into an ambush. As she was moving into position for her shots, two holographic warriors flanked her. Or so it seemed. As Alex moved in to score her hits on three targets, two opposing forces moved in behind her. What we didn't notice was as Alex paused to survey her targets the barrel of her MPW was tucked under her arm and was pointed directly behind her. As the two holographic warriors moved in for the score, Alex squeezed off two simulated bursts of energy. In an instant she not only scored the two hits behind her but also scored the three in front of her. Alex had targeted the two targets behind her by using the rearview function on her helmet.

Our two weeks of weapons training seemed to fly by. Graduation day was close at hand. Over the past six weeks we had learned a great deal from Doctor Detrich and Alex. We owed them a debt of gratitude for all they had done for us.

Several nights before graduation we all got together for a farewell bash. It was our usual bash with our usual crowd, the team, Alex and Doctor Detrich. The night was right. The music was lively. The company was right. It had the ear markings of a lot of fun. It was apparent that Paul and Angie had struck up quite a friendship. As for Dennis, Kym, and Neal well, they were your typical "Mustangs" roaming and playing the field. As for me and Alex, well, we had forged a friendship based on openness, trust and respect.

As the night progressed Alex seemed to be preoccupied with her thoughts. When the guys got into their antics of clowning around, Alex seemed to force her smile and laugh and drift off into her thoughts. She took a pass on several opportunities to dance. I hated seeing her like this. It just wasn't like Alex to be so down. A slow dance came up. I didn't give it a second thought. I stood up, grabbed her by the hand, and said, "Let's dance!"

So off to the dance floor we went. As we danced I could sense a difference in how our bodies met. Alex seemed to nuzzle into me. The way Alex held on to me was a dead giveaway that she had plenty on her mind. As we danced she would look up and smile at me. Her eyes said it all. She wanted to ask me something but she appeared to struggle getting the words together.

As we danced I gently stroked her hair and asked, "What's wrong, Alex? You haven't been yourself tonight."

"Oh, Sam…I…I just hate seeing you and the guys go…We had so much fun together and…well…it's just that you guys are not the average kind of guys. I mean, you guys are down to earth, not wrapped up in all that macho B.S. When I'm with you I can be me, no mind games or who's gonna outfox the other, we're just ourselves…" She buried her face in my chest.

As the dance was coming to an end Alex said, "So I guess you'll be going home on leave…right?"

I smiled and answered. "Well, I'm not sure what I'm going to do. My family is gonna be out of town so I thought I'd head up to Minnesota and get a few days of fishing in."

As if someone hit a switch Alex perked up. "Hey, I've got an idea! You can come to Chetek to my parents' farm. They've got plenty of room, a huge guest room. You can meet my family…And I can introduce you to Tucker! My dad's got connections to get you a charter flight from International Falls to Eau Claire. I can pick you up at the airport. We'll have a great time! Oh please say you'll come, Sam!"

"Well, welcome back, Alex! You were so quiet tonight you had me worried. I'd love to come!"

Alex's face lit up. For the rest of the evening she was a chatter box, laughing, dancing, and back to herself having fun.

Well, graduation day finally arrived. We spent the early part of the day saying goodbye to instructors and technicians. Doctor Detrich refused to say goodbye to us. He felt that goodbye was too permanent.

He preferred to say, "Ya…Und I vill see you later, until ve meet again!"

Knowing Doctor Detrich it wouldn't surprise me if he showed up on my doorstep some day. And if he did I'd be real happy to see him. As we shook hands and hugged I noticed that Angie and Paul were off to one side saying goodbye. There was no doubt that those two had struck a cord. Alex was busy hugging and saying goodbye to all my team members.

When she got to me she smiled and handed me an envelope and said, "I've got all the information you'll need in this envelope: my cell phone number, my parents number, the number to the aviation service at International Falls Airport…Oh ya, don't forget to call me when you get home. I don't want to be worried not knowing if you made it or not."

I just smiled and laughed as Alex reeled off all she had to say.

Home On Leave

It took the better part of the day to get home to Baudette. Nothing ever changed in this small town. No...come to think of it something did change. It appeared that "Willie the Walleye" got a new paint job. Willie was a statue of a walleye pike. A giant walleye pike! Probably thirty feet long head to tail. Over the years that fish had more pictures taken than any super model I could name. Any fisherman fishing the Lake of the Woods or the Rainy River knew that their "Right of Passage" to being considered a true outdoors person meant that they had to have their picture taken with the infamous "Willie the Walleye."

In any event it was good to be home. It was my plan to kick back, do some serious fishing and get my head clear...to get some perspective on things. I just couldn't get Alex out of my mind. She was an enigma to me. Our time together was just so right. Even when we disagreed about something the way we respectfully disagreed was awesome...a debate without an argument. The way we went out of our way to make sure the other's needs were met was remarkable...a caring and selfless way of treating each other. Yet Alex's heart belonged to Tucker.

Those of us who lived along the Rainy River had the privilege of living on a wildlife sanctuary. As one sat and took in the fresh air, peace, and tranquility, it was not uncommon to see all types of critters run the shoreline, water fowl swim by or resident Bald Eagles patrol the river's shoreline. This was a great place and opportunity to sort things out.

I knew in my heart that Alex and I met for a reason. I just couldn't figure how to get this relationship from friends to permanent partners. I was going to wait in the wings to see if Alex and Tucker were going to make it. No matter what, I knew that I had to let things take their natural course. Forcing the issue was the worst thing that I could do. I wasn't going to take the chance and ruin or complicate things for Alex. Worse yet, I wasn't going to risk losing what I had established with her: a great friendship.

I wasted no time launching my dad's sixteen-foot boat and setting off for some serious fishing. I hit a great day for fishing. The larger walleye were in the river and they were feisty. In no time at all I caught a meal of good-sized walleye. As I was cooking my dinner and contemplating my time with Alex the phone rang.

"Hello, D'Angelo's."

The sweetest voice I had ever heard replied, "Hi, Sam, how's fishing?"

Hearing her voice made my heart jump. "Oh, hi, Alex!" I responded. "The fishing's great. I'm cooking some walleye right now…do you want some?"

Alex laughed. "I'd love some. Will you cook it for me?"

I couldn't help myself the words seemed to slip right out of my mouth…"I'd do anything for you, Alex." I thought I'd die. "I mean…I'd be happy to cook for you."

She didn't seem to notice. "Sam, if a charter flight could pick you up in a few hours would come to Wisconsin today?"

"Oh ya I would…I guess."

"Good! Head for the airport.…The charter flight is waiting for you."

"No way! Your dad must be one connected dude."

Alex laughed. "More than you could ever know. Come on, Sam, get your tail down here. We've got a great time planned. I'll see you in a few hours."

I hastily ate some fish, wrapped up several good-sized filets and packed them in ice, showered, shaved, grabbed my gear and was off.

It took me about an hour to get to the airport. Given that International Falls is a one-gate airport I knew I would have no problems getting to Iverson Aviation. As I entered I noticed an air crew, pilot and copilot, sitting in the lounge area. As I walked into the area, one of them looked up and saw me. He said something to the other crew member as he pointed in my direction. As they stood up and straightened their ties and uniforms I approached them.

"Hi, I'm Sam D'Angelo. I'm supposed to catch a commuter flight to Eau Claire. Are you the crew flying me down?"

The pilot smiled and answered. "Yes, sir, we are. I'm Captain Ben Anderson; this is my copilot, Ed White."

I shook hands with both crew members and started to the flight line.

Ed spoke up, "Please, sir, I'll carry your luggage."

"Oh, that's okay, Ed. I've been toting this stuff ever since I left home. Thanks anyway."

As I relaxed into my seat, Gabrielle, the flight attendant, glanced over at me and smiled. "You must be someone very special. We have our orders to make sure you are comfortable and delivered on time to Eau Claire."

"Oh," I replied, "I'm meeting Alex King in Eau Claire…I guess her dad is pretty connected…"

She chuckled. "Oh yes, you could safely say Jon King has connections."

I didn't really understand what Gabrielle meant but I smiled to be polite.

I took the crew's advice and sat back and enjoyed the flight. As I gazed out of my window to the horizon I began to contemplate how my visit with Alex would go. I had no reservations about meeting her family. I felt pretty confident that I would be comfortable with them. By Alex's description we both seemed to come from families with similar beliefs and values. What I was really struggling with was the thought of meeting Tucker.

Talk about mixed feelings. I was in the throws of a gigantic emotional battle with myself. As my pulse increased with each passing moment I thought to myself, Get a grip, boy! You're supposed to be a rough and tough Special Ops guy. Not a love sick puppy!

The anticipation of seeing Alex was overpowering me. I chuckled to myself as my anticipation grew into sheer excitement. I did my best to conceal my excitement. I didn't want to appear overly anxious. I think Gabrielle could read my thoughts. Every time she'd look over at me her grin said, "I know who Sammy likes!" Was I that obvious?

As the jet's wheels touched down and the engines roared from their thrusting I knew that the hour had arrived. To help me out of my private "pity party" I instantly recalled the promise that I made to myself about not interfering with Alex and Tucker.

As I stepped outside the aircraft's door I could see Alex inside the terminal smiling and waving. I smiled, waved, and winked at Alex then headed down the aircraft steps. Grinning like a school boy I entered the one room terminal. The sight of her made my heart race. She ran up and we hugged. That smile, those eyes, I was putty in her hands.

"Oh, Sam, you've made my week! I can't tell you how glad I am that you came. I've got a great week planned out…"

I grabbed my luggage and in a flash Alex led the way to her vehicle. On the way to her vehicle Alex, in her usual playful style, got into step with me and playfully would bump her hip into my side as we walked. At this point I didn't care what we did or where we went. All I knew was that I was with Alex and I was going to savor every minute.

As we approached the parking lot Alex pointed to a new SUV. "There's our ride."

I could see her family's company name on the vehicle. I smiled and answered her, "Ah…King's Enterprise LLC. Are you going to give me a tour of the business?"

"You bet! Dad has that all set up. But first we need to get you home, get you settled in and get on with some introductions."

As we drove north to Chetek we were so at ease with each other…our mannerisms, our free flowing communications, our likes and dislikes…I knew in my heart of hearts that we were supposed to be together.

In a lull in our discussion Alex turned to me and softly asked, "Sam, what do you want out of life?"

I wanted to grab her, kiss her, squeeze her, and tell her

"You…I want you in my life forever!" Knowing that would ruin everything I quickly composed my thoughts. I reached over and gently touched her arm. "I want the woman of my dreams to love me as much as I love her."

"Sam, there is no doubt in my mind that you will find that happiness." I just sighed. Not if it's not you, Alex, I thought.

As we drove along the front property line I was mesmerized by the ivy-covered stone wall that led to the driveway. It stretched for one half of a mile split in the middle by an arch way that resembled the entrance to a royal castle.

"This is absolutely gorgeous," I said.

The stone walls came up to two stone pedestals, lighting built into them, with intricately woven wrought iron lace that spanned across the width of the driveway. The wrought iron archway had the name King centered within it.

The well-groomed stone driveway was lined with huge maple trees like sentries guarding the castle. As we drove under the leafy canopy it gave the feeling of driving through a tunnel. There at the end of the leafy tunnel was a majestic home. Its structure of roof lines, porches, walkout balconies, and dormers was breathtaking. The home was made of the same stone and the front walls were made of natural wood. The landscaping of shrubs, roses, and all types of flowers was near indescribable—small sitting areas with wood and wrought iron benches placed throughout all of the natural beauty.

As we approached the house I could see that the drive way turned into a circle with garages for the vehicles off to the side. It seemed like everywhere I looked there was a pathway that led to a small garden and sitting area. Some of them had hitching posts to tie horses to. There in the middle of the circular drive way was a fountain and pond. Alex explained that the pond contained all types of exotic gold fish just waiting for a visitor to come and feed them.

Off to the side and rear of the home were several buildings that were as equally stunning as the house. Alex pointed at them and said, "Those are the stables. We'll be spending a lot of time there."

I smiled and said, "Fine with me. I'm looking forward to some serious horseback riding."

Alex smiled and said, "I'll give you the grand tour of the back eighty acres."

I laughed. "More like the back eight thousand acres."

We both laughed and prepared to head into the house.

As we walked up the front walkway to the front porch the door opened. It was Alex's mother. She smiled as we approached. As we stepped inside the house Alex's mother greeted me with open arms. Without hesitation I stepped in and hugged the woman.

She turned to Alex and said, "Oh my Alex, he is just as you described him…Tall, dark and handsome! And he gives good hugs!"

"It's a pleasure to meet you, ma'am."

Alex's mother laughed. "Please, Sam, call me Elsie."

The entranceway led to a room that was awesome. The atrium effect, natural woods, the ten-foot-wide granite fireplace and furnishings gave this room a touch that could only be described as "total class."

As we entered the room Elsie said, "Sam, this is the grand sitting room. It is where we as a family meet and share our thoughts and daily experiences. We'd like you to join us this evening."

"I'd be honored to join you and your family this evening."

After being shown to my room, I quickly unpacked and headed downstairs. As I was entering the kitchen I could hear Alex and her mom laughing.

"Are you two behaving yourselves?" I asked.

"We'll never tell," replied Alex. Alex quickly got to her feet and took hold of my hand. "Come on, we have to get you introduced to the gang and the love of my life!"

Hearing this made my heart sink. I forced a smile and answered, "Oh…ya, I've been waiting to meet Tucker."

Alex turned to her mom, "Where's he at?"

Elsie answered, "I think I saw him leading a few horses into stable one."

I was about to meet the one and only obstacle between me and Alex. All my adult life as an Air Force PJ I was trained to adapt and overcome battlefield conditions and obstacles. I felt helpless in this situation. I knew if I tried to overcome this obstacle I would hurt Alex. I just couldn't do that.

As we headed down the well-groomed stone path to the stable I felt like I was being led to the gallows. My pace slowed as I had second thoughts about meeting Tucker. Alex seemed oblivious to my pain. At one point just before we got to the stable I suddenly had an urge to tell the truth to Alex.

I stopped and turned Alex toward me. Looking down at her I held both her hands and began to speak. "Alex…I…"

Alex looked up at me and softly smiled, squeezed my hands, looked into my eyes and caringly said, "What is it, Sam?"

I continued, "I...I'm really glad you invited me here." What a recovery! I nearly blew it!

Alex smiled and said, "I can't tell you how happy you made me by coming."

I fought the impulse to grab her and kiss her and to tell her that I loved her more than anything in life. I took a few deep breaths to gain my composure before we entered the stable.

As we entered I could see the silhouette of someone moving and stacking hay bales. That someone turned toward us with a "surprised-to-see-you" smile on his face. "Alex! Come to help!?"

Alex laughed, then moved quickly toward the cowboy and jumped into his arms. The cowboy lifted her up in his embrace and swung her around as they both laughed. Seeing this made me feel totally out of place. I swallowed hard as my pulse elevated. This was the moment that I was dreading. As the cowboy put Alex down they both turned to me.

Alex looked up at the cowboy and said, "There's someone I want you to meet."

With arms around each other, they walked forward to begin the introductions. My eyes quickly scanned the big guy top to bottom. This guy had to be six feet six inches tall with his cowboy boots on, was lean and well cut, an athlete for sure, and was in his later twenties. To add insult to injury he was a handsome devil. Just the way Alex described her "Tucker."

I figured I'd at least be a good sport about things. I smiled and extended my hand. "Hello, I'm Sam D'Angelo."

The War Begins

As the aircrew made preparations for our landing in the Iraqi desert near the Kuwaiti border I drifted back from my memories to the present. Colonel Beckworth passed through the cabin checking up on his teams.

"How are you boys doing?" he asked.

"Tired from the long flight," we commented. "It will be good to get on the ground, sir."

Beckworth smiled and patted a few of the troops on the shoulder as he passed through the cabin.

Moments later the aircraft touched down and rolled into the flight line area. Outside the aircraft we could see the ground crew hustle in refueling and preparing this bird for flight. As the aircraft's tail ramp was lowered we could feel the cool night air rush in. It struck us to be strange that the desert could be so hot in the day and cool at night.

As we headed off the aircraft several transport vehicles were waiting to take us to command for a briefing. We tossed our gear into the vehicles, piled in and were off to the command center. As we entered the command center we saw several other teams that we had trained with state side. As our eyes caught each others eyes we nodded in recognition of each others presence. Colonel Beckworth joined the other officers at the front of the room.

As we settled in an Army Major General, Prasad Durrani,

stepped forward to address the troops. With his deep booming voice he addressed the teams.

"Men, as you are aware the Iranians have drawn first blood on the United States…a situation that we will soon remedy. You gentlemen are the messengers that are going to deliver our response to such arrogance. Your mission will be to enter into country and deploy our MAGS technology. Each team will be strategically deployed within country to ensure maximum weapons effect. Our teams have been flying high-altitude recon missions around the clock all over the country. The Iranians have all but given up chasing our spy planes. We believe this should give you the advantage you'll need to HALO into your positions. Once on the ground you will GPS your way into positions. There you will find that SEAL teams have been in country and have cached supplies for your weeks stay in country."

The general stepped to the side and signaled his aids to begin the holographic briefing. Instantly a holographic map of Iran appeared. As the general stepped into the map area he paused, looked down, and then addressed the teams.

"Men, as you can see from our virtual tour of this battlefield several teams are going to be deployed deep inside country. Our analysts have concluded that the deeper a team is inserted into country the higher the probability that they will not make it out of country. Before I ask any man to take such a risk I ask that you search your heart as to the cause that your country has called you to do."

As the general spoke I turned and looked at my team to see what they wanted to do. The look on their faces said it all. "This is our job, boss."

Hearing that, I stood up and said, "Ooh Rah! Sir, my team is ready for the job."

No sooner did the words come out of my mouth than Templeton, Brodrick, Swenson, and Gomez stood up and replied, "Ooh Rah! Sir, our teams are ready for the job."

The General's face went from a rock hard warrior's look to a huge smile. He turned to Colonel Beckworth and said, "Outstanding, troops! For the remainder of the briefing we will break into groups. The deep insertion teams will be briefed by Colonel Beckworth and Commander Westfall, Navy SEAL group Commander. For the rest of the teams we'll take a roll call and send you to your respective briefing areas. Good hunting, gentlemen!"

Colonel Beckworth and Commander Westfall left the stage area and approached our teams. Westfall said, "Follow me, men. We'll brief in my command tent."

As we headed to Commander Westfall's command tent, Bronson Templeton called to me. "Hey, Cap. You didn't think you were going to go on vacation without us did you?"

I laughed. "Why, Bronson, I wouldn't think of anything so ridiculous. I was just about to invite you guys to join us for a fun week in the desert."

As we gathered inside Commander Westfall's command tent for our briefing I could sense that the teams were focused and ready for business. Beckworth and Westfall stood in the center of the room while we stood around them in a circle. A holographic map appeared in the center of the room. Within the map were five stars denoting the positions we would be taking in country.

Commander Westfall looked at the teams and said, "Well,

gentlemen, we need to assign each team to one of these starred positions."

"Sir, my team will take this position right here," I said as I pointed to the most interior position.

"Very good, Captain D'Angelo. Now what about the rest of you?"

Each team quickly selected their positions and we spent the next hour discussing deployment tactics as well as extraction from the field. As we were winding down our discussion Commander Westfall said, "Remember, men, your mission is not to engage the enemy. Your mission is to remain invisible to the enemy, observe enemy troop movement, and deploy the MAG technology and get to the extraction point safely. The toughest part of this mission will be your extraction."

Pointing at the holographic map Westfall said, "You must get to this point to reach the chopper that will get you out of country." He turned to me and said, "D'Angelo, you and your team have the farthest to go to get to the extraction point. We will make sure that a chopper loiters for an extra two days to get you out. However, if you don't make it on time you're on your own. The landing zone will be too hot to extract you. Your best bet will be to head for the Gulf, the Straits of Hormuz. You will find our forces guarding the straits. Outside of that I want to wish you all Godspeed and good luck. Now go get some rest. We have a busy schedule of mission preparation ahead of us."

The team was pretty quiet as we headed to our billeting for the night. More than likely they were preoccupied with our mission. The reality of the situation was setting in for each of us.

As we entered the billeting area Paul looked at me and said, "This is the real deal, boss…Exactly what we have trained for."

I smiled and replied, "Damn straight, Sergeant. One thing is for sure: we're going to complete this mission one hundred percent. That includes our safe return home. I'm going into this mission with the highest skilled, best trained Special Ops team in the business. There is no way we are going to fail. It's a matter of fact, pass the word through the team—fail is the worst four letter 'F' word a team member could use. It sure as hell is not an option we can even consider."

The night was full of sounds of activity. Aircraft of all types were taking off and landing. Vehicles moving troops and equipment hustled on and off the base. As I lay in my bunk I let the night sounds play to my advantage and drifted off to sleep.

Over the next two days we spent time training in a holographic simulator. We spent hours each day rehearsing our deployment. The training program was an artificial intelligence program. It learned from your tactics and adjusted the difficulty of its scenarios accordingly. Its sole purpose was to present the trainees with the most difficult situations imaginable…to stretch their capabilities well beyond what the trainees thought possible. By the end of day two we had run the gauntlet. We beat the computer scenarios. We knew that we would be deployed the next day.

At 0700 the next morning I met the team for chow. We all seemed to be upbeat and ready to go. We had a full day of equipment checks and rehashing of our deployment plans ahead of us. We discussed and planned our activities, taking in all possible scenarios. Our goal was to ensure that we were flexible in our planning and would be able to adapt and to improvise accordingly.

All our preparing was for our HALO jump later that evening. The only thing that truly bothered us all was, for obvious security reasons, we were under a communications black out. No messages could come in or go out of the base. Other than that the team was focused and ready for the mission.

At 2100 we headed for the flight line to board a C-130. As we donned our equipment and checked each other's harnesses and packs I could sense the adrenaline in each of us. My senses were acute. I felt so in tune with my surroundings that it was surreal.

My team and I were the first to board the air craft. We were carrying an additional ninety pounds. As we walked, waddled really, up the tail ramp to board the aircraft, Dennis started making quacking sounds.

"Now what?" Neal asked.

Dennis chuckled and pointed to the bottom of the ramp, "Check it out!"

As each troop started up the ramp Dennis timed his quacking sounds to the steps the teams were taking. With each waddle Dennis would quack.

Dennis laughed and said, "Why, it's the great march of the penguins!"

As the last team joined us the crew chief closed the tail ramp and signaled the pilots that we were secured and ready for take off. As we sat down and prepared for the flight Colonel Beckworth came back to address the troops.

"Men, today you will be participating in writing a new chapter in warfare. The weaponry that you will assist in unleashing is a century ahead of any known weaponry. Let history show that we fought gallantly with honor and distinction. I am honored and proud to be your commander. You truly represent some of the finest our country has to offer. Good luck! Godspeed! And most importantly come home safely!"

All teams responded, "Ooh, Rah!"

Colonel Beckworth saluted the teams, turned, and headed forward to the pilot's cabin. A moment later the aircraft engines begin to whine. Outside the aircraft we could see the ground crew hustle in directing us for take off. Several moments later we could hear the rush of the engines and feel the initial rush of speed as we headed down the runway. Instantly we were off the ground heading to our drop zones.

As we flew I looked around the aircraft at each team and their members. As I looked around I couldn't help recall something unique I remembered about each troop. I knew in my heart that there was a real possibility that some of us were not going to make it home. It took something like this to get a person to see the good in his fellow man.

Suddenly the get ready to jump signal was given. This meant that team one, Gomez's team, was up for deployment. We put on our oxygen to get ready for the aircraft to be depressurized and to make our jump.

The crew chief lowered the tail ramp and signaled for team one to prepare to jump. Gomez and team stepped to the rear and prepared to jump. The signal light turned green and the crew chief gave the verbal command, "Go! Go! Go!"

In a flash the Gomez team disappeared into the night.

The crew chief then gave the command, "Team two, prepare to jump!"

The Swenson team moved to the rear of the aircraft. About five minutes later the signal to jump is given.

The crew chief repeated his jump command, "Go! Go! Go!"

Instantly, the Swenson team disappeared into the night. Five minutes later the crew chief followed the same procedure and the Brodrick team was out of the aircraft and disappeared into the night.

As the Templeton team moved to the rear of the aircraft to prepare to make their jump, Templeton turned to me and said, "Hey, Cap! First round is on me when we get back!"

My team all gave Bronson the thumbs-up sign. A moment later Templeton and his team were given the signal to make their jump. They instantly disappeared into the night sky.

The crew chief turned to me and signaled with his open hand, five minutes to drop zone. He then signaled me and my team to prepare to make our jump. Moments later we were at the back of the aircraft preparing to jump. Just as the crew chief gave us the command to jump, I turned to the team and said, "Brothers till the end!'

"Brothers till the end!" they replied. We then disappeared into the night sky.

As we had practiced so many times before, we went through our free fall period, deployed our chutes, and glided to our drop zone. Only this time we knew on the way down that our feet wouldn't touch down in a practice area back home. No vehicles waiting to pick us up and to take us back to base. As Paul put it, "This was the real deal." We were landing in enemy territory.

As we were briefed, the Iranians had deployed hunter killer groups throughout their country with one purpose in mind. To hunt down and kill U.S. Special Operations Teams. Our mission seemed simple enough during our briefing…to get on the ground, get organized, get into position, and hunker down. However, in reality it was going to be tough to complete.

As I hit the ground and got to my feet I wasted no time gathering my chute. As I prepared to bury my chute, one by one I could hear the thumps to the ground close by as the rest of the team made their landing. The adrenaline was pumping so hard in me I felt like I was on fast forward. I had to stop for a second, center myself, and then let my instincts and training take over.

In no time I had my jump suit and chute buried; having done so I immediately donned the rest of my gear. As my helmet's telemetry began to readout and my "Ever Light" system adjusted to the dark conditions, I could see that we hit the bull's eye in hitting our drop zone. There couldn't have been but a hundred yards between me and the furthest member to land, Dennis.

As the team got themselves squared up we met for one last briefing. Hiding in a small rock outcrop area, I began my briefing. With the team standing around me, map in hand and pointing to a spot on the map, I said in a quiet tone, "Okay, men, given the GPS coordinates I am reading we are here. We have to track north and east two kliks to this way point. This is our supply cache. After that we split up to deploy to our respective positions. Synchronize your watches on my mark."

I counted down and gave the signal to synchronize watches. I then began my final comments in my briefing. "Remember, you will be sending cryptic data back to command on your observations. No matter what happens you must complete your portion of the mission. Set up your MAGS no matter what. Once this thing is over we're out of here. Our return route allows us to catch up to each other here," I said, pointing to a coordinate on the map. "We will keep in communications every day. I will key my mic twice at 2100 every night. I'll wait for your responses before we communicate. If you've got a few bad guys in the neighborhood key your mic once the rest of us will wait for you to give us the all clear sign… two clicks of your mic."

After my briefing I gave the signal to move out to our first objective, the cache of supplies. I motioned with hand signals that I would take the lead position of point man. No sooner did I do that than Paul grabbed me by my shoulder, turned me, and with a hand motion put his open hand on his chest in a patting motion then pointed with the same open hand forward signaling he was going to take the point. I responded with a smile and nod, and pointed forward signaling to Paul that he would take the point.

Our maps showed that we could follow the rock outcrop straight to our cache of supplies. We made a cautious yet expeditious beeline for our objective. As we moved toward our objective Paul positioned himself several hundred yards ahead of us. As forward observer he was the eyes and ears of the team. It was his job to get into position, observe the area, and determine if it was safe for us to approach the area.

As Paul found a vantage point to observe our objective from, he reconnoitered several enemy troops. He quietly radioed back to the team. "Top Dog, this is Big Dog One, over."

There is a slight pause and then Sam answered. "Big Dog One, this is Top Dog. I copy, over."

Paul reported his observations. "Top Dog, we have hunter killers in the neighborhood. I repeat, HKs in the neighborhood. I count five…no…check that, I count seven HKs, over."

"Big Dog One, we are vectoring into your position, out."

As we cautiously approached Paul's position we could see the seven HKs hunkered down about one hundred yards from our supplies cache. It was decision time. Do we sit and wait them out and risk not getting to our objectives on time, or do we engage them? One thing was for sure: even with our new composite BDUs, if we didn't at least recover the water supply that was cached for us we'd never survive a week in the desert. Our decision was obvious. We had to take the HKs out.

Using hand signals I deployed the team into position for our attack. Like a pack of wolves stalking and hunting prey we closed in for the kill. As we closed in we used our targeting function on our weapons system to paint each target. Before giving the command to fire I checked the status of each of the team members. When they signaled that they were in position and ready I gave the command to fire.

The night air filled with the muffled sound of the MPWs firing multiple energy bursts, fhsst, fhsst, fhsst.

Instantly, we could see the multiple hits on the targets as the static charges dissipated, the seven HKs fell dead. I gave the command to move forward cautiously. Although we didn't have enough time to bury the dead, we knew that we had to conceal the bodies. As we moved into the encampment I told the team to search for any useful intel. As we searched the area

Kym noticed that the HKs had early generation night-vision technology.

He picked up a set of goggles and said, "Hey, Cap, these guys have night-vision capabilities. We'd better keep a real sharp look out."

I acknowledged Kym's find with a thumbs-up.

As we searched the deceased, Kym, thinking quickly, took a communications unit off one of the deceased troops.

Neal pat Kym on the shoulder and said, "Good thinking, dude. You can keep tabs on the bad guys for us."

I motioned to the team to move the bodies and equipment into the rocky area. It was our hope that these guys would remain missing for a few days. This would buy us the time we needed to disappear and set up in our positions. As we were moving the deceased troops all hell seemed to break lose.

In one quick motion Paul yells, "Look out!" Turned around with what seemed like the speed of light, drew and fired his MPW, fhsst.

There closing in on us was the eighth HK coming in from a one-man recon patrol. Dennis turned to Paul and said, "Damn, Tex! You showed him whose sheriff in these parts."

With a sigh of relief Paul said, "The rear view function on these helmets is awesome. We were had by this guy. He came out of nowhere."

Gathering their thoughts and preparing to split up, the team hurriedly finished their business.

After concealing the deceased we quickly got to our supplies. After we all loaded up with supplies and prepared to leave, the five of us raised our right fists shoulder high in a salute and said, "Bothers till the end." At that we all made our ways to our respective positions.

As we split up the stark reality of being alone hit me. What an empty feeling it was. All that kept running through my mind was that I had to complete this mission and make it home. These thoughts helped me make great time heading to my position. As I arrived at my GPS coordinates I saw that I had a rocky outcrop to hide in. That was comforting. I immediately began deploying my MAGS. I found a great spot within the rocks to set up in. It gave me a vantage point as well as pretty good cover. After deploying my MAGS I hunkered down for the long haul. After settling in I sent a cryptic message to command that I was in position with MAGS deployed.

I must say that my first full day in country seemed like a week. I was exhausted. Considering what we went through the night before I'd say we put in a tough night. I sat back and reflected on how rigorously we trained over the years. Now I could fully appreciate the training and how it paid off.

A sense of upbeat anticipation came over me as 2100 hours approached. I looked forward to hearing from the team. As my watch reached 2100 hours I keyed my mic twice and paused. Seconds later I could hear in my ear piece two clicks, then again two clicks, then again two clicks and finally the fourth set of clicks.

I then spoke, "Big Dog one, copy."

Paul answered, "Roger that, Top Dog, all is quiet, some aerial surveillance, nothing on the ground yet."

I responded, "Copy that, Big Dog one. Stay safe. Big Dog two copy."

In my ear piece Dennis answered, "I copy, Top Dog, no activity here."

I answered, "Ten-four, Big Dog Two. Stay safe. Big Dog Three, do you copy?" I listened expecting Kym's response. However, all I got was a one click of his mic. I paused and waited. About one half hour later, my thoughts were broken by a voice in my ear piece.

"Top Dog, this is Big Dog Three…Do you copy?"

I smiled in relief as I answered, "Big Dog Three, what's your status?"

Kym answered, "Several HKs passing through the neighborhood…be advised they have found the packages we hid (referring to the deceased troops). They are searching for whoever wrapped and hid the packages…over."

I responded. "I copy, Big Dog Three. Any communications chatter? Over."

"Negative, Top Dog. Nothing noteworthy."

"Big Dog Four, what's your status…over?"

Neal responded. "Nothing new here Top Dog everything is copasetic. Over."

Instantly, my ear piece came alive with chatter. Dennis came through loud and clear. "What the hell! Over…Copasetic! Dude, couldn't you just say things are fine?"

I smiled, glad to see the team still had their sense of humor in tact. We signed off until our next communications. I immediately activated my satellite phone and dialed into a cryptic frequency. I began my broadcast to headquarters back in the Iraqi desert. "Broad Sword…Broad Sword, this is Alpha Team Leader over." I paused for a few seconds and repeated the call to headquarters.

A few seconds later Commander Westfall answered, "Alpha Team Leader, this is Broad Sword, copy."

I responded. "Broad Sword, good to hear your voice, I have a status report…we are deployed. We met some resistance on the way in. We engaged the enemy, no team casualties. KIA eight HKs. HK teams are searching for us. We have evaded their search. No activity to report. Will broadcast at same time tomorrow. Alpha Team Leader out."

Broad Sword answered. "Good job, Alpha Team Leader…Keep your heads down. Broad Sword out."

Day two and three brought more of the same. We patiently observed for enemy activities yet there was little to report. Per our usual routine we would communicate our observations then I would relay the information off to Broad Sword. Outside of being a little bored, I was able to catch up on some letter writing. I wrote a few letters to my family and a couple well thought out letters to Alex.

Day four started off about the same as the past several days…no activity on the ground with a few aircraft flyovers but nothing out of the ordinary. As I sat observing my surroundings I couldn't help but notice that the area under my umbrella of invisibility seemed to be robust with small plant life.

As I sat observing the horizon I spotted a heavy convoy moving in my direction. Now what do we have here? This was no small convoy. Major movement of troops and equipment. They seemed to be fortifying positions along a ridge to the north of me…a great vantage point to hunker down in the hills and fire down into the valley area. I noticed that several small groups broke off from the main column and headed south toward the general area where my team and I were deployed.

About an hour later I heard a vehicle approaching. It slowed to a stop about fifty yards from my position. Eight well-armed troops climbed off the back of the vehicle. Each one was wearing night-vision goggles. No doubt this was a hunter killer team deploying. As the troops got off the vehicle they scanned the area. One troop in particular made the hair on the back of my neck stand up. He stopped his scanning and stared at my position. My heart raced as I thought for sure he had made my position. I hunkered down, made multiple target acquisitions...made sure that the blue targeting dot in my visor was squarely on each troop and set my MPW to fully automatic.

The team leader called to his troop and seemed to break his concentration. The troop turned slowly away from gazing in my direction and headed to the area where his team had gathered. Given that my Arabic was limited, I could only make out that the leader had the two-man vehicle crew stay behind to set up camp for the night while he and his team went hunting. I stayed hunkered down; waited, and observed...after all, I had nowhere in particular to go.

At 2100 hours I keyed my mic once to signal the team that I had company. As I sat, listened, and observed, the HK team entered the camp. The team that stayed behind had prepared a hot beverage for the team. I believe it was tea. As the two crew members poured the hot drink for each member the HK team settled in for some relaxation and shut eye. I activated my systems' eavesdropping mode and listened into their conversation. The leader seemed to be the introverted serious type. He seemed to sit back and take in what was being said and then he'd make his comments. From what I could tell, the team was frustrated that they knew we landed but had eluded them ever since. If my translation was correct one of the team members called us "Infidel Gophers."

What seemed to really confuse them was the fact that the U.S. had not started its air campaign yet. They figured we'd be pounding them the same way we conducted Gulf wars I and II.

As the team settled in I noticed that the same troop that had stared at my position earlier that day was doing it again. This guy was spooking me out! I knew he couldn't see me but he sure seemed interested in my position. I sat comfortably behind a few rocks; however, I knew I had to keep an eye on this guy. So to be safe I once again targeted each troop, set my MPW to fully automatic, waited, watched, and listened.

All of a sudden, as if someone had given the troop a hot foot, he jumped up and cursed in Arabic "May the great Satan be crushed!" He then screamed, "The walls are looking at me!" and he began firing in the direction of my position.

Knowing a world of hurt was about to happen, I quickly laid on my left side. Given that my system was in eavesdrop mode the automatic weapons fire sounded like cannon fire. Like a hoard of angry hornets, bullets flew and ricocheted everywhere. What a light show, sparks everywhere. All of a sudden, I felt a hot searing sensation across my backside. I did everything I could do from yelling out. Damn! I felt like I'd been branded with a hot iron.

The team leader jumped up and gave his troop the order to stand down. He then grabbed the troop by the lapels and shook him. He proceeded to read the man the riot act. What I could make out was that the leader reminded the troop that, although they were hunting us, stupid moves like this could give their position away and make them the hunted. He then told the troop to get some rest and to quit acting dumber than the rocks he just shot at.

As I lay in position with my back side burning and stinging. I reached back to feel the damage. Well, to say the least my wound was pretty raw. I was lucky that it was a graze, just enough to scorch me good and leave one hell of a welt. The only problem I could think of with this situation was where the wound was located. Don't get me wrong, I was glad to be alive. It was just that being wounded in the butt didn't seem real dignified.

Just after day break the next morning the HK team broke camp and moved on. Now that I was free to move around I retrieved my first aid kit from my backpack. I grabbed some gauze and antibacterial cream. I laughed as I tried to see my wound. I grabbed a small mirror out of my pack, held it in position and craned my neck over my right shoulder to get a glimpse of the damage. I could hardly make out the extent of the damage. All I knew was it was uncomfortable to sit on my right butt cheek.

As the time passed I couldn't help but feel cramped and anxious. It had been five days since we had gotten into position and yet nothing was happening. I knew that the U.S. had a plan but man! The suspense was killing me.

As dusk approached I glanced at my watch. I thought to myself, "Hmm…a few more hours and I'll check in with the team and Broad Sword. I'm sure their wondering where I was last night." All of a sudden in the distance I could see flashes of light on the horizon and could hear the rumble of heavy explosions. I wasn't sure if it was incoming or outgoing ordinance. All I knew was this was it. The shooting war had begun.

At 2100 hours I keyed my mic twice to signal the team. Instantly they gave the all clear signal to me. I dispensed with the individual communications and spoke to the entire team, "Big Dogs…The party has started. How's the HK situation in your neighborhood?"

Each member responded with the same report. "Heavy HK activity in the neighborhood."

Paul then asked, "How about your neighborhood, Top Dog?"

I paused to think of my response and then responded. "Ah…some activity. Nothing too exciting."

As we wound down our discussion I rehashed our extraction plan with the team. "Remember, Big Dogs, after our mission is completed we are to high-tail it back to our rendezvous site. Keep open communication lines as you head back. We can keep tabs on how each of us doing. Remember, any trouble along the way or if the rendezvous site is compromised head for the extraction point. We'll catch up there. Are you clear on this?"

Each team member acknowledged the directive with a "Roger that, Top Dog."

I responded. "Things are going to happen fast, stay alert and stay safe. See you back at the ranch!"

Each team member acknowledged with two clicks of their microphones.

Shortly after my communications with the team I set up my satellite phone and called Broad Sword.

Broad Sword quickly answered my call, "Alpha Team Leader we copy you. Be advised the dance has started. What's your assessment of the area?"

"Broad Sword, we have heavy build up of troops and equipment both north and south of our positions. They are hunkered down preparing for the long haul."

Broad Sword responded. "We copy that, Alpha Team Leader. Godspeed, get home safe. Broad Sword out."

I responded, "Roger that Broad Sword, Alpha Team Leader out."

As I sat and observed out to the horizon with each passing moment the flashes and rumbling sounds intensified. I could hear aircraft passing over, anti-aircraft guns firing, missiles being launched into the night sky and sporadic weapons fire coming in all directions. Things were happening fast. Yet I knew that in all of this chaos a well thought out and executed plan was happening. I knew that it was a matter of hours before our MAGS would do their part in this war.

As predicted at 0300 hours the holographic show began. I was watching the history of warfare change forever. I watched in awe, an entire army began to assemble right before my eyes. A combination of air drops of men and equipment, choppers flying in and out, as well as several touch and go air drops of equipment. Or so it appeared.

As the holographic program was playing itself out, the Iranian troops from the north and south were totally dismayed. They immediately turned to rush their forces in an all-out attack on the U.S forces. The holographic program moved to phase two. As planned, the program superimposed the image of the U.S forces onto each of the advancing Iranian Armies.

Each advancing army began to charge at what appeared to be U.S. forces.

The battle that ensued was nothing short of destruction in a biblical sense. In this one battle tens of thousands of Iranian troops perished. Not one U.S. troop was lost. It was a staggering defeat in any sense of the word. The Iranian armies inflicted casualties on themselves, and this was taking place all over the country. The Iranian losses of troops and equipment were nothing short of catastrophic.

As the battle drew to a close, realizing the carnage they had unleashed on themselves, the surviving Iranian troops, totally demoralized, dropped their weapons and aimlessly withdrew from the battlefield. Seeing this I knew our mission was completed. It was time to head for the rendezvous site.

I decided to make my move at night. I signaled the team with two clicks of my mic and waited. Instantly I got each team member's "all clear" signal. I responded, "Big Dogs…Do you believe what you just saw?"

"If I hadn't seen it with my own eyes I'd never believe anyone who told me they saw this massacre," said Dennis.

"I almost felt sorry for the poor bastards! They never stood a chance," said Paul.

"The chatter on my captured com unit is the Iranians have claimed that the U.S. violated the Geneva Convention," said Kym. They claim we used hallucinogenic gas on their forces to cause them to attack and kill their own armies. I also caught that the Iranian command and control is in total ruins. All major communications in country have been knocked out. All weapons systems have failed. For all intents the army has laid down their arms…no way of calling in their HK teams. I have caught some chatter that the Iranians have been begging the United Nations to intervene."

"We've witnessed the birth of twenty-second-century warfare. Now it's time for us to get out of Dodge. Top Dog, when do we head out?" asked Neal.

"We go out the same way we came in…under the cover of dark. I'll signal with two mic clicks to let you know when I'm on the way out. Keep com channels open, we can communicate on the run. Good luck…Remember, brothers till the end."

"Brothers till the end!"

No sooner did darkness fall than I alerted Broad Sword that we were heading to the extraction site. I then signaled the team to begin heading out. They all acknowledged with two mic clicks. I instantly began working my way back to my team.

I was focused and motivated to get to my destination. The adrenaline was flowing so hard through my body I believe I could have run and won the Boston marathon. My ever-light system proved to be invaluable. I moved through the battlefield debris and corpses ducking and dodging straggling troops. Several times to avoid detection I had to lie amongst the dead. About one klik from the rendezvous site I radioed to the team, "Big Dogs, Big Dogs, this is Top Dog over."

Instantly, Paul answered, "Top Dog, this Big Dog one, I am on site with Big Dogs two and three. Be advised, HKs are closing in on the site. We will be under cover. Big Dog Four is waiting for you at coordinates, Romeo Whiskey. See you when you get here. Big Dog One out."

I wasted no time dialing in the programmed GPS coordinates to get to our alternative meeting site Romeo

Whiskey. As we had discussed and planned, we would have an alternate meeting point if in fact our original site was compromised. Several hundred yards out I radioed to Neal. "Big Dog Four, do you copy?"

Neal responded. "Top Dog, I copy. You are clear to approach."

"Big Dog Four, I will approach you from your eight."

Neal responded. "Ah…roger that, Top Dog…I see you about two hundred fifty yards southwest of me…welcome home."

As I came into Neal's position I smiled and said, "How about a hug, big guy!"

"Only if you promise to shower," said Neal as he shook my hand. "Cap, we've got us a small dilemma. For all intents this war is over. However, we got some HKs who refuse to give up. Unknowingly they got our boys pinned down. I hate to waste a human life but these boys are standing in our way to getting home. Let's cap their butts and move on."

I paused and then answered. "Let's take a look at the situation. Where are the guys and where are the HKs located?"

Neal took out his map and began to explain, "Well, Cap, see this small ridge right here? The team is undercover a few hundred yards right about here. As you can see the HKs are on high ground with night-vision capabilities. They've got the advantage in this one."

"How many HKs?" I asked.

"I counted six."

I shook my head. "Okay, let's take them. We can flank them."

Neal nodded in acknowledgment and we were off.

Neal and I moved with stealth into position. The unsuspecting troops were huddled up discussing what had just happened to them. From what I could make out all they wanted was to exact revenge on the U.S. for their fallen comrades. For them the war would never be over. As Neal and I closed in on the HKs we began to acquire our targets. My system showed six targets acquired. I ensured my MPW was set at fully automatic then I whispered into my mic, "Fire."

Instantly the air was filled with the sounds of the MPWs rapid firing. Fhsst, fhsst, fhsst.

As each HK was hit by the MPW fire a static discharge radiated from each of their bodies where the energy pulse had hit them. They fell dead.

"Big dogs, this is Top Dog. We are coming in from your high six, copy."

Paul responded, "We copy, Top Dog...Nice work."

Neal and I scurried down the hill to meet the team. As Neal and I approached the team they sprang up from behind some rocks.

"You know, boss, you look pretty good with a beard. It gives you a distinguished look," said Neal.

"I'll consider wearing one when I'm a civilian."

After shaking hands and hugging we started to head to our extraction point. We had only two kliks to go. Paul turned to me and pointed to the lead. I motioned with my hand for him to take the point. I followed behind him and the team cued in behind me.

As we were heading to the extraction point Dennis spoke up, "Hey, Cap, I noticed that you got a bit of a limp...what's up?"

"Ah…it's nothing really…I'm fine."

Trying to change the subject I said, "Let's stay sharp. We're almost home! Let's hustle!"

It was nearing daybreak as we approached the extraction point. I radioed ahead, "Big Bird, Big Bird this is Top Dog, do you copy?"

Instantly I got a response, Top Dog, this is Big Bird, come on in."

As we approached the landing zone a chopper appeared from under a MAGS umbrella. What a sight! Man, did we come alive. The team was pumped…we were going home. As we approached the chopper the crew members jumped out to assist us with our gear. I approached the pilot. "Did the other teams make it in?"

"Every team made it except for one team leader…Bronson Templeton."

My heart dropped. "What happened?" I asked.

"Well, from what I can tell Templeton and his team were vectoring in to the extraction point with some HKs hot on their trail. Templeton got tangled up in some rocks and may have broken his leg. He ordered his team to push on without him. From what his team tells us he held the HKs off while his team escaped. In all likelihood he's dead."

Hearing this really bothered me. I just couldn't bear the thought of leaving Bronson behind. I'm sure his family would want closure. Yet, without his body how would they get it?

As the team boarded the chopper Paul offered his hand to assist me into the chopper. I paused and looked into Paul's eyes, reached into my pocket and handed Paul a letter and said,

"Paul, make sure Alex gets this letter. Promise me you'll get this letter to her."

Paul and the team yelled, "Cap…Bronson's gone…there's little we can do…Come on, let's go!"

I stepped back from the chopper and said, "Your job is done here. I'm ordering you to go home…I've got to get Bronson's dog tags…his family deserves that much. Now get your butts back to headquarters. They need to debrief you."

I turned to the chopper pilot and said, "Have command send a chopper back for me in twenty-four hours. If it's too hot to get in or if I'm not back by that time I'll work my way to the Straits of Hormuz. I can catch a ride there."

At that I signaled the chopper pilot to take off. The air blast from his rotors instantly began to stir up a dust storm. As the chopper began to ascend I turned my face to the side, brought my left forearm up to cover my eyes and looked down to shield my eyes from the dust cloud that was swirling around me. The sound of the chopper gaining altitude made the realization of being alone sink in ever so deeply. However, I knew in my heart that I had to bring Bronson home.

As I looked up at the chopper ascending the dust began to clear. I slowly lowered my eyes from looking skyward. I turned to leave and head out to find Bronson. As I did the dusty haze began to clear. There standing before me were the shadowy figures of four men…my team.

I couldn't help but smile. Actually, a sense of relief came over me. I was really glad they didn't listen to me. We started walking toward each other and before I could get a word out of my mouth Paul reached out with the letter that I gave him and said, "Well, boss, you're gonna have to deliver this yourself."

“So much for following orders,” I said.

Paul spoke up. “Captain, we’ll follow your orders without question. However, this goes well beyond following orders...you asked us to brake a solemn pledge—Brothers Till The End. We had no choice but to back our brother’s play. Now let’s quit quibbling over nothing and let’s get Bronson.”

Paul went to speak when I cut him off...”Ya, ya...I know, Paul...You’re on point.”

The team laughed as we head back out to find Bronson.

We had the GPS coordinates to Bronson’s last known position so we logically headed there. We had about three kliks to cover so we knew we had to stay sharp. Moving during daylight hours was not going to be an easy task. Where we lucked out was a majority of our route was through a rocky outcrop. Where it got tricky was the rocky outcrop had a gap of several hundred meters that we had to cross.

Once again, like a team of wolves stalking prey we move swiftly and silently through the rocks. Paul got to the open ground first and surveyed the area.

He radios back to the team. “Top Dog this is Big Dog One, copy?”

I answered, “Big Dog One, I copy. What’s your status, over?”

“Top Dog, be advised there are multiple bogies in the distance. Come on forward low and slow, out.”

I responded, “Roger that, Big Dog One...Low and slow.”

As we approached Paul’s position he pointed in several directions signaling where the hostiles were located. As we all got into position we scanned and assessed the area. We could see that several of the groups of hostiles were about one klik away. The rest were further away heading away from us. It was obvious to us that if we could see them they'd see us as soon as we got into open ground.

I huddled up with the team to discuss strategy. "Okay…we have few options open to us. We can sit and wait for dark and cross then or we can form a chain formation with the MAGS and slowly inch our way across the opening."

Paul spoke first, "How will the chain formation work, boss?"

"Here, let me draw it out in the sand."

As I drew five connected rings in the sand the team immediately got the picture.

I smiled and said, "What do you think? The only vulnerable part to this plan is when the first link has to move forward they become visible for a split second before they duck into the second links cover. If we do this right, we'll leap frog right across the open ground."

The team agreed with the plan.

"I'll go first. As soon as I've got the MAGS set up you follow in and one by one move to the front of the MAGS umbrella and set your MAGS up. The next man can move to the most forward position and set up and so on until we have a five-man chain formed. When the fifth man is set up call back to the last link, in this case it will be me, I'll shut down my MAGS and make my way through the link to the head of the chain and set up. I'll call back and we will repeat the process right across the open area. Remember, we've got to move quickly."

The team agreed and the plan was set in motion.

The team executed this plan to perfection and the chain of invisibility was formed. They crossed the open area quickly and, most importantly, undetected. As the last man scurried into the rocks the team disappeared into the shadows.

They worked their way to the GPS coordinates that they were given. Paul found a vantage point overlooking the area where Bronson reportedly made his last stand. As he looked down into the area he saw an HK team camped. He immediately keyed his mic once. Hearing Paul's signal, the team and I stopped dead in our tracks. After pausing for a second, I gave the signal to move forward.

As we vectored into Paul's position, Paul, using hand signals, told the team the number and location of the HKs. I moved into position and assessed the situation. As I was scanning the area I noticed a pair of GI jump boots sticking out from behind a clump of rocks. I motioned for the team to view my findings. This had to be Bronson.

I gave Kym the signal to keep close tabs on what's being said. He signaled the team to come forward, whoever was lying there was not dead.

"We're going to move in as soon as it's dark," I said. "Kym and Dennis, keep an eye on these guys. Target acquire them and be prepared to cap them. You got our six as we get into position."

As I drew a diagram on the ground, I said, "Paul, Neal, and I are going to get into position here, here and here. We'll work our way into position. Once in position we'll set up our MAGS. On my signal we'll nail these bastards."

As dusk drew near we moved into position as planned. We deployed our MAGS and got ready for the kill. All of a sudden a small vehicle could be heard approaching the camp. We watch intently as the vehicle approached. As the small personnel carrier rolled into camp the HK team became more animated. It appeared that someone of importance was about to arrive.

As the vehicle came to a stop two high-ranking Iranian Special Forces personnel got out of the vehicle. Instantly, the camp came alive with activity. Two HK team members went over to the prisoner lying on the ground. They grabbed the prisoner under the arms and drug him out into the open. We all could see that it was Bronson Templeton. His face was battered, bruised and bloody.

They set Bronson on his knees with his hands cuffed behind his back. Both Iranian officers approached him. Not surprisingly both officers spoke perfect English. The senior of the two, a colonel, began interrogating Bronson.

"Ah…who do we have here?"

Bronson replied with name, rank, and service number.

The colonel cut him off, "Yes, yes, of course, name, rank, and service number. How entertaining. However, you will tell me what I want to know. I promise you will tell me exactly what I want to know. So let's dispense with the formalities and get down to real business, shall we?"

At that he nodded to the two troops that drug him forward. One of them kicked Bronson in the stomach while the other smashed his left ankle with his rifle butt. Bronson screamed in excruciating pain. The two troops grabbed Bronson under the arms and held him up to continue with the interrogation.

I whispered into my mic, "Stand down. If we hit the two holding onto Bronson the pulses will transmit into him. We have to wait for a clear shot."

Assessing the problem I got an idea. Given that I was located in a position to the front of Bronson and that his captives were focused on him, I decided to quickly reveal myself to Bronson. As they began the interrogation I stepped just to the outer edge of my MAGS umbrella, piercing the veil of invisibility, and stepped back in. I watched Bronson for some sign that he recognized I was there. He began to smile.

The colonel saw that Bronson was smiling and said, "Ah…have we come to an agreement that you will tell me what I want to know?"

"I will answer any question you ask if you answer my question first."

"Okay. Ask your question."

Bronson looked up into the man's eyes and said, "Do you believe in Jesus?"

The colonel slapped Bronson across the face, drew his side arm, and pointed it at Bronson's head. "You infidel dog! I should shoot you for your insults."

Bronson smiled again and said, "Would you like to meet him?"

This time the colonel played along with Bronson. "Okay, my friend. Let me ask you a question. Who is going to introduce me to your Jesus?"

Bronson fell forward pulling away from the two troops holding him up. Instantly the sound of MPWs firing filled the air. As the Iranian troops fell dead we stepped out of the shadows. "We are!"

Bronson rolled to his side and looked up at me. "Damn, Cap, am I glad to see you."

"I believe you're buying the first round when we get back," I replied.

The team quickly un-cuffed Bronson's hands and assessed his injuries. His ankle was shattered.

Neal helped Bronson to his feet. "Let's go, Bronson. I'll carry you out of here."

Under the cover of darkness we began our trek back to the extraction point, knowing there was no guarantee that a chopper would be waiting for us. Each man took a turn carrying Bronson.

It was nearing early morning when we got to the extraction point. As we approached the landing zone a chopper appeared right before us. It was sitting under a MAGS umbrella.

"Your taxi gentlemen," said the pilot.

"Ooh Rah!"

As we made our way back to command one of the medics said to me, "Are you okay, sir? I noticed you're sitting a little gingerly?"

I smiled and responded. "I'm okay, airman. No problem."

As I looked at my team with a deep sense of pride and honor they seemed to collapse into a peaceful rest.

An hour into the flight the pilot called back to us. "We have just entered friendly air space, gentlemen. Rest easy." And so we did.

An hour later we were landing at command. As we approached the landing area we could see several vehicles waiting for us. There was an ambulance waiting to bring Bronson to the hospital, transports to take us to command, and one officer's transport. It was Colonel Beckworth and Commander Westfall. They had come to welcome us home.

As we touched down the medics grabbed Bronson's stretcher to deliver him to the waiting ambulance. As they began to offload Bronson, he smiled, placed his right hand on his heart, and said, "Thank you. I will forever remember the five angels of mercy that pulled me out of the jaws of hell."

"Go on, get well," I said. "We're gonna collect on that first round when you get out of the hospital."

Bronson waved as the medics carried him off.

Colonel Beckworth and Commander Westfall approached the team. We exchanged salutes with them. Colonel Beckworth is first to offer his hand. "Son, welcome home! A job well done! You and your team have distinguished yourselves."

Commander Westfall shook each team member's hand and patted them on the shoulder, commending them for a job well done. "Gentlemen, I know you are tired and hungry; however, we need to debrief you. A great deal has happened. I'd like to get your perspective on things as well as bring you up to speed."

When we arrived and entered the command center we could smell the aroma of hot food and coffee and we knew we were heading for a good meal.

An entire buffet had been set up for us to feast on in the debriefing area. Commander Westfall turned to us and said, "Dig in, boys! I'm sure we can debrief as you eat."

And so we did.

As we ate our meals Colonel Beckworth and Commander Westfall began the debriefing. "Gentlemen, first I want to say that the Iranians have unconditionally surrendered! They have begged the U.N. to intervene and begin sending in aid. Their entire communications infrastructure, radio, TV, micro wave communications, phone system as well as computer networks communications are inoperable. We have permanently knocked out their nuclear plants and have all but destroyed their power grids. In essence we have driven their technological capabilities back to the Stone Age.

"Their entire military complex has been rendered useless. They have no command and control. Their ground and air weapons systems have been permanently knocked out. They are totally blind. Their radar systems are down for good. What we have accomplished will change how wars are fought forever."

"Our marines took the Straits of Hormuz without casualties. Using our new stealth and holographic technologies we landed an invasion force undetected. When it was all said and done the Iranian forces were so confused they dropped their weapons and just gave up without a fight.

"As for the air campaign, well let's just say a new chapter in air warfare has now been written. In what will be classified as the most devastating well-timed and orchestrated air attacks we delivered a death blow to the enemy's entire infrastructure. We hit them with magnetic pulse weapons in all aspects of their technologies. While they were looking to shoot down holographic aircraft we unleashed an armada of aircraft armed with magnetic pulse weapons. With pin point accuracy our planes left nothing electronic in the country viable."

"Now for the ground war, gentlemen," said Colonel Beckworth. "This is where you come in. Our intel shows that the holographic war performed so well that the enemy obliterated themselves. Tens of thousands of enemy troops were killed by their own friendly fire. We have reports that as the holographic army appeared some of the troops dropped their weapons and ran. The enemy became so utterly confused as to who and what they were shooting at that they just quit fighting. When our planes strafed their mobile weapons systems and MAG'd them the Iranian army all but collapsed.

"Gentlemen, as it stands today Iran is utter ruins and chaos. They have no way of communicating within the country. Their army has disbanded. It splintered into independent pockets of resistance. Small armed bands are aimlessly roaming the country."

There was a pause in the discussion and then Colonel Beckworth asked me to debrief my team's activities and observations.

"Well, sir…I guess the best place to begin is how we deployed. First I'd like to give our compliments to the advanced teams. The supply cache was intact and waiting for us. Without those supplies we would never have been able to remain in country as long as we did. However, getting those supplies was another issue."

Both officers nodded.

"As we got to the supply cache we encountered seven HKs encamped close by, too close for us to get into the supplies and get out undetected."

Commander Westfall interrupted, "What was your course of action, Captain?"

"Well, sir, we had no choice but to KIA eight enemy."

Westfall responded, "Did you and your team KIA seven or eight enemy, Captain?"

"We KIA'd eight enemy, sir. The eight came into play when we were concealing the bodies of the deceased troops. He must have been returning from a one-man recon. Sergeant Venegas caught him in his helmet's rearview function before he could get the drop on us. Venegas took him out. That's our eighth KIA, sir."

Colonel Beckworth interjected his thoughts, "Captain on that subject, how did your weapons systems function?"

I smiled and answered. "Sir, the only word that comes to mind right now is awesome. Awesome is the best description for the weapons system. The technology was robust. Our ever-light system coupled with the forward viewing and eavesdropping system gave us advantages that the enemy using night-vision technology could not compete with. The GPS guidance and mapping system was pin-point accurate. The MPWs targeting and firing capabilities functioned perfectly. Sir, given the training we received I'd say we owned the battlefield."

Beckworth nodded his head as he took in all that I had to say. "Thank you, Captain. I'm sure when you and your team debrief with our weapons research and development group your input will be most enlightening to them."

We all smiled, taking this to mean we would all be heading back to Area 51.

We proceeded to recount the events of the engagement, and when we finished Commander Westfall moved around the room to address us. "Let's see if I've got this information straight. You and your team deploy deep into enemy territory and successfully deploy weapons systems, in three separate engagements KIA a total of twenty-four enemy combatants, after reaching your extraction site you and your team traversed several kilometers back into hostile territory during daylight hours where you crossed several hundred meters of open ground, rescued an injured comrade, traversed back to the extraction site, and successfully got back to base?"

"That's about it, sir."

"Captain, I must say that in my entire military career I have never heard or witnessed such an act of cunning and bravery. You and your team's act of duty, honor, and selflessness will be remembered as the true meaning of what the Special Forces code and training is all about. Gentlemen, we salute you."

We all stood to attention as both officers offered a salute to us.

—

Totally exhausted and dirty from a week's stay in the desert, we headed back to our billeting area.

I was the last to come out of the shower. As I was drying myself off the team was standing at the sinks across from the shower stalls. As I went to dry my right side I turned to my right. Paul happened to glance back through the mirror. My wound was in plain sight.

Paul turned quickly and said, "Boss, that's some gash you have on your butt!"

Now the others turned to see what's happening. Immediately the team came over to me to investigate.

Right away Dennis started in, "Come on, boss, show us your tushie!"

I kept my backside covered. "Go on! Get out of here!"

The team began to press me even harder.

"I knew something was wrong," said Paul. You've been limping since we all met up. How did it happen?"

I once again tried my best to get the team to forget it. "Let it go, I'm okay."

Neal, the voice of reason, chimed in. "You know, given

the filthy conditions we were in you could have picked up micro organisms that will turn to God knows what kind of an infection. If you don't get that looked at you may end up dead."

I sighed, "Gee, Neal, you have such a great bedside manner. Okay guys I'll go to sick call in the morning. But for now just let it go. Okay?"

The next day at 0700 I headed for sick call. As I entered sick call I was greeted by an airman first class with a clipboard.

"Good morning, sir. Do you mind filling out this form?"

I smiled. "Sure. No problem."

I completed the form, handed the clipboard back to the airman, and gingerly took a seat in the waiting area. Several minutes later my name and rank was called. I stood up and followed the attendant back to a waiting room. Moments after that two female personnel showed up at the door of my examination room, a sergeant and airman. The sergeant introduced herself and her team member.

"Hello, Captain D'Angelo, I'm Sergeant Marshall and this is Airman Lane. As a matter of Air Force protocol we are here to take and record your vitals and to get a description of your medical problem. This will assist the physician in treating you."

Things went very well up until the point of when the sergeant asked me, "Nature of your medical problem?"

I paused to collect my thoughts and said, "Oh…I've got an abrasion that I'd like the doctor to look at."

The sergeant wrote down my description of the problem. She then asked, "Location of this abrasion, sir?"

I sighed and answered. "Let's say it's on my right side and leave it at that."

The sergeant wrote down what I had said. Then the moment that I dreaded would happen happened…the sergeant asked, "Please, sir, could I see the exact location of the abrasion?"

I looked at the sergeant and said, as I pointed to the anatomical figure on the chart the sergeant is filling out, "On the right side. In this area."

The sergeant patiently smiled and said, "I'm sorry, sir, but you will have to be more specific than that. Air Force regulations require that all medical forms be filled out exact and precise."

By this time I was becoming nervous and frustrated. I decided that my only option to avoid the embarrassment was to pull rank on the sergeant.

"Listen, Sergeant, I know you're trying to do your job and I can appreciate that. However, these captain bars are telling those sergeant stripes that this discussion is over. So take what information you have and please send in the physician."

The sergeant, knowing she was outranked, left the examination room. Several minutes later, in walked Lieutenant Colonel Marsha Dodge, MD, and her two assistants, Marshall and Lane. The look on my face must have said it all…Awe crap!

The doctor looked at my chart, smiled and said, "Well, Captain I understand you have an abrasion, is that correct.

I nervously smiled and answered, "Ah…Yes, ma'am."

The doctor continued. "I see that it's in the general vicinity of your right side is that correct?"

"Yes, ma'am."

The doctor responded. "Ah…good. Now, Captain, would

you like to tell me exactly where this abrasion is located on your right side?"

I swallowed hard and whispered, "On my right buttocks, ma'am."

The doctor turned to her aids and said, "Did you say your right buttocks, Captain?"

I turned beet red with embarrassment and answered, "Yes, ma'am."

Well, my being tortured by this medical crew was far from over. The doctor then sets the stage for my utter humiliation.

The doctor smiled at me and said, "Captain, these colonel leafs are telling those captain bars to drop those pants, bare your wound, and bend over this exam table for me to examine your wound. Am I clear?"

I winced and complied, "Yes, ma'am."

I quickly turned, dropped my pants, and bared all.

"Captain, you've been shot! When did this happen?"

As the doctor took a closer look at my wound I explained how I received it.

"Why didn't you report this to your medic team when you were being extracted from battle?"

"Well, ma'am, I just didn't think a scratch like this was worth mentioning. After all it really isn't a bullet wound…is it?"

The doctor quickly replied, "You have a chunk of flesh missing from your posterior, you bled profusely, and you wonder if you've been shot! Yes, Captain, you were wounded in battle! What I don't understand is why this wound is not raging with infection. This has to be reported. You're one lucky man, Captain."

My humiliation was far from over. As the doctor cleaned and dressed my wound she instructed her aid, Sergeant Marshall, to fill a syringe full of antibiotic and to bring it to her. With me bent over the table, "full moon" in view, the doctor instructed Sergeant Marshall to administer the shot. The sergeant pinched the flesh on my butt, quickly jabbed the needle into my flesh, and slowly injected the antibiotic.

After receiving my shot, I dressed quickly. As I turned around and looked at the medical team I could see from the gleam in their eyes that they enjoyed every minute of my humiliation. The doctor offered her hand for a shake. I obliged.

"Captain, I understand that you men did a great job out there. Thank you for your courage and service."

"Thank you, ma'am."

"Make sure you see a doctor at your next duty station.

"Yes, ma'am. I will."

As I headed back to my quarters the team came rushing over to me. Just like school boys they had smiles on their faces as they jostled with each other and made their way to me.

Dennis started in first. "Hey, how'd it go with the doc?"

"It's nothing…good as new. You guys seem pretty chipper. What's up?"

"Pack you bags, boss!" said Paul. "We're going home this afternoon!"

"You're kidding me."

Neal answered, "It appears that this war was over about forty-eight hours after it started. Boss, we are going back to area fifty one to debrief with Heir Detrich and team!"

"Ooh Rah!"

The Trip Home

As we packed our gear I couldn't help think that the war happened so fast that maybe this whole thing was a dream and that I'd wake up and find myself in my bunk back in the states. Yet, the pain in my backside reminded me that it was indeed reality. The journey home was going to be a long one.

As the aircraft took off I settled into my thoughts. I had a new perspective on life. Seeing death the way that we did, I now realized how fragile life really was. I was glad to be alive. From this day forward I was going to live my life with purpose and meaning. I had a newfound appreciation for the small things.

As the jet gained altitude I relaxed into my seat and drifted back to my memories of Alex and me at her parents' home. I went right back to my first visit there…shaking hands with my nemesis, Tucker.

I chuckled to myself as I recalled the apprehension I felt the day we walked into the stable. I slowly drifted back to that day…

—

As we entered the stable I could see the silhouette of someone moving and stacking hay bales. That someone turned toward us with a "surprised to see you" smile on his face and said, "Alex! Come to help?"

Alex laughed and then moved quickly toward the cowboy and jumped into his arms. The cowboy lifted her up in his embrace and swung her around as they both laughed. Seeing this made me feel totally out of place. I swallowed hard as my pulse elevated. This was the moment that I was dreading. As the cowboy put Alex down they both turned to me.

Alex looked up at the cowboy and said, "There's someone I want you to meet." With arms around each other, they walked forward to apparently begin the introductions.

As they moved toward me my eyes quickly scanned the big guy top to bottom. This guy had to be six feet six inches tall with his cowboy boots on, was lean and a well-cut athlete for sure, and was in his later twenties. To add insult to injury he was a handsome devil. Just the way Alex described her "Tucker." Sammy boy, this guy has got things sewn up. You haven't got a chance in hell of winning Alex's heart.

Thinking quickly I figured I'd at least be a good sport about things. So I decided to smile, I extended my hand and introduced myself. "Hello, I'm Sam D'Angelo."

The cowboy shook my hand, smiled and said, "I've heard a great deal about you, Sam. I feel like I already know you. Alex has been talking about you non-stop since she met you."

Good Lord, Alex, you have a strange way of treating the love of your life!

The cowboy continued, "I'm Jon, Alex's older brother."

Stunned, I took a double take and said, "Oh…Ah, it's a real pleasure to meet you, Jon."

Totally confused, I then asked, "When do I get to meet Tucker?"

Jon laughed. "Oh, Tuck…well he's out back. Alex, I guess you'll have to do the honors of introducing the boys."

Alex took me by the hand and started to move forward. My feet would hardly move. I felt like I was stuck in quick sand. I fought my impulse to tell Alex how I truly felt about her.

Alex turned to me and said, "Come on, cowboy! Get a move on. You're gonna meet Tucker!"

I forced a smile and headed to the end of the stable to the rear doors. Alex led the way through the doors with me in tow.

We stepped to the outside of the stable and Alex yelled, "Tucker!"

Tucker turned.

Alex ran up to him and puts her arms around his neck and turned to look at me. With a little girl's smile of glee on her face, Alex said, "Tucker, this is Sam."

Stunned, speechless and in near shock, I swallowed hard. There as big as life was the bane of my existence. Just as Alex had described him…about six feet four inches tall, muscular physique, the athletic type and handsome. However, Tucker had long ears, four legs and a long tail.

A flood of emotion over took me. I didn't know where to start. I knew my way around horses, so I approached Tucker and began to scratch and rub him. I spoke to Tucker as if we were long lost friends. He instantly took to me.

Alex lit up with joy. "I told you that you two would get along famously!"

I turned to Alex, pulled her close to me, and looked into

her eyes. As Alex looked up into my eyes, I realized what she had been telling me all along. Instantly, the most powerful force known to mankind, love, pulled our lips together for a passionate kiss.

As we came up for air Alex smiled. "What kept you, cowboy? I was really beginning to wonder."

"It's a long story. Is there somewhere we can sit and talk?"

Alex led the way to her favorite garden area. With arms tightly around each other we slowly walked to the King estates' west garden area.

I began to explain why I was so slow at the draw. As I described my sleepless nights and heart aches because of how I thought Tucker was in fact the "Love of Alex's life…the very man she'd spend the rest of her life with." How I was willing to step aside so she and her Tucker would live happily ever after.

Hearing my story made Alex roar with laughter. She had to beg me to stop telling the story so she could catch her breath. Watching this show didn't bother me in the least. I rather enjoyed seeing my Alex happy. All I cared about is that I had won Alex's heart. Tucker had now been bumped to second seat.

It was nearing the supper hour at the King home. Alex looked at her watch and said, "Let's head in. I'm sure Mom has got a great dinner planned."

I smiled and gently kissed Alex. "There's more of that to come. I've got some serious catching up to do."

Alex smiled and said, "You bet you do, cowboy."

As we walked into the rear entrance of the house we could hear voices and laughing coming from the kitchen area.

"Dad's home! Come on let's introduce you two."

As we entered the kitchen there was a small team of people preparing the evening meal. Although the hired help was doing the cooking there was no doubt that it was Elsie's kitchen. Elsie and Jon Senior heard us enter. Elsie and Jon turned and smiled at us as we made our way across the room.

Alex spoke first, "Dad, this is…"

"Sam D'Angelo," said Jon as we shook hands. "Son I feel like I already know you. Alex hasn't quit talking about you since you two first met. Welcome to our home."

"Thank you, sir. It's a pleasure to meet you."

Jon smiled. "Please, son, call me Jon."

I smiled and nodded my head.

At that Alex and I headed off to freshen up for dinner.

As Alex and I entered the dining room Elsie motioned to Alex for us to sit at the left side of the table. The seating arrangement put Alex closest to her dad and me closest to Elsie. Brother Jon was seated across from me.

As we took our seats Alex commented to me, "Oh my. You must be a real special guest. Mom has the best china set out."

At first, things seemed a little quiet as the family ate their meal. However, things started to liven up when Alex broke the silence. "Dad, I was wondering if Sam and I could hold the wedding in the west garden?"

Alex's dad noticed the stunned look on my face and calmly said, "Tell me Alex, when did Sam propose marriage to you?"

Alex giggles, turns to me, and with puppy dog eyes and with a sweet tone to her voice said, "You will marry me won't you Sam?"

As Alex was asking me to marry her, Jon Senior was sipping water, and he nearly showered the room. Coughing and sputtering, the poor man had all he could do to contain himself.

Across from me brother Jon and Elsie were in a fit of laughing as well.

I took Alex's hand in mine, looked into her eyes, smiled, and asked, "Will you marry me, Alex?"

Alex smiled at me, patted my hand and said, "Oh don't be silly…I asked first."

The room erupted into laughter. Like two love birds we quickly kissed and hugged. The wedding was on!

After the meal Jon Senior looked to me and said, "Sam, we have a family tradition of adjourning to the "Grand Sitting Room" for an after dinner beverage and good discussion. We catch up on the day's activities. You're family, now so please join us."

Elsie walked over and hugged me and said, "I'm so happy that you and Alex have found each other. I've never seen her as happy as she has been since you two met."

Alex and I shared a love seat. As the beverages were served Alex's dad proposed a toast to our engagement. He wished us happiness, health, prosperity and a long life together.

We told stories and laughed late into the night.

—

I arose before breakfast and began a martial arts workout. I found a perfect spot in the garden area directly behind the house. I recalled what my grandfather taught me. "When you perform your art, draw your strength for your surroundings. Son, you must become one with nature."

When I returned to the house, the family men were there. "Good morning, Sam!"

"Good morning. Wow, that coffee smells great!"

Jon Senior grabbed a cup and handed it to me. "We couldn't help but watch you out there…quite impressive."

I smiled and humbly replied, "Thanks…what I was doing was a Korean martial art called 'Tang Soo Do.' My grandfather brought it home from Korea, taught my dad and his siblings, and my dad taught it to me, kind of a family tradition."

Jon Junior speaks up, "Great tradition…I'd like to learn."

I smiled and said, "When the time is right I'd be honored to be your instructor."

Jon Senior asked, "Will you be teaching my grandchildren this tradition?"

"Oh yes. It's my hope that my children pass it on as I passed it on to them."

Alex and I went on a horse back ride and picnic later that day. As we took in the natural beauty around us Alex said, "Sam, would next June be too early for the wedding?"

"Alex, tomorrow wouldn't be too early for me."

The Landing

As the flight home progressed and passengers had a time to rest, many of the troops began milling around the cabin visiting with their buddies. The commotion slowly caused me to drift back from my memories. Relishing my memories, I sat back and blissfully smiled. I knew that I was going home to my Alex.

As I came around from my trip down memory lane Paul, sitting across from me, said, "Did you have a good rest, boss?"

I grinned and nodded my head.

"We'll be landing in Germany in about a half hour, Ramstine Air Force Base I think…They say we'll be laying over there for a few days. This should give us a chance to take in some serious German beer drinking."

I smiled and chuckled, "I'm not sure that's a good thing…If we kill too many brain cells before we get home people will think we're suffering from combat fatigue."

As the aircraft touched down and rolled to a stop we prepared to disembark the plane. There were transport vehicles waiting to ferry the troops to their respective quarters. As I deplaned I noticed several officers waiting at the bottom of the aircraft ramp. As I approached the bottom of the ramp way I saluted a colonel waiting for me.

As the colonel shook my hand he identified himself to me. "Hello, Captain D'Angelo. I'm Colonel Ron Wills. I'm the base public relations officer. I'm here to escort you and your team to billeting. I'll explain your itinerary for the next five days when you've had a chance to settle into your quarters."

As we entered the billeting area Colonel Wills said, "Gentlemen, please get settled into your quarters. We will meet in the conference room to my left in fifteen minutes."

After the brief break, I entered the conference room and approached the colonel. "Sir, I know that this briefing is important, but my team would like to call back to the states to our families and loved ones. Would it be possible to do that sometime today?"

"That's what this meeting is about, Captain…a great deal of political turmoil is unfolding as we speak. Men, first order of business is to send you to our base medical center for a routine physical. After that you will be debriefed by a joint committee of military intelligence and review board. They are very interested in debriefing your mission. After that you will grab some rest and relaxation here on base for a few days before we send you home. Now as for your calling home…well, the bad news is, the base is under a full alert. We are in total lock down. No one goes off the base. All communications in or out have been blacked out."

We all groaned.

Colonel Wills continued. "The political fallout from this war is tumultuous…There have been massive anti-U.S. demonstrations all across the European Union. It is reported that these demonstrations have been spreading like wildfire around the world. It is reported that this wave of demonstrations has picked up momentum back in the states. The U.N. Security Council has called an emergency meeting to discuss sanctions against the U.S. The world is demanding the disarmament of our new weapons systems. They feel that the U.S. is a threat to world security.

"The Security Council believes that the U.S. has gained such a technological advantage that we will move against any nation that disagrees with us with impunity. They outright fear that the U.S will dominate the world. There are rumors floating around the council that we captured alien technology from a downed UFO. Gentlemen, to say we shocked and awed the world would be a total understatement. We have paralyzed them with utter shock and fear.

"It appears that we did such an unbelievable and efficient job that the Iranians have convinced the world that we nuked them to start this war so we could use their country as the test ground for our new weapons systems. They've convinced the U.N. that we used hallucinogenic gas on their troops and indiscriminately slaughtered them. They are screaming foul because their nation's entire infrastructure—communications, industrial, power grids, the works—has been destroyed. We drove the bastards back to the Stone Age! What really goaded the Iranians is that we nailed their nuclear capabilities, totally ruined their plans to dominate the Middle East. To complicate matters the EU is up in arms that the nuclear fallout from the blast is blanketing a majority of the continent. They believe there will be long term negative affects on their population, live stock and agriculture. If this isn't enough the Chinese are about one step away from severing relations with the U.S. They have been leery of us for over a half of century, and now they are down right paranoid of us. Gentlemen, this is one of the worst crises that our nation has ever faced. The outcome is anybody's guess."

After the briefing we decided to head to the base NCO (Non-Commissioned Officers) Club for a few drinks and a meal. As we sat in our small private group sipping our beer and pondering what Colonel Wills had told us, Dennis broke the silence. "I mean think of it. The Iranians detonate a fifty megaton nuke, fire on us, virtually starting this mess, we respond and kick their butt, and now they have the world convinced that we're the bad guys! They're the victims?"

I sat quietly as I listened and let Dennis blow off some steam. After all, these boys had just been through an intense week. We all were wound for ninety and needed to unwind. I smiled at the team and lifted my glass for a toast as the team did the same.

We touched our glasses as I said, "No matter what happens, brothers till the end!"

"Brothers till the end!"

The next day we reported to the base hospital for our physicals. What we didn't expect was our physicals would take the better part of the day. We were prodded, poked, blood drawn, questioned by all types of medical staff both internal and mind science professionals, and had full body scans and eye and hearing exams.

At one point in the physical process we met in a waiting room. Neal, being the physiologist, said, "Cap, this is no routine physical. These guys are most definitely looking for something."

"They are sure to find it whatever it is. Why they studied

my wound for over an hour. I had a small team of docs studying my butt."

"How'd you like all the questions the shrinks had to ask?" said Paul. "If I didn't know better I'd swear they were trying to Section Eight us for being crazy!"

"They wanted to know if I had recurring dreams." Kym smiled and paused.

We all looked at Kym and waited for him to give his answer.

Dennis laughed. "Come on, man! What did you tell them?"

"I told them that I keep having a recurring dream that a bird flies into my patio door window at home. Poor thing falls right to the deck and just lays there. No matter what I do to help the bird nothing in the dream seems to work. So in one of the dreams I tried something new. In trying to revive the bird I rubbed a little gasoline on his beak. Instantly the bird revives. He begins chirping and singing and preening his feathers while he sits on my hand. Then all of sudden the bird drops over dead."

"That's it? What happened to the bird?" asked Neal.

"Oh…the bird ran out of gas!"

The team erupted into a laughing fit. Neal grabbed Kym in a loose head lock and rubbed his knuckles across the top of Kym's head. "You're full of crap, man! With a story like that they'll Section Eight you for sure!"

Later that afternoon, with our physicals completed, we met in the base gym to lift weights and go through our usual martial arts workout together. To say the least, we were anxious to go home. We did our best to keep our minds occupied to pass the time.

The next day at 0800 hours the team reported to base headquarters for their debriefing with command. Given that we had debriefed with Commander Westfall we thought that this debriefing would be routine.

When we entered the briefing room we were greeted by several senior officers, Department of Defense, officials and military intelligence officials…lots of smiles and hand shaking. It was obvious to us that this was not going to be your run-of-the-mill debriefing. There was far too much horsepower present in the room for that.

The most senior officer identified himself to us. "Good morning, men. I am Lieutenant General Earl Grayson. I'm coming in from NATO Headquarters. With me today are representatives form the DOD and military intelligence. I've called this review committee together today to review and discuss your mission. I have read Commander Westfall's report and must say it was most interesting to read. However, I'd like to hear about your mission first hand. My distinguished guests also have an interest in your debriefing. Shall we get started?"

For the next three hours we again gave a play-by-play description of our mission—how our weapon systems functioned, how we deployed and used the MAGS technology, the tactics we used and what we observed. As we spoke, two court reporters captured every word that we said. General Grayson would frequently interrupt the conversation and re-state what he believed was said. He wanted to ensure that he got the story exactly as it happened.

As we concluded our debriefing, I looked at the general

and said, "Sir, it is my opinion, and my team concurs, that Lieutenant Templeton should receive a citation and recognition for his bravery and selflessness. He was willing to die so that his team could survive."

"Captain, your recommendation is duly noted. We will forward your recommendation through command for evaluation and processing. Rest assured that as we speak a team is interviewing Lieutenant Templeton and his team."

As the meeting concluded the general and his committee members all shook our hands. General Grayson looked at each team member and said, "Gentlemen, you have performed your duties brilliantly. Your unit can be proud of your service and accomplishments."

We saluted the general and were off to do some serious R and R. For the next two days, with nothing but time on our hands, we rested, exercised, and met at the NCO club for our nightly game of pool and, of course, some serious beer drinking. This was, however, not exactly the R and R we had hoped for. Outside the base world opinion concerning the U.S. was deteriorating. Finally, the order to pack up and head home was issued.

We boarded the aircraft and prepared for the eight hour trip home. To kill some time the team started bantering with me about getting married in four weeks. As usual Dennis led the charge.

"I don't know, boss, tying the knot at such a young age…Think about all the fun you'll miss out on."

I laughed. "Oh yeah, every night sitting in the local tavern drinking beer with you, wishing we had dates. Now what could be more fun than that?"

The team laughed.

In good fun, the team prodded and poked fun at me for about the first hour of the flight, then they all began to settle in for the flight's duration. I slowly drifted back to my first visit to Alex's parents' home.

I began to recall the day Alex and I began planning our wedding. I smiled as I recalled our conversation…

—

"Sam, I thought it would be nice to have you and the guys in full military dress. You know, the gloves, swords, the works. There's just something about a man in uniform that is so attractive."

"Well I'm okay with that, but what about Jon?"

Alex laughed. "A tux will be just fine. Jon won't mind at all. I'm sure he'll be honored to be part of the wedding party."

As we sat and discussed our plans I noticed that Alex was writing in her PDA. I smiled and kiddingly said, "Are you taking this all down?"

With her trademark grin Alex smiled and winked at me then turned the screen of her PDA for me to see. I smiled and as I was nodding my head I read what was written on the screen out loud. "Mrs. Sam D'Angelo."

Alex kissed me and said, "I like the way that sounds."

The evening hour was fast approaching. Alex looked at her watch and said, "It's time for us to head in. Mom and Dad have planned a barbeque for this evening. It should be a lot of fun. Let's hit the trail, partner."

I jumped to my feet. We quickly packed up and were on our way home.

As we rode home Alex noticed that I was in deep thought. “A quarter for your thoughts?”

I laughed. “Whatever happened to a penny for your thoughts?”

Alex laughed. “Inflation, my good man, inflation.”

“Alex, I’ve been thinking…”

Alex smiled and teasingly said, “Come on, cowboy, out with it. Don’t be shy.”

“Well, your family is a well established and well off family. Obviously, some day you’ll be an heir to a portion of the King estate. Well…I mean…umm.”

Alex laughed, “Come on, Sammy, you’re killing me! Out with it.”

“Okay…I want us to make it on our own. You know, work hard, make sacrifices and build our own empire.”

Alex shook her head. “Dad and Mom are definitely gonna love you. I think we should talk to them about our independence this evening. But there’s something I need to tell you.”

“And that is…”

Alex hugged me tightly, looked into my eyes, and said, “I have a dowry that matures in a few years. We can use it to get a start in life.”

“A dowry?”

“Yes, mom and dad put a little something away for us kids for our future.”

I smiled. “And just what does the little something add up to?”

Alex giggled, “Oh I don’t know ten maybe fifteen…”

Excited, I cut Alex off. “Ten to fifteen thousand dollars,

not bad. Let's make sure that you keep it invested for your old age."

Shaking her head in agreement Alex let me ramble on for a moment then smiled and said, "Sammy, you're missing a few zeros and you've slipped a decimal place or two in your figures…That's ten to fifteen million dollars. My dowry is worth ten to fifteen million dollars."

I stood there speechless.

Alex stood on her toes and kissed me, "Come on, cowboy, let's continue with this party, shall we?"

Landing in Georgia

As the aircraft began its decent to land at Dobbins Air Force Base we began to stir with excitement. We were finally home! Dennis turned to me, "Yo, boss! We got a pretty hectic schedule when we get back to Hunter."

I smiled and nodded. "Yes we do. We have to get back to our unit, sign in, stow gear, debrief with command and the rest of the teams, then head right back out on leave. You boys are gonna give me away to my bride at the end of the month."

Kym laughed. "Hey Cap! What do you want us to do if she gives you back to us?"

As we disembarked from the aircraft we were greeted by a cheering crowd. There was a joint armed forces band playing an upbeat victory salute to the troops returning. As me and my team and other team leaders and troops headed for the transportation awaiting us, I noticed Colonel Martinez off to the side. As we noticed each other, Colonel Martinez headed toward me and the team.

As he approaches me he smiled, we salute and he said, "Ah, Captain! It's good to see you and your team. Listen, son, there's been a slight change in plans. We are going to lag behind here at Dobbins for a few hours. I thought you and your team could join me for some refreshments and discussion before we head back to Hunter."

I smiled. "That would be great, sir. We'd be happy to join you."

At that we got into the Colonel's transports and were off.

As Colonel Martinez and I where heading to base operations the Colonel asked, "Tell me, son, how bad were you hit?"

Trying to deflect the question I replied, "Oh it was nothing, sir, just a scratch. Really I'm fine."

Colonel Martinez looked at me, "Scratch, hell! When one of my boys is hit it's a big deal…Where did you get hit?"

I cleared my throat, "Really sir it was just a scratch…I guess you could say I was grazed on my….side…I guess."

As we all entered base operations several of General Theo Cornelius' staff was there to greet us. As the men shook our hands and exchanged greetings Colonel Martinez asks the aides, "Are we set?"

They answered, "Yes, sir."

Colonel Martinez then asked the team to join him in the hanger next to base operations.

As we entered the large aircraft hanger we could see a huge parade gathering of joint services. Colonel Martinez turned to me and said, "Captain please join this formation. March your team to the front and center position of this parade formation."

I saluted the Colonel and replied. "Yes, sir."

I called my team to attention and in a single file marched to the front and center position as we were commanded. As we got into our position and turned to the front there standing before us was General Theo Cornelius.

As the parade stood at attention General Cornelius addressed the group. The general's initial comments were centered on service to country, duty and honor. He commended all armed services members for their dedication and professionalism in achieving such a decisive victory. Then he began to personalize things. He began mentioning how a fire team, without hesitation, volunteered for a mission in which the possibilities of surviving it were slim. The general went on. "This particular fire team successfully infiltrated into the deepest point in hostile territory fighting their way in, completing their mission to perfection and then fighting their way out to be successfully extracted. This same team, with one member wounded, knowing that a comrade had fallen, without hesitation or concern for their personal safety, chose to re-infiltrate hostile territory on a search and rescue mission and successfully rescued their comrade."

As the general approached me and my team his aids followed him. He first approached me. He smiled and said, "Captain Samuel D'Angelo. Jr., it is my honor to award you with the armed forces Distinguished Service Medal."

As the general pinned the medal to my uniform, photographers took pictures.

"In addition, it is my honor to award you with a Purple Heart Medal for wounds sustained in battle."

The general pinned the medal to my uniform, then shook my hand, and then saluted. The general proceeded down the line congratulating and bestowing the Distinguished Service Medal on Paul, Dennis, Kym and Neal.

As the parade was dismissed General Cornelius invited us back to base operations for a social gathering. The team and I, anxious to call our families and love ones, obliged the general. As we entered the base operations planning room we were greeted by DOD officials, Pentagon staff and several high ranking officers. There was champagne and hors d'oeuvres waiting for us. As we mixed and mingled with the crowd I was repeatedly asked about my wound. I did all that I could do to duck the question. I was quick to work my way over to Colonel Martinez and mentioned that the team and I were anxious to call home. The colonel was quick to get us outside lines to our families and loved ones.

We got to the phones and began our calls home at last. My parents were excited to hear from me to say the least. They told me that the town fathers were planning a homecoming for me.

I finally got through to Alex. "Cowboy! You'll never leave me again without saying so-long! When I got word that you had shipped out I cried all the next day thinking that I may never see you again and that we didn't say see you later!"

I winced as I tried my best to console Alex and promised to be home soon. We agreed to meet at my parents' home in Minnesota.

Heading Home to Minnesota

After the team and I squared away our business back at Hunter field we prepared to head home on leave. We all caught a chopper flight back to Dobbins Air Force Base and then headed to Atlanta Hartsfield Airport. As we entered the airport we high-fived each other and prepared to head our separate ways. The team assured me that they'd meet me in Wisconsin for the wedding.

As I sat in the waiting area for my flight I listened to the television broadcast as well as to the opinion of the people around me. Why even the newspapers had put a rather negative tone to the war. I did not like what I was hearing. The news commentators were claiming that the war was unnecessary that there was evidence that we may have in fact staged events to provoke the war with Iran. The commentators also asserted that the former administration had squandered billions of tax payer dollars in developing weapon systems so horrific that he had set the U.S. on the path of becoming a conquering nation. They claimed that the evidence was clear that U.S. was aiming to dominate the world, to dictate global policy. Overall public opinion was split concerning the war.

As my flight to Minneapolis was in route two men were discussing their views on the war. Things got so heated between them that the attendants warned that if they continued arguing that the pilots would be forced to make an emergency landing and the two would be arrested.

We finally arrived, and as I entered the terminal there in front of me were Alex and my parents. We kissed and hugged. I pulled my mom in close for a hug and kissed her forehead. As she wept she said, "My son is home."

"I love you, mom. Everything is okay now."

My dad grabbed me and hugged me and shook my hand. "We're proud of you, son. You guys did a great job for our country. It's a relief for all of us that you're okay."

My dad noticed that I was walking with a slight limp. "Having a little trouble with your leg, son?"

In an effort to change the subject I quickly answered, "It's nothing, Dad. How's fishing been?"

Over the next several days we all spent time fishing the Rainy River and horseback riding. One morning Sam Sr. headed into town to purchase his daily Minneapolis newspaper. Per his regular routine, he returned home and sat down with a cup of coffee to read his paper. "Joint Chief welcomes home and honors war heroes." Not paying to much attention to the picture, Sam Sr. began to read about the heroics that this team went through. How the team was engaged in a perilous mission deep into enemy territory. How the leader, despite his being wounded and after successfully completing the mission, led his team back into hostile territory to rescue a fallen comrade. Then he glanced at the caption under the picture. There he saw the name of Captain Samuel D'Angelo being awarded the Distinguished Service Medal and the Purple Heart.

He called to his wife to read the newspaper. She gasped

as she read the article. "My Sammy was wounded! That's why he's limping!"

"Now, Marilynn, we can't press Sam on this. If he wants to talk about it he will in good time."

Marilynn smiled "Trust me, Sam. I know just how to get the boy talking. Give me that paper."

Sam Senior and Marilynn headed outside to the gazebo where we were having our morning coffee and discussing our day's plans.

"Mind if we join you?"

Mom nonchalantly put the paper in front of Alex and said nothing. As we visited and made small talk Alex picked up the paper and read the headline. Immediately it caught her attention. She intently read the article…Then she looked at the picture and read the caption.

The morning calm was broken. "You were wounded? Why didn't you tell me!"

Alex jumped into my lap and started asking question after question, "Where were you hit, was it bad, when did it happen? Speak up, boy, you got some explaining to do!"

I smiled, hugged Alex, looked into her gorgeous blue eyes, and calmly said, "It's nothing. I got nicked that's all. I'm as good as new."

My mom sat back and watched me get the third degree. Alex was relentless with her questions. I had to give in sooner or later.

As they sat and waited for my explanation the portable phone rang. My mom answered, "D'Angelo's…Yes…Okay…Well, I'll make sure we're all there. Thanks for the call."

Sam Senior asked, "What's up?"

Marilynn smiled, "The four of us have to be at the court house at noon today. That was the mayor. They would like to honor Sam today…The community has seen the news release." She smiled at Sam, "It appears you've become a celebrity. The town is anxious to see you."

I sighed as I looked down, "Oh man…They didn't have to do this…I mean it's nothing really. We just were doing our job."

"My hero," said Alex. "Now about this wound."

I smiled. "Listen, gang, it's nothing. I was barely nicked."

"How were you nicked and where were you nicked?"

I sighed. "Okay here's how it happened."

I described how the hunter killer team camped in front of my position and how one of them got spooked and decided to take it out on the rocks where I was hiding. How the HK fired his automatic weapon at the wall of rock where I laid hidden. And how one of the bullets ricocheted and grazed me on my side.

With teary eyes Alex looked into my eyes and gently touched my right side and said, "Here?"

"No."

Alex gently moved her hand to my hip area. "Here?"

Again I smiled and said, "No."

I took Alex's hand and placed it on my wound. "Here."

In a fit of laughing Alex said, "My Sammy was shot in the butt!"

That afternoon we headed into town. As our vehicle approached the outskirts of town we were met and escorted by several police cruisers…lights flashing and sirens sounding. I looked at Alex, shook my head, and groaned.

"Come on, cowboy. This will be a piece of cake."

As the motorcade pulled up in front of the courthouse there was an ocean of people there to greet their hometown hero. "Oh, man…I thought this would be a small insignificant gathering. It looks like everyone and their uncle has shown up for this…News cameras. Give me a break."

"Son, this is your time. Enjoy it," said Dad.

As we exited the vehicle the crowd began to cheer and I blushed. Alex, mom and dad stood off to the side as I approached the front of the crowd. The mayor and I shook hands and a group of protestors started heckling and jeering. "Murderer, baby killer, warmonger…"

Tension seemed to grow throughout the crowd as the protestors blew their whistles and screamed their chants. Many of the war supporters began to become restless, annoyed with the protestors.

I smiled at the mayor and said, "Do you mind if I address the crowd?"

The mayor smiled at me, "Please do. I apologize for the distraction."

"They're not a distraction, Mr. Mayor. They are democracy in action."

As I took the microphone the crowd quieted. Like a lion waiting to pounce on its prey, the protestors anxiously awaited my comments.

"Good afternoon. I would like to thank each of you for taking time out from your busy schedule and for being here. I am deeply humbled by your presence. I'm not one for long-winded speeches so I thought I'd get right to the point."

I smiled and calmly said, "Friends, please understand that

what we have here today is democracy at its best. Today we hear the voices of consent and dissent. It is this very activity that defines why we live in the greatest nation on earth. This very freedom is why so many in the world reject us. Like so many people before me and in the tradition of a free nation, I humbly serve our nation. We must never lose sight of the fact that in preserving this great democratic freedom many that have served our nation have made the ultimate sacrifice. They gave their life so that we could preserve our freedom and to ensure that future generations would always be able to make their voices heard. We must not reject a voice that does not agree with our own views. Rather, to honor the brave souls that gave their lives for us we must continue to encourage and respect open dialogue and debate."

The audience erupted into a cheer and applause. They drowned out the protestors' noise. The mayor turned to me and asked, "You're not running for office, are you, son?"

I laughed, "Not on a bet…looks like it's too tough of a job."

As we were leaving the area I was mobbed by news cameras, reporters, and well wishers. The news reporters called to me to stop and talk. So I did.

One of the reporters asked, "Tell me, Captain, isn't what you said just the ole two-step around the issues. That in fact a majority of the nation doesn't support the war?"

"No sir. It's what gives you the privilege to write and say whatever you want."

The others standing there all began to laugh. "Listen, folks, the real heroes are out there in the world…the soldier, airman, sailor and marine that are never seen or heard about…the ones who complete their mission without complaint. They're the real heroes. I don't see myself as a hero. I was doing my job that's all. The real heroes are the ones who plan, execute, and support the war efforts, whether they're wearing a military uniform or civilian clothes. Tell your story of heroics about them. I am sure that a story about me would bore your readers."

One reporter yelled to me, "Captain we understand you were wounded in action. Would you care to share your story?"

I smiled and made no comment. We got into our family's vehicle and drove off.

"Son…that was a powerful speech," said my father. "You did yourself proud."

The rest of my trip home wasn't as restful and private as we had hoped for. The daily intrusions were immense. People were showing up at the door and the phone rang constantly and at all hours of the day. If it wasn't a reporter looking for an interview with me it was a well wisher or, worst yet, a heckler who wanted to jerk my chain. At one point my dad got fed up with the nonsense. He refused to answer the door and took the phone off the hook. We distanced ourselves as best we could from the commotion and enjoyed our time together.

The Wedding

"This isn't like the guys. They're general early to any events we've been to. I hope everything's okay...Maybe they got recalled or something. I'd better check my cell phone for messages."

Alex started to laugh, "Whoa! Sammy, relax, the boys will be here."

We spent some time mingling and introducing our guest to each other. Suddenly one of the guests pointed up and exclaimed, "Look at this!"

There in the sky were four skydivers crisscrossing with each other with multiple colored smoke streaming from them as they were freefalling. Alex and I looked at each other.

As the four skydivers got critically close to the ground their chutes popped open. The crowd gasped with awe at the sight. The four skydivers glided gently to the earth and landed there in the backyard. As they gathered their chutes and gear, Alex and I rushed to greet them.

"What an entrance! I was beginning to wonder where you guys were."

"That was great!" said Alex. "Whose idea was it?"

The team pointed at Kym.

Alex smiled as she hugged him, "Kym, you romantic! That was awesome! Come on, let's meet the guests!"

After the introductions we all sat down for a meal. At the head table were both sets of parents and the bride and groom. Sam Senior tapped the side of his glass and calls to the audience.

"I'd like to propose a toast to the bride and groom."

All eyes were on Sam Senior. He walked over and stood between Alex and me. He smiled at his soon-to-be daughter-in-law, "Alex, could I have your hand please?" Alex smiled and offered her hand to Sam Senior. "Son, could I have your hand please." My dad placed my hand on Alex's hand. "Alex, we welcome you into our hearts. May God keep you and Sam in all His ways and bless the work of your hands."

He then turned to me and wished me the same. However, before he released our hands he smiled at me and said, "Oh yes, one last thing, son. Remember and cherish this day. For it this is the last time you'll have the upper hand in this partnership!"

As the evening came to a close and the guests were retiring, Alex and I spent time discussing life together. As we entered the house and headed for our rooms Alex smiled and said, "This is the last night we will sleep in separate beds."

I smiled and hugged my bride-to-be good night. As we turn to head to our rooms, with her trade mark girlish twinkle in her eyes, Alex asked, "Sam…I was wondering…Could I shine your shoes for tomorrow?"

I raised my eyebrows in bewilderment, "Huh…why would I have my bride shine my shoes? I love you, Alex. I would never dream of having you do such a thing."

Alex smiled and replied. "I love you, Sam…Let's start our partnership off on the right foot…Think of it as my way of showing humility in our marriage."

I shook my head and smiled. "Well you don't have to prove

anything to me...but, if that's what you want to do then I guess it's okay."

With a gleam in her eyes Alex smiled. "I'll leave them right outside your door."

I went and got my already spit-shined shoes and gave them to Alex. We hugged and retired for the evening.

—

The bridal party and best men were busily hurrying about preparing for the big event. I made my rounds to ensure that all was ready. I made a last-minute phone call to the florist to ensure that Alex's bouquet was prepared and delivered on time. My best men and I were prepared and waiting well in advance.

As we gathered in the garden at the rear of the house the team playfully bantered with me. Dennis couldn't resist being playful. "Hey, Sam, do you want us to call 911 if you faint?"

"No, have Alex give me mouth to mouth. I'm sure that'll revive me."

As we all made small talk and waited for the wedding to begin, I handed each man a small, neatly wrapped gift. I smiled and said, "From Alex and me...To our brothers."

As the time drew near we took our places.

The minister looked over to the orchestra and nodded. Instantly the musicians began playing the bride's entrance song. The wedding party faced the rear of the gathering as the audience rose and faced the rear of the gathering. As the music played Alex and her dad passed under a trellis full of roses. The sight of Alex was breathtaking. As she walked forward her gown seemed to flow along with her. Through her veil I could see her gorgeous features, her stunning blue eyes, her curly auburn hair, olive complexion, and her beautiful smile.

As Jon placed Alex's hand into my hand he said to me, "Take good care of my little girl, son."

I smiled and replied, "I will, sir…I will protect her with my life."

Jon smiled at me and replied, "I know you will, son."

As the minister concluded he asked for the rings. I looked to Jon and nodded.

Alex whispered to me, "Okay…what's up?"

I winked and smiled. "You'll see."

Jon turned and motioned to two individuals. The audience turned to the rear to see what was happening. Alex turned to see what is going on. To her surprise she saw Tucker, all groomed and decked out in his finest show halter, being led down the isle to the front of the gathering. There around Tucker's neck was a sky blue ribbon that matched the color of Alex's eyes with the rings attached.

"Awe, Tuck…you look great."

I retrieved the rings and handed them to the minister.

As the wedding vows were completed the minister asked the audience, "If there is anyone here that believes that Sam and Alex should not be wed let them speak now or forever hold their peace."

The silence in the audience was deafening. Just as the minister was to pronounce Sam and Alex husband and wife Tucker gave a loud whinny.

The minister replied, "Well, it appears that Tucker may be objecting to this marriage. How say you, Sam and Alex?"

I looked back at Tucker and said, "Not this time, Tuck. I'm her number one guy."

The minister smiled and then pronounced us husband and wife. As the ceremony concluded with our kiss, the minister asked us to kneel so that he could ask God's blessing on the marriage. As we did, those in the audience could read a message in bold print on the bottom of my shoes: "Help Me!"

The date was August 23, 2050, my retirement from the Air Force. On this day my mission was to collect my personal belongings and vacate my office. Alex and I were finally going to retire at our Chetek ranch.

As I passed through the security check points on the way to my office well wishers stopped me and congratulated me on my impending retirement. For me it seemed surreal. It seemed like yesterday I was on my way home from Gulf III.

With a smile on my face I entered my office area. My entire staff was there to greet me. My senior staff member greeted me, "Good morning, General!"

"Colonel, tomorrow morning you will address me as Sam," I replied.

"Well, sir, we just want you to know that it has been an honor and privilege to have served with you."

I paused and looked down as I became choked up with emotion. As I looked up fighting back my tears, I smiled and softly said, "The honor and privilege is all mine…You are some of the finest professionals that I have had the privilege of leading. I leave this office knowing that we did our best to uphold the true warrior's tradition. At the end of the day we can hold our heads up and stand tall, for we met our mission with confidence, commitment, and honor. We kept watch as the children of this great nation lived in peace and harmony."

As I entered my office my mind began to race, recalling the many events in my life and the nation's that led to this very day. My eyes scanned the room and I chuckled to myself. "Best place to start is at the beginning." I began packing with a picture of me and Alex at the shores of Lake Superior on our honeymoon.

As I held the picture I recalled the memories of those early years together with Alex. How we did not want our trip to end. How both of us discussed how "All good things must end."

As my thoughts drifted back in time I recalled the good news that the team and I were to be stationed as trainers at Area 51. I remembered how excited Alex and I were, knowing that we wouldn't be apart…

—

As an added bonus for me, early in my career it appeared that my leadership style caught the eyes of the joint chiefs. They saw potential in me and thought they'd begin my development for the future. I was given the responsibility of being the liaison between the Pentagon and the science group at Area 51.

I recalled the difficult times we faced after Gulf War III. The global community virtually shunned us. Things did not bode well for the U.S. both at home and abroad. Political and economic turmoil ensued as emotions flared. At home the nation was sharply divided for and against the war. The president did his best to educate the public as to how the events took place and our justification to go to war, but it seemed the harder he tried the more public trust and support he lost.

To make matters worse a coalition of key political figures was formed to protest the direction that U.S. world policy had taken and was focused on realigning U.S. policies to come in line with global opinion and direction. It was a move to disarm our new weapons systems and rejoin the world community.

The coalition was led by Massachusetts U.S. Senator Thomas N. Thornton and co-sponsored by New York U.S. Senator Gail R. Stoneham. As world political and economic pressure grew the coalition's popularity gained momentum. The tide of public opinion was rising against the administration at that time, so much so that the president announced he would not seek reelection in 2012.

The repercussions for what we had achieved in Gulf War III had devastating consequences throughout the world. It couldn't have come at a worse time for the U.S. With world opinion at an all-time low, it pushed global opinion to the brink. Even our closest allies were shocked by our new weapons technologies and seriously questioned our intentions.

Consensus throughout the world was that, given that the U.S. had used nuclear weapons in the past, it was now plausible they did indeed use a nuke to stage an incident with Iran. That in fact the U.S. was looking for an excuse to use their awesome advanced technology on Iran, to use Iran as a testing ground. That its true intention was to dominate the world, to finally impose its ideals and will upon the world. This made the world body unnerved and unsettled, knowing that the U.S. could at anytime enter into their countries virtually uncontested. The E.U called for a unified political and economic front against the U.S.

These events caused the United Nations to rethink its charter, thus forming a new political and economic organization, based in Brussels, called the New World Alliance (NWA).

Given the French's distain for the U.S. they had no problem starting the NWA movement. Initially the NWA consisted of the European Union, Russia, and their former states, India, Southeast Asian countries, China, North Korea, and several Middle Eastern countries. Israel, Latin and South American countries and several African Nations remained open to the U.S. However, it did not take long for other nations to eventually be goaded into joining the NWA. The U.S was told to find its own way. We were virtually shunned and pushed into isolation by the world.

The state of the union worsened by the day. Over the ensuing months foreign investment capital was being withdrawn from the U.S. Our world trade was stymied…it came to a screeching halt. Our former trading partners refused to ship to us and refused to accept our shipments. The economy began to wobble and falter. The stock market went into a downward spiral. The value of the U.S. dollar was devalued world wide to a value of dimes on the dollar. In an act of desperation the U.S. government brokered a deal with the major world economies as to an orderly wind down of their investments, giving the U.S. a cushion from falling into utter ruins.

Although we accepted our fate, the U.S. government warned the world that we needed time to prepare for alternative solutions. Without question we were backed into a corner. We hand no choice but to warn the world community that if our needed resources were shut off, such as oil, we would be forced to secure a source by any means necessary. We made it clear to the world that if pushed we would forcibly take it if necessary. The U.S. government secured a guarantee from the global community that for ten years we would receive our required resources, and during the ten-year period that we would pay a fair market value for all resources received.

—

During the first year of isolation, as economic conditions deteriorated, the U.S. government was forced to cut back on social programs and services, armed forces, and research programs. This news was especially hard felt by me, Alex, and the team—Area 51 was being decommissioned as well as the team was being broken up.

As I recalled our last night together as a team, I remembered when we got together for one last hurrah. The team was determined not to let the evening go out on a sour note.

As Alex and I entered the lounge Dennis spotted us first. "Come on, you two. You've got some catching up to do!"

"What's your pleasure…I'm buying?"

Alex smiled. "I'll have some orange juice."

"That sounds good. Now what do you want in it?"

Alex politely smiled, "Just OJ that's it."

Dennis and Paul had red wine delivered to the table for everyone. They raised their glasses and called for a toast. "A toast to friendship and…Brothers Till the End!"

As we all raised our glasses Alex hesitated to pick up her drink. She looked up at me and said, "Sammy, I can't drink the wine…I'm pregnant."

A little dizzy, I stood up and raised my glass, looked each team member in the eyes, smiled and said, "To friendship, brothers till the end, and to the uncles of our first born child. We're pregnant!"

"Ooh Rah!"

The day after our farewell party Alex and I were off to Washington, D.C., to the Pentagon, to begin a new chapter in our life.

I was promoted to the rank of major shortly after my arrival, and Alex's transition from her duties at Area 51 took no time at all. She moved right in to a leadership position within King Enterprises. It was up to her and her brother Jon to run the business. As for the team, well, Alex made sure that they didn't stray to far from her and me. King-Sci kept them on a retainer as consultants.

The National Imperatives

The first few years of isolation were devastating. Institutions and business that formed the bedrock of our economic system wobbled and nearly collapsed. The political upheaval that ensued spilled over into the 2012 elections. The Thornton and Stoneham ticket won by a landslide margin, and President Thornton was quick to move the country in a bold new direction. Both he and his vice president vowed to regain the world's respect and expeditiously lead the nation back to regaining our rightful place at the global table.

The U.S. government moved quickly in developing its priorities for continued survival. It took a great deal of heated debate on both sides of the aisle as to how to best handle the situation, but the House and Senate eventually banded together to support the president's vision for the new direction the U.S. would take, a direction that not only would help us survive as a nation but would advance us well into the future.

In the years 2012 - 2020 the U.S. was nearly driven into a third-world status. Cities' infrastructure, transportation systems, communications, health care systems, financial institutes, and business environments were all nearing collapse. However, all of what we faced brought the best out of us as a nation. We were forced into what became known as "Creativity by Crisis." President Thornton led the nation to pursue five new objectives:

Priority One: Ensure that all citizens were safe within the borders of the U.S. Rethink our defense paradigm and policies to be defensive and non-offensive. Develop defensive systems so advanced that the need for offensive weapon systems and weapons of mass destruction would be obsolete.

Priority Two: Ensure that all citizens were adequately fed, clothed and had ample housing…agriculture would once again become the nation's backbone.

Priority Three: Ensure that health care was available for everyone—preventive care, advanced medicines, and treatment to ensure that disease/pandemic outbreaks were kept in check.

Priority Four: Research and develop new forms of energy as well as how to develop, discover and replenish our resources. Turn to space for resources, develop hyper-conductivity for power and communications transmissions to develop computer technologies so advanced that known technologies would be considered obsolete. Advanced technology was to become our future.

Priority Five: Rethink our transportation paradigm. Advance it as far as possible. Create super high speed rail transportation systems as well as redesign personal transportation systems. Eliminate the need for petroleum.

As the president addressed the nation he made a convincing and impassioned plea for trust, patience, and calm. He asked all Americans to put aside their differences and join together in rebuilding the greatest nation on earth.

National Security: A New Paradigm

With the global upheaval that the U.S. was facing President Thornton was faced with enormously complex and difficult Department of Defense issues. How should the U.S. reshape their defense policies, practices and most importantly, at what levels should the U.S. staff its armed forces…what would their mission truly be?

President Thornton wasted no time in getting to this issue. He challenged the DOD to come up with a bold plan that met his objectives. He knew that time was limited and that the U.S. needed to come to grips with what had been taking place in the world. The balance of power obviously had shifted away from the U.S. to the newly formed New World Alliance.

The NWA had pledged to all members that wherever U.S. forces had withdrawn, its coalition forces would ensure the peace. China wasted no time in pledging its support throughout the Pacific Rim. As the U.S. drew down its Korean and Japan based troops China was quick to ensure they were ready and willing to ensure the peace. China went as far as letting North Korea know that in the event that they were to disrupt the peace in the area that they, China, would swiftly move in defense of South Korea and or Japan. Let's just say that the Chinese government had no problem convincing the Kim Jong Il government to step away from their ambitions of unifying the Korean peninsula.

China did an impressive job both diplomatically and economically in structuring a defense and economic pact throughout the Pacific Rim. All Pacific Rim Nations benefited from China's efforts. The Chinese were so successful that Taiwan opted to join the pact. Australia had no other choice but to grudgingly join. China was leading the way for the Pacific Rim Pact to achieve super economic growth, a growth never thought possible and they ensured security in the region. China opened its doors for business, doorways that led to a treasure trove of economic markets never thought possible. The NWA did not miss their opportunity to join the pact. In short order, like a rushing river, a deluge of capital began to flow into China's economy.

The DOD wasted no time in developing several options for the president. During this time I was appointed to General Cornelius' planning team. General Cornelius was adamant about not retiring from service until a plan was devised and implemented. His team wasted no time in researching and preparing a comprehensive defense strategy. It was shortly after the plan was completed that the general and his team would make their presentation to the president and his cabinet.

The Plan

The day before the presentation General Cornelius stopped by my office. "Major D'Angelo…Sam, do you have a few minutes that you could spare for an old warhorse like me?"

Taken by surprise I replied, "Ah…Yes, sir, please come in, have a seat. Would you care for something to drink?"

The general smiled, "No thank you, Sam. I just came by for a chat so I'll get to it. My days are numbered, Sam…I'll be retiring from service shortly after our presentation to the president and his cabinet."

I blushed as I looked for things to say.

The general continued in a somber tone, "Sam, I'm concerned that our nation will lose sight of the warrior's code…Promise me, son, that you will never let them forget it. We both know in the depths of our hearts and spirits that our nation's survival in the future is dependent on it. It's your generation that must carry the baton now…I am sure that in the future you will feel isolated in keeping the faith, but don't despair. Follow what your heart tells you and you'll always come out on the right side of things."

I was nearly overwhelmed by what I had just heard. It was clear to me that the general had just vested the future of the warrior's code in me. I scrambled to get an answer to my lips. "I won't let them forget, sir."

General Cornelius smiled, shook my hand, and

uncharacteristically hugged me and wished me success in the future. My mind raced as the reality of being handed the warrior's scepter set in. The general had made his choice as to who was to preserve the way of the warrior.

The next morning at 0800 hours, General Cornelius, myself and his staff motorcade to the Whitehouse for our meeting with the president and his cabinet. I was invited to ride with the general to the Whitehouse. On the way to the Whitehouse the general mentored me.

"Major…Remember, when I give my presentation show no sign of emotion at the table. Do not let those in the room know what's on your mind. Be fluid and highly adaptable in your thinking. Be open to all aspects of the discussion. Do not paint yourself into a negotiation corner by staking your position at the table. Show them that you are the true diplomat and statesmen that I believe you are."

I listened intently and grasped firmly onto every word the general spoke.

"Sam, remember the key to success in any negotiation is to seek and understand the interests of those at the table in the matter at hand. If they argue against any part of the plan, attentively listen to their concerns, ask questions, strive to understand their point of view without creating an adversarial environment. Your goal should be to create options that satisfy both yours and their interests. Most of all, know what your best alternative to making an agreement is. Compromise when you have to, but always strive for a collaborative agreement. You just may get everything you want."

"Thank you, sir. I will."

The Meeting

As I entered the room I was slightly taken back by the presence of the president and his cabinet. It was quite a sight to see these distinguished individuals in real life and all in the same room. I tried to regain my center.

Trying not to look like a tourist among celebrities I looked nonchalantly around the room. As I did, I glanced across the table and noticed that the vice president was looking directly at me. I smiled and slightly nodded my head in acknowledgement. To my surprise the vice president returned a smile and a nod.

As the meeting progressed General Cornelius eloquently presented his comprehensive twenty-year defense strategy and plan, a plan that spoke to the harmonization of technological advancements with the advancement of a highly skilled Special Operations force, a medium-sized force technologically equipped and trained to function at ten times its size and capabilities.

The president listened intently to the presentation and observed his cabinet's reaction to the plan. They had plans of their own. Like a pack of hunting raptors, with the vice president in the lead, they did their best to corner the general in their debate.

"Let me see if I got this straight, General. You are suggesting that in addition to creating a virtually impenetrable shield around our nation we should maintain a highly trained, futuristically equipped armed forces capable of being deployed anywhere in the world in short notice. Does that about sum it up?"

"In essence, Madam Vice President, that is it. However, you seemed to have glossed over the root reason for maintaining a highly trained combat-ready armed force. Our very survival as a nation depends on our ability to not only defend ourselves but also to project our military might. In the history of the world no nation or people have avoided being conquered without this capability. It is this very capacity that keeps invaders from our shores."

As the vice president listened to the general she shook her head in disgust. "General, General, General…it was this very line of antiquated thinking that has gotten us kicked out of the world community."

She then turned to the president. "Mr. President, it is time for us as a nation to demonstrate to the world that we can live up to our stated objective of wanting to live peaceably within the world community. We cannot achieve this if we don't fundamentally change our defense strategy. We have the technology that will allow us to achieve our goals. It's time to de-emphasize our use of armed forces."

As the president paused to ponder his thoughts the vice president employed a new tactic: a direct appeal to his team. In a lull in the conversation as members of the cabinet had sidebar discussions, the vice president called over to me. "Excuse me, Major…"

I looked up from reading my notes. "Yes, ma'am."

The vice president smiled. "Given that you and your

colleagues are potentially tomorrow's leaders, how would you recommend that we move forward?"

I did my best to be calm. As I looked around the room my eyes caught the general's. He nodded. I knew that he trusted what I had to say. I smiled as I prepared to answer the vice president. All eyes were on me as they anticipated my response.

"Well, ma'am, I'd like to begin by restating the issues as I believe I understand them."

"Please do, Major."

"Well as you can see, Madam Vice President, I believe that both your vision and General Cornelius' vision for the future are compatible. The focus of both plans calls for leveraging our technology. I believe that a mobile weapons platform is complementary to the land based systems. As for the issue of maintaining a highly trained Special Forces capability, I believe the respective strategies are also compatible."

As the president listened to my analysis he sat slightly looking down with his hands folded, forefingers pointing up and to his lips and elbows on the arms of his chair.

"And how is that compatible, Major?" asked the vice president.

General Cornelius looked to me and smiled. I showed no signs of being stressed by the vice president's pointed response. I calmly began making my comparison.

"Let's draw the parallels together. You agree that the root of your concerns stems from the issue of expeditiously returning our nation to its rightful status as a key member in the global community?"

"Yes, Major, and there is no way under the sun this will

happen if in fact we appear to be a warring nation. We can't return to being the world's police force."

"I agree, ma'am. Are you concerned with the notion that we will continue to maintain a powerful military, or are you concerned with how the global community views our maintaining a powerful military?"

The vice president paused. "I would say both. You must admit, since World War II we have projected an image of military might to the world. Lord only knows how we've used it. We have spent trillions of dollars on defense. Think of the social good we could have done if we had spent it on improving our society—poverty, education, health, the list goes on."

"I understand. I also believe that our national security is paramount to you, ma'am."

"It goes without saying, Major."

I continued. "In light of this let's review the timeline in which we will be researching, developing and deploying our new technologies. Given the timeline and projections as to when the new systems will be operational, it appears that it will take ten to fifteen years to achieve. As such, would you not agree that during this transition we could be at our most vulnerable if we did not maintain a strong armed forces capability?"

The vice president paused for a moment and pursed her lips. "You make a good point, Major. What are you driving at?"

"Ma'am, given that during this time we would be approximately sixty percent through General Cornelius' plan, wouldn't it make sense for us to transition into our new armed forces structure at the time of completion? I do not believe that the composition of our forces is the issue, only how they are deployed. If we are measured in how we act I believe we can project strength at the same time demonstrate our true desire for peace. In fifteen years we will be in a better position to evaluate how we should develop and deploy our military assets."

The vice president looked to the president, "Mr. President, I believe we have a new option on the table."

The president smiled. "Good work. Have your respective staffs work out the details and have the plan on my desk ASAP."

The group concurred and the meeting was adjourned.

As the members in the room were bidding each other farewell the vice president made her way over to me. She looked at the name tag on my uniform, smiled, and offered her hand to me for a shake.

"D'Angelo…I'll keep that name in mind."

"Thank you, ma'am."

The meeting was a defining moment in my career. I had taken a giant step forward in my personal growth and development. As each diplomatic challenge came forward I met it head-on.

—

As I stood gazing out the window a voice beckoned me back from my memories. "General. Excuse me, sir…sir, Doctor Wallace is on line one."

I activated my communications module and heard a familiar voice, "Happy retirement dad!"

"Sami! How's my girl?"

"I'm just great! How's my dad doing today?"

I chuckled, "I'm packing up my things and will be heading home this evening. I should be in Eau Claire around 1930. Will you have my granddaughters at the airport to meet me?"

Sami laughed, "Dear God, they'd have a fit if I didn't bring them. Hurry home!"

I no sooner hung up from my call and my administrative assistant entered my office. "Sir, Doctor Armstrong is on the line."

"Hello, Jonni. How's my girl?"

"Happy retirement, Dad! Just wanted to tell you the boys and I will be at the airport to greet you tonight…I've got to run."

As I deactivated my communications module my mind raced back to the days my girls were born. In an instant I recalled their births, their first steps, their school years and their medical school years. They had grown up to be doctors, Sami a Neurosurgeon and Jonni a Doctor of Veterinarian Medicine.

I sighed as I returned to my packing and my mind drifted to earlier days…

Feed the Nation

As I entered the house Alex called to me, "We're in here."

I entered the study to find Alex working on her computer and Sami playing with her toys. "How's my girls today?"

Alex turned and smiled, "We're doing great."

Sami stood to her feet and reached up to me. I playfully scooped her up and swung her and placed her on my hip as I stepped forward and bent down to kiss Alex. "Still working on your puzzle I see."

Alex smiled, "Ya…we are so darn close to unlocking this thing. If we find the key to unlock this enigma we will solve one of natures' mysteries. What's driving me crazy is that we've found the darn switch, we just don't know how to turn it on. Bumper crop production every year, super disease-resistant crops, just think of the good we could do for ourselves and the rest of the world."

I smiled and patted Alex on the shoulder. "Keep working at it, hon…if anyone can solve this I know you can."

"Sammy, when you get a minute could I ask you some questions about your Gulf III deployment?"

"I guess so…what does my deployment have to do with your project?"

"Just a hunch."

A moment later I took a seat beside Alex. "Okay…I'm all yours."

Alex smiled and raised her eyebrows as she replied, "Okay, my team has been investigating the effects of the MAGS umbrella on the human psyche and body as well as its effects on plant life. We have poured over the data from Gulf III concerning the deployment of the MAG System and we found a recurring theme in all the reports from those of you who were deployed in country…Sammy, what did you mean in your report that 'everything seemed robust' while you were under the MAGS umbrella?"

I paused to recapture my thoughts, "I don't remember…You've got to remember we were all pretty geeked up when we deployed. We were in great shape for the mission."

Alex smiled. "That's true, but the description you gave in your report was pretty explicit. You and the team gave real descriptive reports of your observations."

I paused. "Well, I did my best to give as accurate information as I could. Thinking back I guess it just seemed that as we deployed I didn't need a lot of sleep, kind of kept one eye open at all times. Given the little sleep I got I felt refreshed and rested. As for being isolated, well, we really trained for the mission. I guess I was ready for being isolated. However, during the mission I felt that mentally I was in good shape, I had a sense of well being. Nothing seemed to bother me, mentally or physically. You know, clear headed and no aches or pains. Heck, we were cooped up under the MAGS for days yet everything seemed rosy. Why, even the small plants in my encampment seemed greener in color…Does any of this help you, Alex?"

Alex smiled, "Yes, I believe so. I'm just putting the pieces to a difficult puzzle together. I'll keep digging. I'm sure the answer will pop up soon."

Over the next several days Alex poured over the various fire teams debrief reports. Her eye caught a statement that Neal had made in his report. "I thought I could start my own garden."

"Hi, Neal, it's Alex…"

"Hey, Alex, how are you feeling?"

"I feel fine. I'm not due for another two months…Neal, could I ask you a few questions about your deployment in Gulf III?"

"Sure, Alex."

"Neal, what did you mean in your report that you thought you could start your own garden?"

Neal paused. "Ah, let's see…Oh yeah, the damnedest thing seemed to happen in my encampment. After a few days under the MAGS umbrella I noticed that plants seemed to pop up everywhere around me. I mean everything seemed so green and lush under the MAGS. I thought that I was imagining this, but when I broke camp I noticed that the plants in my area had grown about six inches, yet nothing outside my area had grown. The plants left a perfect impression as to where my MAGS was deployed."

Over the next several days Alex pondered, hypothesized and made calculations as to the effects of the MAGS on plant growth. She knew that she was close.

Later that week Alex awoke from her sleep. "My God, that's it!"

Startled, I jumped out of bed and yelled, "I'll get the car, you get Sami!"

In the dimly lit room I managed to find my sweatpants and shirt and began to get dressed. Watching the mayhem, Alex's giggled and turned on her bedside lamp. There I stood confused and frazzled. "Come on, Alex. We got to get Sami to the sitter and head for the hospital."

"Look at you, Sam! Your shirt is inside out and on backwards—"

"Aren't you having the baby?"

"No, silly! I figured it out! I know how to turn on the switch! I've got to call Jon. We've done it."

After Alex called Jon and explained her findings she turned to me. "Sam, we've been looking at this all wrong. We've been working on the assumption that the magnetic umbrella caused the growth. You know, bending the light caused some kind of greenhouse effect. It finally dawned on me that it wasn't the light being bent around the plants; it was the redirection of the earth's magnetic field. Sam! Just by chance the area in which you and the team deployed in required you to modulate your MAGS frequencies much differently than the other teams'. All the other teams reported deploying their MAGS at much higher frequencies. You and the team reported frequencies well below the average. That's the missing piece of the puzzle! To get to where we need to be there has to be a balance between three variables—the earth's magnetic field at a given latitude and longitude, the MAGS frequency, and the plant's natural harmonics to the earth's magnetic field. The trick is to balance these variables. Each plant species has its own optimal harmonic level. Tune the MAGS frequency to this level and you have maximum plant growth and output."

The next morning Alex began building computer models

of her findings. As she built a model she forwarded it to Jon. He in turn had his science team begin building working models for the Agri-MAG System. Jon wasted no time getting Paul, Dennis, Kym and Neal involved in the project. It was their expertise in working with the MAG System that was crucial to King-Sci's success.

The initial lab results exceeded the teams' wildest calculations and expectations for success. Initial results calculated that the magnet pulse energy could in fact energize plants to enter into super hyper production. King-Sci mastered the art and science of setting up MAGS and adjusting the output harmonics/frequencies to what the scientist called "the plants natural rhythm to the earth's magnetic field." To their awe and amazement the field experiment plants produced 1000 fold their natural capacity to produce fruit and fiber.

King-Sci's success with Agri-MAGS technology went well beyond fruit bearing plants. The technology touched every aspect of agriculture and forestry. The Agri-MAG System revolutionized the forestry industry. The new technology caused trees to grow to maturity for lumber ten times faster than they normally would take. On average, pine trees are ready for harvest within approximately fifty years. Under cultivation with the Agri-MAG System deployed pine trees were capable of being grown and harvested within five years.

What astounded the scientific community was that all products grown using the Agri MAG System technology were of a quality so high that it surpassed quality standards for agricultural and forestry products. A profound short-term gain from the hyper agricultural gains was the increased production helped ease the nation's energy crisis. Ethanol production went through the roof…we could finally wean ourselves off foreign oil.

One of the most amazing discoveries with this new found technology was that MAGS could be arrayed to direct and or divert weather. The MAGS technology was not capable of total weather control, but it had a profound effect on certain weather patterns. They could be used to coax or direct rain and snow to drought stricken and arid areas therefore creating a natural form of irrigation. Most importantly, the researchers found that the MAGS could also be used to expedite storm systems through areas to prevent disasters such as flooding and wind damages. The MAGS could cause the storms to dump precipitation well before it impacted heavily populated areas.

Through all of this the King-Sci Corporation was catapulted into the national spotlight. Their work was hailed as being in the same category as Edison's invention of the light bulb.

President Thornton was quick to ensure that the U.S. shared its new found bounty with the world. Yet only the third world nations would accept the offer. The NWA refused to allow the U.S. back to the global table. They viewed the U.S. generosity as a ploy to regain their world leadership position, a position that the NWA did not want to share.

Give Me Shelter

As I packed my collection of pictures I came across a picture of my father-in-law, Jon, and President Thornton. The picture was taken at the president's meeting with high-profile corporate members to seek solutions to the nation's economic problems as well as ensuring adequate shelter for all. It was here that the American Pride movement began. Americans focused on rebuilding America, putting our differences aside to achieve the higher goal of reestablishing America's greatness. And so we did as the world looked on in awe and envy.

Given the new focus of the U.S. and an increase in national pride, many who lost their jobs enlisted into the modern form of the Civilian Conservation Corp, formally known as the CCC in the great depression. The new group was called "Develop America Corp." The DAC, as they were called, was used in all facets of rebuilding America—housing, roadways, railways, communications systems, assisting in agriculture and forestry services.

As I recalled those days I smiled with a sense of pride of being a part of such a great nation. As I packed my last item a sense of finality came over me. Yet, I knew that it was just the end of one chapter in my life and that I was to begin writing a new one.

I said goodbye to my staff and colleagues, and headed to my waiting staff car. I was finally on my way home. As I was driven to Andrews Air Force Base I could see a huge American Flag flying in front of one of the federal buildings. What a sight. The stars and stripes seemed to roll in waves as the summer breeze blew past it. The sun shining on the flag seemed to make it glow with iridescence. I whispered to myself, "All the history that she represents...I hope I was able to help."

My driver looked up into the rearview mirror. "Excuse me, sir?"

I smiled, "It's nothing, son...just an old man talking to himself."

As we drove, I looked out over the landscape recalling many of the events and national accomplishments that had taken place over the past forty plus years...The only way to describe them was "awesome."

As The Years Passed

As events raced through my mind I smiled with contentment. The world had virtually shunned this nation. They did it punitively, with the intent to inflict harm on us, and how did we react? Like true champions. The one thing the NWA and their ilk totally underestimated was that we may squabble and bicker amongst ourselves, but when outside forces come to bear against us, like a family, we put aside our differences and unite. The very reason the American culture will retain its greatness.

In a flash I recalled how far we as a nation had come. How we as a people achieved our lofty national objectives. Ensuring every American was afforded adequate health care. How our scientists discovered that magnetic pulse energy killed germs and viruses. The scientists became so proficient they were able use technology to eliminate a number of different cancer cells in living tissue. Radiation and chemotherapy were nearly obsolete. One of the most astounding uses of the technology was the rapid healing of wounds and broken bones. The applications in surgery were limitless.

How for years it was a secret that the U.S. found their rare magnetic element on an asteroid. And that, given the shortages of precious raw materials NASA came up with a plan to mine near earth asteroids. How they moved larger metal-laden asteroids closer to earth to mine them robotically. The intriguing part of the plan was that they had no idea what they were going to discover. To their surprise several asteroids were loaded with precious metals.

Researchers also found that by creating a "magnetic plasma conduit" that they changed power transmission forever—virtually no resistance in transmitting power. Researchers had successfully created "hyper conductivity." This opened the door to the future of communications, computer power and speed, and super high speed transportation systems.

As for our nation's transportation paradigm, well let's say that the U.S. was moving into the next century in its thinking. It was apparent the way we thought about transportation had not really changed in the past 150 years. Railways still ran on steel wheels on steel tracks. Roadways were built for fossil fuel powered vehicles with wheels. Researchers pioneered the way into mass transit systems powered by magnetic propulsion. Magnetic levitation systems made up of hubs and spokes leading into major population areas were designed in such a way that it took minutes to get to destination versus an hour by driving in a conventional manner.

What was most impressive was that the transportation system development plan indicated that in the later years (the late 2050's early 2060's) highway infrastructure was to be developed to allow for magnetic powered transportation. All major highways were to be under-laid with a spider web of hyper conductive conduits that allowed for newly designed magnetic levitated cars to navigate on. The prototypes were already being tested. They were fully computerized cars that made them programmable. They could virtually drive themselves to the desired destination. They would be capable of GPSing right to your front door. As for safety, each vehicle had the capacity to communicate with other moving vehicles. They were to be virtually crash proof. Initially all vehicles would have wheels to allow for driving on off system roads and terrain. Wheels on vehicles would be for the off road enthusiast and needed to function on roads that had not been integrated into the national road system.

During these years the U.S. flourished. Like a Phoenix rising from the ashes the U.S. succeeded in rising to a super advanced culture. As we did, the world stood by in disbelief. Over this period, with the exception of the lean years, the U.S. never lost sight of its charitable nature. Despite world opinion the U.S. shipped food and health care abroad to needy nations. However, most nations were goaded by the NWA to reject our help.

—

As my vehicle approached the runway where my aircraft awaited me I drifted back to the present. I smiled as I quietly summarized our nation's accomplishments. We'd come a long way. We had achieved a greatness that would go unrivaled for years to come.

In a flash I summed it up. Technology and agriculture had abounded, our medical community had made super advancement, education had abounded to the point where we'd reached a one hundred percent literacy rate and we had advanced in the arts and sports. What an astounding accomplishment for a nation.

What was so mind boggling for most people in this nation was that the U.S. was on the brink of ruin and decades later had become the world's most affluent nation. The U.S. became so affluent that the oil rich nations could not compare. NASA's mining project brought untold wealth home to the nation. The amounts of precious metals that were recovered from their mining project allowed the U.S. government to distribute the wealth back to the population in the forms of:

- Free education
- Free health care
- Tax relief (Taxes were all but non-existent; to keep the capitalistic system viable only token taxes were paid into the system.)
- Public services of all kinds were improved to levels of near luxury.
- Crime rates dropped to record lows
- Society advanced because advanced technologies, education, the arts, and sports abounded. Street gangs shrank into oblivion. Drug and alcohol abuse diminished to near nothing.

During this period of prosperity the U.S. society came to grips with its diverse opinions concerning its culture and religion. The various cultural and religious sects quit squabbling among themselves. They came to realize that we are all in this together. They adopted a true doctrine of tolerance, love, and respect for their neighbor. They encouraged all to look beyond a person's humanity and accept them as they were. To respect their right to live life as they wished.

As I disembarked my vehicle I was greeted by several of the joint chiefs and an honor guard. As I approached the stairway to my aircraft I was saluted by all. I smiled as I returned the salute. I shook each of the joint chiefs' hands, said my goodbyes, and boarded my aircraft. With a heavy heart I settled into my seat. I so loved serving this nation. Yet as the aircraft was making altitude my heart grew heavier. I did my best to keep the warrior's code alive, but felt I did not fully achieve that mission.

As I settled in to the flight I once again allowed my thoughts to drift. I looked out into the blue sky and began to reminisce. My thoughts raced back to the years I spent in the Stoneham administration. She won the presidency with a margin nearly as wide as her predecessor, President Thornton. To say that President Stoneham was ambitious would be an understatement. She pressed forward with energy unrivaled by any president before her, ensuring that we did not lose momentum with the former administration's national imperatives. In addition, she held true to her word. I played an integral part in the design and implementation of the nations new Costal Defense Command (CDC). President Stoneham was sure to use me as a team member on her diplomatic corp.

It was President Stoneham that set the U.S. on a new social course. Although she allowed the military to maintain a sharp offensive and defensive focus, she made no hidden secret of the fact that once the CDC was fully functional she would begin the process of deemphasizing the offensive capabilities of our armed forces. Given my popularity with the president I managed to convince her to keep a small-yet-relevant Special Forces group active. However, over time the nation's youth lost interest in becoming a Special Forces Warrior. They just couldn't see the need.

As the flight progressed I drifted in and out of my thoughts. As I sat looking out my window into the blue sky it reminded me of my many trips across the Pacific Ocean to China. As I pondered my diplomatic missions to China my mood swung from contentment to one of concern. In a flash I recalled the many passionate pleas I made to the various administrations concerning China and her true intentions: world domination.

As I drifted deeper into my memories I recalled my days when I was the key note speaker at the War College. How I did my best to lay out China's intentions and plan for dominating the west. What was obvious to me but did not seem to register with the U.S. Government Services was that China was growing into an economic super giant. The world was addicted to China's economy. They just kept pumping their wealth into China as they extracted wealth from China's economy. I could see that with all this newfound wealth China was technologically advancing at a hyper pace.

I recalled the many discussions I had pointing to the fact that with the U.S. in isolation China had set its doctrine to world dominance. I recalled how I made a compare and contrast of how the Chinese philosophy of Ying and Yang—soft and hard was at play. For millenniums the Chinese had understood that there was a season to act with strength and a season to act passively. Their true strength was found in their ability to patiently wait for the time to act.

I recalled making an impassionate plea to all who would listen concerning China's history for being a conquering nation. That in fact they were awakening from a long sleep and revitalizing their abilities to conquer. My concern for the nation was that it was apparent that as the U.S. grew in a softer, more socially driven direction, China was growing itself in a hard direction, a disciplined and militaristic direction. Returning to her roots as conquerors.

I recalled the ridicule that I received when I recommended that the solution to the problem was to retool our defense strategy from a purely defensive to a combination of offensive and defensive tactics…return to the warrior's code. To return to making our presence known in the air and on the high seas. It was my contention that living peacefully amongst the world community was paramount, but in protecting our way of life as a nation we had to demonstrate how powerful we were and our willingness to use our power to keep aggressors at bay. My love of my country was always my motivation. I placed such a high value on preserving our liberty and freedom. I knew from the depth of my soul that I was right. It pained me deeply to be ignored.

My thoughts drifted from one diplomatic mission to the next. I recalled how each time I would visit China the Chinese delegation assured me that they wished only peaceful relations with the U.S. I instinctively knew better.

I recalled one event. On January 20, 2035, I led a diplomatic delegation to China to discuss economic issues as well as set the stage for negotiating an arms limitation deal. It appeared that with all of their newfound wealth China was researching, developing and arming themselves at an alarming rate. The world nervously looked on. Many delegations from the various NWA members discussed their concerns with the Chinese. All they got were assurances that China wished to live peacefully in the world community.

It was apparent to the U.S. government that this particular summit was an opportunity to earn credibility to get back to the global table. China knew that the U.S. still maintained its nuclear arsenal and had extraordinary means to deliver their warheads with pinpoint accuracy. The Chinese understood and respected the U.S.' strength. They understood that the U.S. was still a formidable opponent.

I recalled when I was the lead diplomat on one specific mission and was to be accompanied by several aids and one DOD rising star—a Mr. Darius Dillon.

As I finished my briefing I opened the floor for discussion. "I believe the mission is straight forward. Do you have any questions?"

Dillon spoke first. "Yes, General. Why are we taking such a strong position on the issues? I mean, don't you think that we can achieve greater results if we take a softer approach? You know, a more cooperative approach?"

I smiled and replied, "I'll explain, Darius, but first I'd like to explore your line of thinking. How do you see the issues?"

Darius was encouraged by my comments, "Well, general, I believe that we are holding all the cards. I mean, we've got what they want. Technology, food and natural resources. Sir, the U.S. is an impenetrable fortress, a cornucopia of resources. I believe that if we use the carrot vs. the stick approach we will get the Chinese to give us exactly what we want."

"Darius, how would you guarantee that they would hold true to their side of the bargain? After all, we have no way of verifying their true intentions."

"Well, sir, first is our satellite intelligence. The Chinese know that our spy satellite system is robust. They know that there isn't much we can't find out about their build up. Obviously, sir, it requires trust between the parties…I mean the Chinese have not shown any ill will toward us as a nation and they are a century behind us in military technology. Even with their enormous army they are no match for us. They just can't get to us and they know it."

I smiled as I listened. "Darius, never underestimate your opponent. The Chinese are a patient people. They are inclined to make slow and steady progress. Where we in the west make our long range plans out to, say ten years, the Chinese are making plans fifty to one hundred years into the future. We are not negotiating a deal for today. What we negotiate today has far-reaching affects for generations to come. The Chinese are testing our strength and resolve to use our strength. We will approach these negotiations with resolve, tact, and quiet confidence. It's not what we say at the table. It is what we do not say that the Chinese will listen for."

The Chinese were open and receptive to my visit. They liked me because they felt I projected a strong presence and was trustworthy. As usual I was greeted by the Chinese delegation at the airport; however, like me they had a few new members on their team. I did my best to eloquently introduce my team. My Chinese counterpart did the same.

As the talks progressed I paid particular attention to how my team functioned. I couldn't help but notice that Darius and a young Chinese officer, Captain Khan, seemed to hit it off. I had cautioned my team to be especially careful in what they said and to whom they said it.

The talks progressed as I predicted. The Chinese wanted more resources and most of all wanted the technology to go with it. They wanted our Agri-MAGS technology. I did my best to keep the Chinese demands at bay. However, there came a point in the talks when things became intense. It appeared that Darius had misspoke in a side bar discussion with Captain Khan concerning disarmament and Agri-MAGS technology.

As I recalled the incident I vividly remembered how the Chinese aggressively demanded at the table that the U.S. live up to what it had suggested. That in fact, my credibility as a diplomat was in jeopardy with the Chinese if in fact the U.S. did not deliver on its promise.

I recall how I gave Darius a verbal thrashing. Then I sent him back to the DOD for reassignment. A reassignment to be buried in a menial job and to be lost to obscurity.

To say that my diplomatic skills were put to the test would be an understatement. I recalled how I was pushed and prodded by the Chinese as to their insistence that because one of my team members put the issue on the table it could be interpreted that I put the issue on the table. I understood the Chinese's philosophy of staying fluid in battle, as the bamboo shoot bends and yields in the storm. For when the storm has passed the bamboo always returns to its original upright position. I did exactly that. I weathered the storm and regained my credibility with the Chinese. In fact the Chinese ended up with a deeper respect for me. They truly feared my capabilities.

A voice over the aircraft intercom interrupted my thoughts, "General D'Angelo, we are about twenty minutes from landing, sir."

A sense of excitement came over me. I couldn't help but smile as I thought of seeing my family and of course my lifelong friends and brothers. I sat back and smiled as I recalled how the years seemed to fly by. How Paul, Dennis, Kym, and Neal all were so instrumental in King-Sci Corporation's initiatives in

MAGS technology. How our bond as brothers grew stronger as we all grew older.

As the aircraft landed and taxied to a stop I could see an anxious crowd waiting for me. All of my family and close friends. As I exited the aircraft the crowd grew more excited. I could hardly contain my smile and I waved and winked to my well wishers. As I entered the terminal I moved toward the crowd before me and as if Moses was parting the Red Sea, the crowd opened in the middle. There standing before me was the love of my life, my Alex. As we embraced the crowd encircled us and seemed to swallow us up with hugs and tugs…Lots of "Papa, did you knows," and "Dad we were thinkings." I basked in the love and attention.

The Retirement Years

Alex and I wasted little time in establishing the next chapter in our life and began managing our ranch. We were content in how our lives had gone, how our family had flourished, and how our nation lived in peace, prosperity and harmony. Yet world events seemed to deteriorate.

Over the years and because of China's economic appeal to the NWA, the world appeased the Chinese's ambitions. The U.S. was comfortable in its cocoon of safety and prosperity. We became complacent as to the NWA's problems.

World events got extremely complicated. The Chinese were on the move. First they annexed Taiwan. Southeast Asia in general folded right into China's control. In the early years they dropped the hammer on North Korea. They promised the South Koreans that if they unified with the north they would allow the new government to be established by the south, therefore, guaranteeing the south of maintaining its current structure and economy. Then the Chinese turned their eye to the big prize—Japan. The Chinese had a score to settle from the WWII days. The Chinese systematically choked off Japans trade and resources until they complied with China's doctrine for the Pacific Rim countries.

What complicated the matter was that as the decades passed and China's world stature grew, several disasters hit the Chinese empire—famine, pestilence and several natural disasters, earth quakes, fires, and floods of biblical proportions. This caused them to look toward the U.S with deep envy and distain.

The White Crane

Since the year 2050 the U.S. had sent their emissaries to Beijing to diplomatically express their concerns over China's expansionist activities throughout the Pacific Rim as well as their continued violation of U.S. territorial waters.

On February 24, 2060, Secretary of State Sonja Zared and her deputies hurriedly exited their meeting with the Chinese president and his cabinet. It was obvious she was concerned as to the direction her meeting had gone. By the look on her face there was no doubt that she wanted to get on her aircraft and airborne ASAP.

As the secretary's aircraft cleared Chinese air space she instructed her deputies to establish a holographic link with the president. One by one the president and his cabinet appeared for the meeting.

The president addressed the group first, "Ah, hello, Ms. Secretary. I hope you had a productive meeting with President Lin."

There was a brief pause as the secretary gathered her thoughts. "Well, sir, to put it bluntly, the meeting didn't fair very well."

The president chuckled and then responded. "No sugar coating this one. I knew I could count on a straight-to-the-point assessment from you."

The secretary smiled as the group responded with a laugh.

The president continued, "Obviously you are troubled by this meeting. What's your take on things?"

The secretary paused and then began to give her assessment.

"Well, sir, we were basically left waiting on the president's front stoop. Just before our meeting was to begin one of the president's deputies informed us that the president had other pressing matters to attend to. The S.O.B. kept us waiting one hour. To add insult to injury as we took our seats for the meeting I had the distinct feeling that I was nearly sitting on the floor. I swear they cut the legs off our seats. Lin and his cabinet on the other hand seem to sit tall in their seats, kind of an elevated position.

"In any event, as we began our dialogue Lin had that arrogant bastard Khan stand behind him to his right. To say that our discussion was chilly would be an understatement.

"On issue one, China's Pacific Rim dominance, the president retorted with, 'History demonstrates that many empires have risen and fallen. The U.S. should embrace the fact that a new world leader has risen.'

"Issue two faired no better. When I addressed the issue that China's fishing vessels have continued to encroach our fishing grounds, nearly depleting our resources, and on several occasions had to be escorted out of U.S. territorial waters, he laughed at me. His response was, 'We have nearly two billion people to feed.' When I suggested that we could increase our exports to China he retorted, 'Give a man a fish he eats…you have fed him. Yet, give a man a boat and nets he feeds himself and his village. Give us the technology and we will feed ourselves!'

"When I addressed the fact that his so-called fishing fleet was a covert eavesdropping mission the president laughed and retorted, 'So some of our younger fisherman like to listen to U.S. rock music.'

"Things got testy when I broached the subject that China's navy was sailing particularly close to our territorial waters. When I brought up the subject Lin looked to Khan for the answer. Khan barked his response, 'You do not dictate how China sails the open seas!'

"The final straw, sir, was when I addressed the issue of our High Plane Weather Satellite System mysteriously disappearing in a flash of light. The look on Khan's face told it all, but he recovered from the surprise quickly. His response was as predicted. 'You lose a satellite and question us on your loss? It sounds like you must improve on your engineering of such instruments.'

The secretary chuckled. "I believe they thought we would have no idea they hit the satellite. What they are struggling with is they're not sure if we know how they did it."

The president listened intently to the secretary's assessment then commented, "Ms. Secretary, in your estimation is China moving toward a war footing?"

There was a long pause as the secretary gathered her thoughts then she answered. "China is looking to become the premiere world super power. All that stands in her way is the U.S. For years they have eyed the U.S. with a contemptuous eye. Sir, we are on a collision course with the Chinese."

"We will meet as a full cabinet upon your return. I will inform key members of congress and the senate."

Beijing

As Secretary Zared left the meeting with President Lin, Lin turned to Khan and said, "How soon will we be ready?"

Khan smiled with confidence and answered, "Not long, sir. Our planning and resources are ready. Now it's a matter of timing."

There was a pause as President Lin pondered his thoughts and then he spoke.

"I would like a complete briefing. Let us reconvene our meeting in one hour at the defense ministry. General Khan, you will brief me and my cabinet on your plan."

As the meeting concluded Khan turned to his aids, "Go prepare for our presentation. This is the most important presentation of our military careers."

As President Lin and his entourage entered the theater-styled briefing room Khan's staff hurriedly completed setting up for their presentation. With the theater lights dimmed Khan stepped up to a podium under a spotlight. He paused as he looked up into the audience. "Mr. President and most honorable guests, I am honored to address you today. It gives me great pleasure to present to you the plan and road map to our nation's glorious destiny and future. Gentlemen, I present to you Operation White Crane."

As the theater lights went out a brief documentary film narrated by Khan began. The documentary depicted how China grew from a futile nation to an economic giant and military world power. The documentary moved methodically through how China developed their technological achievements without being detected by foreign nations' intelligence or satellites. Khan beamed with satisfaction as he discussed how the Chinese for years utilized cold war underground facilities for research and development of their weapon systems as well as the development and training of his ultra elite Special Forces division the Black Dragons. All were trained in the true warrior's tradition.

The documentary covered China's accomplishment of being the second nation to send a manned mission to the moon, to have deployed a space-based research station, to successfully land research probes on Venus, Mars, Jupiter, and Saturn's moons, and how this research led China's military complex into a new era of weapons research and development.

As Kahn explained, China made an historical leap in weapons research and in the development of a Neutron Beam Weapon System—a weapon system so powerful and accurate that missile warfare was now obsolete. The system could detect, track, and destroy an object the size of a baseball from several hundred miles away. Not only did the Chinese harness the "Neutron" into a beam weapon system, but they also developed a Neutron Beam Propulsion system for their aircraft and navy vessels.

Khan's presentation went on to describe China's revolutionary changes in stealth technology. The development of "Nano Stealth." As depicted in the documentary, Chinese scientists had developed a nano fabric that was so advanced that it was overlaid onto every aircraft, vessel, and vehicle making them totally invisible to radar. When a radar signal reached its target, the nano fabric would catch the signal, absorb it, and pass it through the targeted vessel, giving no echo response to the radar sending unit.

The Chinese had also revolutionized sea travel forever. They had finally solved the problem of vessels having to plow through water by creating a Neutron Slip Stream Propulsion System. Vessels now traveled on a Neutron slip stream and skipped across the water in excess of airliner speeds—five hundred plus miles per hour. In addition to the speed, the Chinese had revolutionized a new shape for seagoing vessels. Seagoing vessels were a cross between a UFO saucer and a tear drop, the ultimate aero-dynamic shape. All weapon systems, decks, and support systems were neatly tucked away under the outer hull while traveling at high speeds. When needed these systems would pop up from under the vessels' hull.

Finally was China's development and deployment of a space-based weapons systems—satellites and hyper-space planes. The Chinese had successfully developed and deployed a killer satellite system capable of seeking out targets and delivering a neutron beam blow to any space-based target it was directed to knock out. In addition, they had developed and deployed a fleet of hyper-space planes capable of taking off from land, entering low earth orbit, loitering over a target for extended periods, and dropping in undetected on their target to unleash a lethal and devastating blast of neutron beam power. These space planes traveled in excess of Mach twenty. They could get anywhere in the world in less than one hour.

China had finally done it. They had engineered their way around the awesome magnetic pulse weapon systems of the

U.S. The excitement in the theater was electrifying. As the first segment of Khan's presentation came to a close, the president and his cabinet stood to their feet and applauded. Khan smiled with deep gratification. Khan then begins to address the audience as to how China would deploy these assets.

He began with a real-time satellite feed of the U.S. West Coast. "Gentlemen, as you know the U.S. Coastal Defense Command has deployed a sophisticated network and array of pulse weapons along their coast lines—to date an impenetrable defense. As such, these weapons form a protective umbrella over the U.S. This array of weapons can deliver trillions of watts of pulse energy into the air or at sea level."

Khan then had his team focus a satellite video feed over several key points in the mountains along the west coast.

"As you can see we have pinpointed the location of the U.S. CDC's mountain based defenses." As the satellite feed focused in on the installations it was easy to discern that these installations were buried deep inside the mountains and well protected by security forces as well as the mountains themselves. Nothing short of a direct nuclear blast would knock them out, or so it seemed.

"Ah, you have pinpointed their coastal defense locations." Khan smiled. "It would appear so; however, our ground intelligence has proven otherwise."

Khan switched the satellite feed to the U.S. Northwest, Puget Sound, and worked his way down the coastline. As he did he stopped at various ports and focused on a series of loaded container ships.

He paused and addressed the audience, "This is where the U.S. has hidden their coastal defenses."

The president responded with surprise. "Are you sure? How can you be certain?"

Khan smugly smiled. "Our ground and satellite intelligence have followed sixty such vessels up and down the U.S. seaboards. These vessels are moved and placed into position in an elaborate shell game. They are scrambled in and out of ports, never unloaded; they only make crew changes and are always docked in secure areas. Make no mistake, the mountain facilities are viable weapon systems; however, the real fire power comes from these vessels."

The president smiled. "American ingenuity…not so brilliant after all."

This drew a laugh from the audience.

Khan continued with his discussion. "As for the northern tier, the U.S. relies on fighter bases along their border with Canada. We have intelligence as to the exact location and numbers of assets at each fighter base across their border as well as within their country. As for the U.S. ground forces capabilities, well, they are inept at best. They are incapable of sustaining a ground campaign. Our intelligence has infiltrated their ranks and has observed their military's demise over the past fifty years. Their 'Citizen Solider' program is a farce. For nearly fifty years the U.S. has evolved from maintaining highly trained, equipped, and disciplined ground forces to a highly technologically automated defense strategy. Over the past five decades the U.S. has shunned those who advocate strong defense strategies, maintaining a superior fighting force in favor of their more socially acceptable defense strategies. Their weekend warriors train like children playing dress up. They look good in their uniforms yet are indifferent toward entering battle.

"Throughout the U.S. military complex not one warrior exists. They are all politicians. Their true warriors are all aged and in their graves. Mr. President, our forces will cut through the U.S. forces without hesitation. The U.S. is asleep, no one is on watch, and most importantly, they lack a warrior's spirit and discipline. The time grows near to when we should strike."

President Lin listened intently and pondered what he had heard and seen. He nodded his head as he began to speak.

"General Khan, with great cunning and skill you have observed and studied your opponents' strengths and weaknesses. As we all know, the American people are an unusual people. They seem to be at their best when things are at their worst. Their history is rich with events when they united as a people. In the great wars that they fought they would, in the midst of their bickering, debate, and debauchery, unite and move in solidarity to defeat enemies. How will you defeat such a driving force—the will of an unconquerable people?"

"Sir, it is true that at one time the American people were unconquerable, a nation of hard-working dedicated people with an indomitable competitive spirit. However, for the past fifty years they have softened and spiraled into decay. Their affluence and freedom to do as they please has become an intoxicant. Our advantage in all of this is that for fifty years the U.S. has not engaged in battle. They have lost their warrior's edge. They are soft and undisciplined. Their very strength has become their most profound weakness—democracy.

"Their democratic process, majority rules, has led them to lose their discipline for moderation and balance. To them life has become one big social event. They have caused their own society's decay. They worship leisure and having fun more than living a disciplined life. They have learned nothing from history."

President Lin smiled and nodded in agreement. "Okay, General, you have made your case for moving forward with your plan. Now let us review Operation White Crane."

Khan smiled. "Thank you, sir. It is an honor to do so."

Khan began his discussion with an historical overview of how the ancient Shaolin Monks studied how various animal species fought and defended themselves, the ultimate test in survival, and adapted these techniques to human applications. Khan then made this analogous to warfare.

"Sir, as you can see our ancestors devised various offensive and defensive strategies for coping with an enemy's strengths and exploiting their weaknesses, the ultimate in vanquishing an enemy's spirit. After carefully studying the U.S. defenses we have concluded that we will defeat the U.S. as a white crane defeats a cobra snake.

"First let us review the U.S. strengths. As the cobra, the U.S. can strike a lethal blow with lightning speed. Both the snake and U.S. weapons systems are capable of pinpoint targeting accuracy as well as rapid striking capabilities. Now, compare how lethal the blows can be. Neither the cobra nor the U.S. weapons have to strike a vital spot on their enemy. All they have to do is make a hit. The results are total devastation. Think about the similarity. No matter where the snake hits, its venom will travel through their enemy's body with devastating results. It is the same for the magnetic pulse that hits its target. It will travel throughout the target's system, destroying it.

"Now let us discuss the white crane's strengths. First is the crane's balance and agility. The crane's acute sense of balance gives it the advantage of quickly adapting to an enemy's attack. For example, when the crane steps at the cobra it has the capacity to evade the snakes strike by jumping or stepping back out of the way of the strike. Second is the crane's ability to present a misleading target to its opponent. That is, when battling a cobra the white crane fluffs its feathers, creating a much larger target for the snake to strike at. If the snake is successful in hitting the target all it gets is fluff, nothing vital. Third is the crane's spear-like beak. A formidable weapon that the crane can use with deadly speed and extraordinary accuracy.

"Now, sir, I will draw the parallels as to how our plan will draw the snake into battle and how we will defeat it. Our plan is a three-pronged strategy, involving our obsolete navy, our space-based assets and our new navy assets.

"Over the past ten years our navy has continually probed the U.S. reaction to our movement toward them. As you know we have divided our Pacific fleet into three groups. Every four months we rotate one of the groups into position just outside the U.S. territorial waters. Over the years we have collected valuable intelligence as to how the U.S. Costal Defense Command reacted to our moves…always the same. They go on alert, dispatch a small interceptor force, ships and aircrafts, activate their targeting and weapon systems and eventually stand down and keep a watchful eye on us.

"In phase one of our plan we will have our three naval groups merge east of the Hawaiian Islands and move toward the U.S. west coast—at the point of executing the plan we will obliterate the islands. We also will have our hyper-space planes loitering in orbit over their designated targets. Consider our naval movement as the white crane fluffing its feathers as it steps toward the snake. As our old expendable fleet heads toward U.S. territorial waters we will time the launching of our new super naval fleet toward the U.S. with the U.S. first strike. We will get the snake to commit to striking.

"Phase two happens instantaneously. As the snake unleashes its deadly venomous strike it is in its most vulnerable position. It is fully extended revealing its true striking capabilities. It is here where the crane makes its move and strikes the snake at the base of its skull, killing it instantly. In provoking the U.S. to strike it must activate their space-based SCRAM-1 system to activate their targeting, holographic and pulse weapon capabilities and they must mobilize their air force and navy assets. In doing so our space-based weapons system will locate, target and destroy the U.S. SCRAM-1 system, our hyper-space planes will drop in on their targets, literally destroying the U.S. Costal Commands weapons platforms, ships and land-based pulse weapon systems, as well as totally destroying the U.S. Air Force and Navy assets. Sir, we have for the past ten years collected GPS target data on virtually every military installation and asset worth noting. Nothing will escape destruction.

"Phase three of our operation will be our submarines that will be positioned off the U.S.'s West, East, and Gulf Coasts and will deliver missile strikes to key military and population areas delivering air bursts of a pacification agent. Its affects are instantaneous. There are no residual effects that our landing forces will have to deal with and its effects are not permanent. We will land in several key ports and airports to secure them. I estimate we will have two hundred and fifty thousand troops ashore and deployed in a matter of days. My Black Dragons will airlift over the mountain range and move into the Midwest to secure the agricultural centers. We will crush any and all resistance swiftly and brutally. The message will be clear to the entire population, resist and die; cooperate and live."

The president and his cabinet were impressed with every word spoken by Khan. He exuded a confidence that seemed to overpower the audience.

The president cleared his throat and addressed the group. "General, you have presented us with a brilliant plan and strategy. History will record this as the greatest military action ever accomplished. Let us move forward with Operation White Crane."

Washington D.C.

On February 25, 2060, at the White House the president and his cabinet members met. The president addressed the group.

"Good morning. You all have received my agenda for today."

The group nodded their heads in acknowledgment.

"Let me begin by saying that all options are on the table. Do not hesitate to make a recommendation, no matter how far fetched you believe it is. These are indeed drastic times. If our assessment is correct our very existence as a nation is at stake."

There was a slight pause as each cabinet member did his and her best to grapple with what they had heard.

"Okay, let's begin with the big picture. What is it that we have that would drive the Chinese to such drastic measures?"

First to speak was Secretary Zared. "Well, sir, given that the Chinese are struggling to keep their population fed, my guess is they want food."

"Okay, what else?"

The vice president spoke up, "Well, Mr. President, when you look at our technological advancements over the past fifty years, one could guess that they want every possible application of our technologies."

The president nodded. "Good, let's keep this brainstorming rolling."

The Army Joint Chief, General Marlene O'Brien, offered her opinion, "Well, sir, I think it is all of these issues, our wealth, our food, our technologies, all of these things and more, but I believe it's more basic than these. In my opinion they want a good old fashion fight. You know, the two toughest kids on the block duking it out to see who the number one bad boy is. I believe it's that simple."

"You're saying they just want a fight…a fight to test how tough they are?"

"Yes, sir. Think of it. What's the worst outcome if they lose? They know we won't nuke them. Hell, we disarmed our long-range nukes twenty-five years ago. They know we won't invade. We haven't got the means or the forces. Besides, an invasion of China would be outright suicide. And they know that we have mothballed nearly all of our long-range air, sea, and mobile land assets. They have a standing three-million-man army with a population of two billion and rising exponentially. They could lose three hundred million people and wouldn't even notice it. Yes sir, I believe they have called us out for a fight, plain and simple."

The president looked around the room at each cabinet member. "Do you all concur with General O'Brien?"

As the president looked at each member they nodded their head in agreement.

"Great! They want to fight for the sake of fighting. It's the most bizarre thing I have ever heard. General O'Brien, given that our military strategy and design is strictly a defensive design and strategy there is no practical preemptive strike that we can initiate, correct?"

"Yes, sir, that's correct. It would take years for us to get back into offensive fighting form. No, sir, what is needed is for us to evaluate how we can use our defense as our offense."

There was a pause in the discussion then the president spoke, "Okay. Let's get prepared for this."

The president began to mobilize his cabinet members.

"Okay, CIA we need as much up to date intelligence on the Chinese leadership, civilian and military, their profiles and capabilities, all you can get ASAP. General O'Brien, come up with a plan as to how to mobilize our forces without tipping our hand, some kind of national training exercise. NSA, as we prepare I want you to keep an ear open for chatter entering or leaving the country, and by all means don't forget the debacle at the beginning of this century with President Bush. The man was fighting a war and the congress wanted to crucify him for gathering intelligence. Under no circumstances are you to violate anyone's rights. Stay in bounds to what the congress agreed to. Okay, Home Land Security, make sure we are prepared for the worst possible event. Make sure you also do not tip our hand."

The president paused for a moment as he pondered his thoughts. "Okay, that will be it for now. We'll meet to discuss scenarios and strategies later today."

As the meeting concluded General O'Brien approached the president.

"Sir, about ten years ago we retired a General Sam D'Angelo. I'm not sure if you knew this, but, twenty-five years ago he wrote a thesis that predicted that China and the U.S. would some day square off in battle. Would you like to read his thesis?"

"Yes, General. Maybe his work will shed some light on how to deal with this problem."

At that the meeting ended.

As General O'Brien exited the White House she turned to her aid, "Major, I want you to do some research for me and the president. I want you to research a paper written by a General Sam D'Angelo. Get me a copy ASAP."

At that the two headed to the Pentagon. One hour later General O'Brien received both an electronic copy of Sam's thesis as well as a hologram of his presentation at the War College.

General O'Brien called her staff into her office, "Major Kage, I would like you and Colonel Larson to join me in my office ASAP."

"Yes, sir, we'll be there on the double."

As the three officers settled in to view Sam's prediction they reminisced as to where they were in life when Sam made his presentation.

General O'Brien smiled. "I was a junior officer when General D'Angelo made this presentation."

The two men laughed as they responded, "We were just heading for college."

As the three watched and listened to Sam's presentation they were captivated by him. At the time of the presentation Sam was fifty years old, though the only sign of aging on him was he was slightly graying at his temples. His speech exuded confidence and charisma. His eyes sparkled with vibrancy and energy.

As the presentation ended General O'Brien smiled, "Gentlemen, I want hard copies of General D'Angelo's thesis—

a copy for the president, the joint chiefs and the president's cabinet. Colonel, I would like you to ensure that we are set up for a holographic viewing of this presentation. It packs one hell of punch. Let's get organized and get over to the White House for our meeting."

Two hours later General O'Brien and her aids entered the cabinet meeting room at the White House.

The president smiled, "Ah, General, I understand that you've found some interesting archival materials. Shall we begin the meeting?"

"Yes, sir. My staff will run the hologram of General D'Angelo's presentation."

As Sam's presentation played out before the president and cabinet they seemed to be glued to every word he said. Sam's image stood before the audience as big and as real as life. He spoke with such confidence and respect for his listeners. The president began to take notes at one point in Sam's presentation.

"As I learned so many years ago as a young martial artist, the true meaning of the arts is not to want war. The concept and objective of the martial arts is to develop a defense so strong that you would never have to enter battle. That is, never have to face the ultimate test of life or death. This concept leads to the question, why learn and practice something so lethal if your intent is never to go into battle? Why bother with such hard work and discipline. The answer is simple yet very complex—self-preservation.

"The martial artist's quiet confidence tells any and all assailants that an attack will be dealt with swiftly, brutally, and finally. We will call this indomitable spirit the warrior's edge.

Now, let us draw a parallel between this age-old philosophy of self-defense to designing a national defense strategy. The survival of any nation depends on its capability to defend itself. Like the martial artist, we as a nation seek to exist in the world at peace with our neighbors, a live and let live philosophy. We seek to advance our society as well as flourish as a people. As the martial artist we have developed a powerful system of defense. In doing so we have put would be aggressors on notice, aggress and be defeated.

"However, unlike the martial artist, who constantly practices and improves technique, we have become complacent, believing that our current technology will forever keep us safe. Are we so arrogant to believe that the world has sat back and just accepted that our defense cannot be defeated? What we have lost sight of is the warrior's edge. Technology alone cannot prevail indefinitely. The most important component in any defense strategy is the skill and spirit of a nation's fighting force. History demonstrates that nations that lose their warrior's edge are doomed to failure. Just ask the Romans when the Barbarians showed up at their gates.

"It is my assertion that only through continued technological advancement and the superior training and development of a nation's military human resources will the nation maintain their warrior's edge…"

For the next forty-five minutes Sam outlined what he saw as the future battle with China. As the presentation came to a close the president took a deep breath as he collected his thoughts.

"Okay, I would like to first summarize what I believe I heard then I'll open the floor up for discussion. First, assertion that General D'Angelo made was that as China grew in world economic stature that their defense research, development and spending would grow exponentially. Secondly, the super economic growth that the Chinese would experience would eventually lead them to dominate the Pacific Rim. Third, as the Chinese economy becomes the new world center of gravity they would draw in world wide investment capital therefore dominate the world economic stage. Fourth, at the rate the Chinese economy was growing twenty-five years ago they would consume world resources at an exponential rate basically causing world wide shortages. Fifth, given that the Chinese military complex is expanding in its capabilities they will continue to grow their nuclear arsenal in an attempt to use this as a future bargaining chip.

"Finally, there was the issue of natural disasters. As General D'Angelo pointed out, given the worldwide resource shortages that would be caused by the Chinese's unchecked growth and consumption of resources—food, energy, and natural resources—any sustained natural disasters, floods, or drought would push the Chinese to aggressively seek them out. It was D'Angelo's assertion that they would turn their eyes to the west."

Sam's depiction of the future had a sobering effect on the president's cabinet. He looked across the room to his Secretary of Defense, Darius Dillon. "Okay, Dillon, as Secretary of Defense what do make of D'Angelo's assessment?"

"Well, sir, I must admit that D'Angelo made some broad statements as to how things could play out. I guess he made a wild guess about the future…lucky guess, I suppose."

The room erupted with chatter.

General O'Brien couldn't contain herself, "Oh for cripe sakes, Dillon! Have you taken leave of your senses? The man was spot on. Hell, he almost told us how and when they would come after us."

Secretary Dillon laughed. "Oh come on, General! Economic growth, arms build up and all that hoopie ju about the warrior's edge. I know D'Angelo was one of those Kung Fu guys...Let's face it, it was this line of thinking that kept him from climbing to the top."

"Mr. President, I recommend we get General D'Angelo involved in our planning. He made numerous visits to China with our ambassadors. He knows how the Chinese think and act. I believe he can help."

Hearing this Secretary Dillon angrily snapped back, "For all we know the man is dead! Besides, as I recall his tactics were outdated. The man could not accept that our modern defense strategies evolved from old warfare tactics. Think about it, O'Brien, at the turn of the last century army generals couldn't accept the fact that the military was becoming mechanized. Had we listened to them we'd still be riding horses into battle and firing single-shot weapons. D'Angelo couldn't accept the change. Of what possible use will he be? Mr. President, we have such a technological advantage over the Chinese that they haven't got a chance."

Dillon turned to the CIA Director Mark Shaw, "How do you see it, Shaw?"

"Well, to tell the truth we've kept a good eye on the Chinese. Our intelligence shows that they have made inroads on pulse weapons and new propulsion systems. However, our intelligence reveals that these systems are years away from perfection. Hell, we found that over the past five years they have upgraded their missile systems, which by the way are useless for intercontinental delivery to us. They have built five new aircraft carriers all nuclear powered and have a brand new fleet of fighter jets for these carriers, all non-stealth and jet fuel powered I might add. They have built a dozen missile frigates and have added to their nuclear sub and destroyer fleets.

"Mr. President, the Chinese know that if they head toward our shores our CDC will obliterate their fleets and sweep their fighters out of the sky. As I see it the Chinese have no effective way of invading us. They have to get across an ocean with a massive fleet undetected, land their forces on our beaches, and establish a beach head. Then there is the slight problem of the holding the beach head while we pound the ever loving hell out of them. It is both preposterous and insane to think that they could do it. I believe that they are posturing, rattling their sabers if you will, to pull as much resources out of us as they can…kind of a blackmail ploy."

There was a pause in the discussion as the president pondered what he had heard.

"Tell me, General O'Brien, how would you invade us?"

"Well, sir, it's true that our CDC MAG Pulse system can detect anything coming at us and put up an impenetrable screen at sea level or in the skies; however, if I were to take a shot at it I'd probably infiltrate Special Forces units through Vancouver to seek and destroy the Alaskan and Puget Sound MAG Pulse systems creating a corridor for my fighter squadrons to get through. At the same time I would have my Special Forces units take several of our smaller northern tier air bases used for quickly refueling for my fighters. Also, following in behind my fighters would be my fighters armed with small tactical nukes. I'd look to punch a good-sized hole in the CDC systems. After that I'd look to swarm the shores with overwhelming forces and push my way into the country."

Secretary Dillon exploded with anger. "For cripe sakes, woman! Have you lost your mind! You are insane to think such a thing!"

"Hold on, Dillon," said the president. "I asked the question. Remember, all possible scenarios and options on the table. To think they wouldn't attack is the one option I will not accept. All indications are that they are up to something…It's our job to figure out what it is and to stop them if they try."

The president turned to General O'Brien, "General, get D'Angelo. I want to meet with him as soon as possible."

"Yes, sir, I'll get right on it."

"Okay, we will meet after I have met with General D'Angelo. I suggest we get our ducks in a row. You all know what we will need for our next meeting."

As General O'Brien entered her office in the pentagon she turned to Major Kage. "Major, get me D'Angelo's holo-com number. Look's like I'm gonna pay him a visit."

That afternoon in Sam and Alex's home in Chetek the holo-com chimes sounded. Alex was working at her computer when she looked to the holo-com icon and said, "voice only," instantly shutting off the visual to the communications system.

She answered, "Hello, D'Angelos."

"Oh, Hello, Doctor King, this is General Marlene O'Brien is General D'Angelo available?"

Taken back for a moment, Alex paused as she heard a name

that she hadn't in ten years—General D'Angelo. "Ah, of course, please hold on I'll get him for you."

Alex looked at the hold holo-com icon on her computer. As she did the computer activated the communication system hold function. She then asked the computer to "locate Sam and transfer call." Instantly, the computer transferred the call to Sam in the horse barn.

The holo-chimes rang in the barn office. A pleasant computerized voice spoke. "Sam, there is a call for you."

"Thank you, Audri. Please inform the caller I'll be right there."

I immediately headed to the office in the barn. As I entered the office I instructed the computer to initiate the call. "Audri, visual on, please."

Instantly General O'Brien's image appeared.

"Ah, hello, General D'Angelo, I'm General Marlene O'Brien. Did I catch you at a bad time, sir?"

I smiled as I held up a brush and curry comb. "No, not at all. I was grooming my horse Buddy."

"Well, sir, you're certainly dressed for the part."

"Oh? What gave me away, the cowboy hat, flannel shirt, cowboy boots, or this U.S. Cavalry belt buckle?"

General O'Brien laughed. "Sir, you look dashing!"

"Well, General, I'm sure this isn't a social call, what can I do for you?"

General O'Brien soberly responded. "Sir, I've been asked by the president to invite you to a meeting with him this Thursday. I am authorized to have a military transport pick you up and bring you here to D.C."

"Well, I don't want to keep the man waiting, but I've been

out of the game for ten years now…I'm not sure I've got much to contribute…Oh, what the hell. If the man wants to meet I'd be happy to do so."

General O'Brien smiled. "I look forward to meeting you, sir"

"General I have a favor to ask of you"

"What's that, sir?"

"General, please call me Sam, I've been inactive from the military for ten years now, and I've grow accustom to my civilian name. For the years I spent in the military it seemed like everyone had the same name. You know, Sir, General, Sergeant."

We both laughed as we ended the communication. I returned to grooming Buddy.

"Well, Bud, they've called me to the White House to meet with the president."

I no sooner finished my sentence when a familiar voice spoke from behind me.

"So, cowboy, they can't live without you."

I turned and smiled. "Ah…well, I'm sure they don't need these old bones for much. I'm sure it's one of those diplomatic meet-and-greet gigs. He's probably got some dignitary coming to town that I may have rubbed elbows with."

Alex laughed. "Oh my humble and modest Sammy. It couldn't be that they need your expertise on some important issue now could it?"

I smiled at Alex and we embraced. "Did I ever tell you that you have drop dead gorgeous eyes and the prettiest smile?"

The White House

As my limousine pulled up to the White House front entrance I reminisced about the many times that I had come through this very entrance, the numerous meetings and briefings that I attended within the halls of this most prestigious house. As I headed up to the entrance I was greeted by several of the president's staff.

"Hello, General D'Angelo…The president is waiting for you in the oval office. This way, sir."

As I entered the oval office I was greeted by the president. "Ah, General D'Angelo. It's a pleasure to meet you."

As we shook hands I smiled and replied, "It's an honor to meet you, sir."

The president then began introductions. "General, you and General O'Brien have met."

I smiled and shook her hand. "Hello, General, it's a pleasure to meet you."

"General, this is Secretary of State Zared and Secretary of Defense Dillon."

I smiled and offered my hand to shake. Secretary Dillon forced a smile and slowly offered his hand to me. "Hello, D'Angelo. It's been a few years, hasn't it?"

I smiled. "Twenty some odd I'd guess."

"Well, gentlemen, getting to the point. General, we have a situation that we need your read on. However, to ensure that we don't reveal the true reason why you're here I've planned a dinner and photo op honoring your years of service. This should give the press corps what they need."

The president paused for a moment and then looked at my eyes.

"General, it appears that your predictions about the Chinese may be coming true."

I looked down for a moment. "I'm sorry to hear this, sir. Are you sure?"

"Well, General, the signs are all there."

For the next three hours we reviewed the intelligence reports and data. I listened intently as the discussion took place.

The president looked to me and said, "General, I know that this was just a summary discussion, however, it truly is revealing wouldn't you say?"

I paused and then replied, "Well, sir, I'd say that it most definitely piques suspicion. Knowing the Chinese the way that I remember them, they are skillful, cunning and methodical in their planning and execution. They are a patient people. They won't rush into anything without meticulously studying their opponent. Given the data, I can say that there's a high probability that they are planning to make a move on the U.S. Obviously, they've found a way to neutralize our defenses."

Hearing Sam's assessment Secretary Dillon sighs and rolled his eyes.

"Very profound, D'Angelo. I think we have figured that out for ourselves."

The president sternly looked at Dillon and then intervened.

"Well, I guess that settles it. General D'Angelo, consider

yourself re-activated to your former rank of General. General O'Brien you are to ensure that General D'Angelo has full access to all the intelligence information and resources that he requires."

"Yes, sir. We will set up a direct cryptic secure link to General D'Angelo's home. I believe it's the best way to maintain his cover."

As the meeting ended the president shook hands with me.

"I look forward to our dinner this evening. Remember, General, you have twenty-four hour a day direct access to me. Anything you need call me directly."

"I will, sir, and thank you for your trust in me. I won't let you down."

The Planning Begins

When I returned home from my trip to D.C. I was greeted at the door by Alex. As I stepped inside the entryway I dropped my bags to the side. I opened my arms and stepped toward Alex. With her wide smile and open arms she stepped toward me for an embrace, squeezed me and nuzzled into my chest. As we embraced, I kissed her forehead.

"Well, cowboy! What an honor…And from the president himself…I'm so happy for you, Sammy. You really deserve the recognition."

I grinned. "It was really an honor to meet the president and to have him present me with the award. I feel like celebrating. What do you say we saddle up the boys and take a ride?"

Alex laughed. "You're on, cowboy. Let's hit the trail."

As we rode our favorite trail Alex could see that I was heavy in thought.

"Okay, out with it."

I shook my head and laughed. "Well, it's so secret that I'd have to make you pinky swear that you could never tell."

Alex laughed and then reached out to me with her little finger extended.

We locked our little fingers and playfully laughed. I paused and smiled. "I've been reactivated by the president."

Alex gasped. "Sammy…why now? I mean, you gave them your life why do they need you back?"

As we rode I explained the situation.

"You tried to tell them this years ago and their just coming around now?"

"I guess I didn't say it in a way they could relate to…at the time our CDC seemed impenetrable."

"Hold on, Sam D'Angelo! You were right! That was no happenstance prediction you gave. Your love and concern for this nation and what it stands for was the motivation behind your well-researched and thought-out predictions. You had vision, you showed them a way to be strong yet peaceful."

"I love you, Alex. You've been my strength and inspiration for all these years."

—

As the days passed I pored over the satellite photos and intelligence data, I just could not get past how the Chinese could get across the Pacific Ocean with overwhelming forces, establish a beach head on our shores and move inland to their objectives. It just didn't add up.

"General O'Brien, I've studied the Intel and keep coming back to the same question."

"What's that, Sam?"

"How can the Chinese get to our shores without us detecting them and obliterating their forces. I keep coming back to the same obvious answer—they have perfected invisibility, total stealth. They probably have got both long and short range stealth aircraft as well as naval stealth."

There was a pause in our conversation.

"Well, Sam, to tell the truth I haven't been able to get past this very point. It would be totally asinine to rush at us in a head-on charge. Even if they had an endless stream of assets we would obliterate them without breaking a sweat."

"I am also suspicious of their weapons and delivery capabilities. The Chinese would not make a move unless they had a proverbial stick as big if not bigger than ours. In all likelihood they've got their beam weapons operable and have a way of getting it here. The question is how."

"Hmmm...Over the past several years the Chinese have spent billions in upgrading their air force, army and navy assets. But none of them are stealth capable."

"General, are you sure they don't have some new super stealth capabilities?"

General O'Brien laughed. "Well Sam, as the saying goes, you don't know what you don't know. Here are the facts. First, our Costal Defense MAG-DAR picks up every naval vessel well beyond the horizon before they even realize we have spotted them. SCRAM-1 then GPS's their location. Even if they could cloak their air craft and vessels our MAG-DAR can cut through the cloak and find them. So the obvious conclusion is they can't get by our MAG-DAR. Second, we have swept the skies. We know where every satellite and piece of space junk they have floating overhead is. Our high frontier fighters can MAG Pulse them out of the sky. And lastly, over the past five years our CDC has brushed the Chinese back as they approached us—"

"How's that. You did what?"

"Oh...the defense department believed that if we flexed our muscles, so to speak, the Chinese would get the hint. So, as the Chinese moved toward our territorial waters we activated our defense systems, painted them, let them know that they were in our sights and locked onto, sitting ducks if you will. Our strategy seems to be working."

I sighed. "Please tell me this isn't true. Whose idea was it to do this? No, don't tell me. Dillon's, right?"

"You disapprove Sam? Why?"

"General, they were studying the timing of our response, learning your tactics and pinpointing our defenses. Each time you activated our defense system you went through the same steps—you MAG-DAR'd them, activated SCRAM-1, the CDC went to yellow alert status, weapons were pulse readied and you scrambled air and naval assets. After the whole rehearsal was done you stood down. That about covers it, right?"

"Yes, Sam…That about covers it."

General O'Brien paused to gather her thoughts then asked, "Sam, could I ask you a personal question, strictly off the record?"

"Why of course you can ask me what's up between me and Dillon."

General O'Brien laughed. "Was I that transparent?"

I laughed. "No, Marlene. If I were in your shoes I'd be dying to find out what was up." I recounted the incident between the Chinese and Dillon.

"The damn fool was going to give up something without considering what he was getting in return. Let's just say as lead negotiator I wasn't going to stand for anyone on my team setting up side deals. So, I dressed the man down and sent him back to the DOD to be buried in an obscure position."

"Well, Sam, I have to say that Dillon has never really learned from that situation. Don't get me wrong, he's a brilliant man, sometimes too smart for his own good. His problem is that once he picks a direction he seems to get so focused on achieving his goals that he loses sight of the big picture."

"Well, General, I guess it's time to get down to some brass tacks. Looking at the Intel I don't think we've got a lot of time before the Chinese make their move."

As we discussed tactics and debated possible strategies General O'Brien soberly commented, "Cripe, there is no way we can fight this fight outside our borders is there?"

I pursed my lips, frowned slightly, and shook my head and replied.

"No, General, it looks like the fight is coming to us. We have to pick where we're going to fight it…I think I've got an idea. I'd like to include a few more people in designing this plan. With your permission I'd like to mobilize my former fire team to assist in the planning phase."

"Your former fire team? Are you sure they're up to this, Sam?"

"General. these guys are up for anything that poses a challenge."

The general laughed. "Well, Sam, to tell the truth at this point I'm open to about anything. I'll inform the president and cabinet as to our progress. How soon can we reconvene our planning session?"

"Well, I'll have my team here and briefed to the mission. Within three days I'll contact you at 0800 hours three days from today."

General O'Brien's Debrief

The following afternoon General O'Brien attended a White House briefing. The president had each group report.

"Tell me, Secretary Dillon, how is your team's planning progressing?"

"Secretary Zared has been in contact with the Chinese ambassador. She has had some interesting dialogue with the ambassador."

The president looked toward Secretary Zared. "Sonja, what have you learned?"

"Well, sir, Ambassador Chin was adamant about ensuring strong relations with the U.S. In a goodwill gesture he encouraged the Chinese government to ensure that their commercial fishing fleet and naval fleets all move further out into international waters. Sir, they complied. Our intelligence reports that not only did they move out further but the size of both fleets has been reduced."

CIA Director Shaw nodded in agreement.

The president listened and considered what he had heard. "Okay…what's your take on things, Dillon?"

"Well, sir, as I believed all along, our current defense policies have worked. The Chinese know that we have the technology and will to defend ourselves. Sir, it's my opinion that they've looked down the barrel of our gun and blinked…they are in no position to take us on."

The president nodded his head.

"You may be right, Darius. However, we had better be on our toes. Keep moving forward with our preparations. If nothing else the drill will do us good. Now, how about you, General O'Brien, what have you and General D'Angelo come up with?"

"Sir, General D'Angelo and I have concluded that we should prepare to fight a war within our borders."

"Please explain."

"We have studied the Intel and believe that the Chinese have developed a stealth that our MAG-DAR cannot detect. We believe that they have perfected a beam weapon system and that they in fact want to invade and ultimately occupy our Midwest agricultural areas."

The president pondered what he had heard as he looked at his cabinet members.

"I like the divergence in the plans that you all have brought forward. General O'Brien, when will you and General D'Angelo complete your plans?"

"Well, sir, General D'Angelo has requested that we reactive his former fire team and I concur with him. He believes his former team will be of great service in formulating our tactics and strategies."

"Oh, great! The geriatric brigade to the rescue!" said Dillon. "Of what possible value will these dinosaurs add? They have been out of touch to our political reality for years."

"These men were in the field of battle when you where just getting out of diapers. Their military records show that they served with distinction I believe they will contribute a great deal to our planning process."

“Okay general, bring D’Angelo’s team onboard,” said the president. When do you think you’ll have a plan ready for our review?”

“We will begin work within two days. I’ll have a better estimate after our first meeting.”

“That’s fine, General. I’ll wait to hear from you in a couple of days. For the rest of you, keep researching the data and refining your plans.”

The Team Reunion

The team arrived at my home in Chetek. The reunion went as always, upbeat and playful. Alex seemed to become energized every time the team showed up. They reminisced past fun times but always planned for the future. Their age had little bearing on how they lived and enjoyed life.

I wasted no time getting my team briefed and up to speed on the mission. We spent hours pouring over the data. "As you can see from the Intel, all indications point to the Chinese bringing the fight to us."

"If this was fifty years ago we'd have kicked their butts so far back that they'd be saying hello to their ancestors," said Dennis. "Where do they get off trying to pull off a stunt like this?"

Paul looked to me. "Tell me, boss, if we're making plans for preparing for an invasion, things aren't looking very good, are they?"

"To tell the truth, things are looking bad. Just look at the readiness and fitness reports concerning our military infrastructure. Over the past fifty years we went from having the world's best trained, best equipped and highly motivated armed forces to weekend warriors with a small contingency of military forces. We have built our entire defense strategy around technology. A fighting force became secondary in this strategy.

"The framers and architects of this strategy refused to consider this day. They became so enamored with the technology they lost sight of how wars are fought—through the raw skill and courage of the men and women fighting it. Sorry, gentlemen, I see this as our nation's day of reckoning. It's our job to prepare a reception that the invaders will never forget."

Over the ensuing days me, the team and General O'Brien discussed and debated strategies. We worked diligently to bring our work and planning to a decision point. Finally, we arrived at our destination, a plan. General O'Brien was pleased.

"Okay, gentlemen. Let's review our action items and the essence of our plan. First, Sam and team, you will accompany me to Nebraska to our joint army air force base, General Theo Cornelius Air Field, to review and evaluate my troops there. Second, Paul, Dennis, Kym and Neal, shortly after our Nebraska trip you'll return to the West Coast to commence with our deep sea intelligence gathering. Third, we will commence preparations for broadcasting our holographic troop and assets movement and placement. And lastly, Sam, you and I will brief the president tomorrow morning. Now for our plan…"

Briefing the President

The day after the planning session, General O'Brien and I presented our plan to the president, joint chiefs, and cabinet members. I listened as the general took the lead in the presentation.

"So from our perspective we thought it would be best if our plan dovetailed into the Defense Departments plan, a contingency plan if you will. In the event that the Chinese do land on our shores it is a safe bet that they could only do so by neutralizing a significant portion of the CDC.

"The Intel that we have has convinced us that they will come at us from the west. However, we will remain guarded as to our most northern regions. As you know, as a condition to our mutual defense treaty with the Canadians they have granted us the freedom to deploy, at will, MAG Pulse Cannon defenses in their most northern regions. As part of asset deployment we will discretely move assets into position; however, we see this as a low probability route.

"We have secretly begun to resurrect mothballed mobile equipment and have strategically placed it, under MAGS cover, throughout the West Coast, Midwest, and along the east and west foot hills of our West Coast mountain range. Our east and gulf coast defenses are in good shape. Our Intel shows only minor offshore activity by the Chinese. Also, we will resurrect our helo-gunship fleet. They will be strategically deployed with our other assets.

"As for our troop deployment, General D'Angelo, his team, and I will be evaluating their readiness. I will have General D'Angelo explain tactics."

"Thank you, General O'Brien. Mr. President, after careful scrutiny of the Intel we are convinced that the Chinese have a highly trained and disciplined Special Forces unit that they will use to secure their objective—our agricultural centers in the Midwest. We have studied the profile of their leader and find that he is an extremely disciplined and highly skilled leader, a traditionalist from every sense of the word."

"Who is this leader?"

Sam looked to the president then to the Secretary of Defense.

"His name is General Tzu Sun Khan."

Secretary Dillon immediately responded, "That's inaccurate. Our Intel said that he fell out of favor with the Chinese high command years ago. They shipped him to the hinterland near the Mongolia border to babysit some God-forsaken outpost. He's been behind a desk ever since. He's a politician not a commanding general."

"Mr. Secretary, we are confident it's Khan. Given what we have learned recently we believe the Chinese staged a ruse to appear Khan fell out of favor when in all actuality he was sent to what appeared to be a barren outpost, an outpost that had cold war underground facilities, where we believe he trained and developed a lethal and murderous group that he named 'The Black Dragons.' We believe it was Khan and his Black

Dragons that put down the food riots in 2053, indiscriminately slaughtering thousands."

The president asked, "Anything else we should know about Khan?"

"Our Intel on Tzu Sun Khan is that he is a descendant of the infamous Genghis Khan. He is a student and practitioner of ancient Chinese war techniques. The Art of War. He is convinced that it is his destiny to conquer the west."

"Do we have any idea as to how many of these Black Dragons Khan commands and why the color black?"

"Yes, sir, we believe Khan has fifty thousand under his command, and as for the color black, well, for the Chinese the color black has connotations of 'Final' or 'The End.' I believe Khan and his Black Dragons are considered the Chinese's final option."

As the committee pondered the information Secretary Dillon asked, "General D'Angelo, how do you know that Khan will come to the Midwest ag centers? Why not send in the 'regulars' to take over the agricultural country?"

I looked to General O'Brien and she nodded.

"Well, Mr. Secretary, first, we believe that the Midwest is key to the Chinese, the very reason they're invading. Wouldn't you send in your best to secure the objective? We also know that Khan wants to put his troops to the test. What better way to test them then to take on U.S. Special Forces? It's our intention to leak information that I am in the Midwest commanding Special Forces. Knowing Khan and his drive to fight like a traditional warrior I'm sure he'll want to take on an old war horse like myself, warrior versus warrior.

"As for our tactics, we'll keep our assets and forces under

MAGS cover and deploy them after the Chinese have played their hand. General O'Brien will command and lead these forces. Our holographic troop and asset movement should create enough of a diversion that Khan will move to his objective more guarded. We'll slow him down with General O'Brien's Special Forces—"

"Special Forces?" said Dillon. "Where did they come from, O'Brien?"

General O'Brien grinned as she gave her answer.

"Well, sir, over the past five years I have been training and developing a small contingency of Special Forces, about one thousand troops. I submitted this through you, sir, and you okayed this as a part of my budget."

Dillon cleared his throat. "Hmm, oh yes, that's right, General."

I continued with my briefing. "As I was saying, General O'Brien's Special Forces will provide hit and run tactics on the invading forces. They will lead the Chinese forces in a chase to our forces positioned in the Midwest right here." I pointed to the position on the holo-map.

"Mr. President, it's our intention to lead the invaders into this quadrant here where we will contain and if necessary destroy them. Hopefully, we will convince them to surrender."

Secretary Dillon immediately challenged the plan. "Let's see if I got this straight, if the Chinese make it to our shores it in all likelihood means they have devised a defense against our weapons systems or at least destroyed them. And you're suggesting that we're going to draw them into the Midwest, contain them, and defeat them? How?"

General O'Brien pointed at several key points on the map

as she responded. "General D'Angelo and I believe that if we can draw the Chinese into this area we will be in a position to MAG Pulse the hell out of them. Remember, sir, Khan is a true traditional warrior. He is itching for a true traditional fight. He is driven to prove himself and his troops capabilities in a so-called glorious battle, just like his conqueror heritage. He'll come."

The president listened and considered his options.

"I like it. We have covered this issue from about every point on the compass. Let's hope that we never have to exercise our military options."

The president looked to his Secretary of State. "Madam Secretary, I want you to put a full court press on our diplomatic front. Make sure that the Chinese know that we seek strong relations with them. Director Shaw and Secretary Dillon, scrutinize the Intelligence. I don't want to trigger something that didn't have to happen. However, under no circumstances should we ignore the possible impending event, am I clear?"

The Tensions Build

June 10 I sat in my daily briefing with General O'Brien.

"Sam, things are not looking good. Secretary Zared has briefed us today. She has reported that the Chinese are patronizing us, virtually playing with us. Dillon and Shaw reported that once again the Chinese naval fleet has been moving toward us and then backing away. The same ole stuff."

I rubbed my chin. "General, to tell the truth I'm not surprised. I believe that all of their posturing has bought them time to keep preparing and testing our reactions. General, I think my team has stumbled upon something. Maybe it's nothing, but we should look into it. I'm not sure if this has any significance but my team was eavesdropping on a communication between a submarine and missile frigate. Does the name 'White Crane' meaning anything to you?"

"White crane, white crane. No, Sam, I've never heard of it. Does this refer to a person or maybe it's a new vessel? I'll check with intelligence to see what they have. In any event I thought I'd wish you and Alex a happy fiftieth wedding anniversary."

"Oh, thank you Marlene…You know, General, call it a hunch or may be it was the pizza I ate late last night, but something isn't right. My guts tell me something is up. Why would the Chinese step up to the table with an olive branch in one hand and a stick hidden behind their back?"

"Well, Sam, I guess we ate the same pizza last night. All of this activity has put me on edge. So just to be sure I was ready I've kept two hundred thousand troops within arms reach. Over the last two months many have been slowly deployed with our hidden assets. As you know, we were going to keep our force level up by initiating a national military training program. Well, we have kept our troops in training for the two months. We're just slow at releasing them back to civilian status."

The Wedding Anniversary

On June 27, 2060, Alex and I celebrated our fiftieth wedding anniversary. It was a festive day. However, noticeably missing was my closest friends—the team. As the party progressed Alex and I were asked what the key was to our success. With arms around each other we looked at each other then to our audience.

"Well first of all, Alex and I are just too stubborn to quit. But I'd say the true key to our success was we never lost sight of wanting to put the other's needs ahead of your own."

Alex nodded and smiled.

"Fifty years ago when I first laid eyes on Sam I knew in my heart that I'd spend the rest of my life with him. Fifty years of sheer happiness. Does everyone know the story of how I got Sam to marry me?"

Alex went on to explain the infamous Tucker affair. The audience roared with laughter.

The Dragon Rises

On July 4, 2060, I awoke at my usual early morning hour. As always, I started my day off with a rigorous workout. I always began my workouts with my traditional one hundred push-ups and sit-ups. As I stepped outside the house to begin my martial arts workout I paused to watch the sunrise. I looked all around to take in the sights and sounds—sun rising, birds singing and flowers blooming. As I did I pondered how all these natural things happened every day for eons of time. How living things came into existence and then, in the true cycle of life, passed away making room for the next generation. As I pondered these things a deep realization of my own mortality set in. In an instant I pondered how fulfilled I felt in living the life that I had lived.

At seven a.m. Alex and I sat down for breakfast in our gazebo. As we did our holo-communications systems' chimes rang.

I smiled. "I'll get it, Alex. Looks like we're starting the day off early."

As I stepped into my private study I gave the command, "Audri, visual on," and answered the call.

"Hello."

"Sam! It's happening! My God, it's happening! I never thought this day would come. They have swarmed all over us. They've hit us from about every possible direction!"

"General, General, one thing at a time. Where did they attack?"

"Sam, a few minutes ago the CDC reported that our MAG-DAR picked up the entire Chinese navy moving toward our West Coast shores. The president gave the order to warn the fleet to turn back or we would MAG Pulse them. Well, when they were well inside our territorial waters and presented a clear and present danger, the CDC annihilated them. They just ignored our warnings! They kept coming at us. Their carriers launched their fighters, their missile frigates targeted our vessels, and we believe their subs have been lying off our shores for some time now.

"All hell has broken lose. As we MAG pulsed their fleet they pounded the hell out of the CDC. Sam they've got beam weapons! In one coordinated move they have knocked out the CDCs mountain and sea based assets. They're gone, Sam! They have virtually obliterated our naval and air assets. They own our skies! Anything we put up they shoot down. They hit us from above with an advanced aircraft that moved so fast that our ground to air systems couldn't find them. MAG DAR can't locate them. They have a stealth that we can't find. They are virtually invisible to us. These advanced aircraft came in from orbit, dropped in on top of us. They have knocked out SCRAM-1! We've lost our holographic capabilities along with our advanced targeting and spying capabilities—"

"Marlene, don't worry too much about SCRAM-1. We have a friend that will take over for SCRAM-1. It will take us a while to get a hold of him, but trust me, I'm sure he'll answer our call."

"Who is this friend Sam?"

"His name is Overlord. What about the president and congress, are they okay?"

General O'Brien continued.

"The president and congress are fine. They're in emergency bunkers. The president has been trying to negotiate with the Chinese. They won't hear of anything but an unconditional surrender from us. The Chinese are now systematically knocking out our communications infrastructure. However, they can't get it all, just mess it up a bit."

My instincts kicked in.

"Okay, General, it's our turn—"

"Sam, I just got word that the Chinese subs launched missile attacks on our major coastal cities. They have air burst some sort of nerve agent on these locations. The news is sketchy as to what's happening. It appears they have used some sort of pacification agent on key areas. The people in these areas have been reduced to lethargic and passive. They've lost their will to fight."

"Okay, we need to get ourselves collected and get as much Intel as we can. The best place to start will be to get an up-close assessment on the Chinese fleet. At least the CDC pounded them before they got to us. Let's get a link to my team. We'll have them get an up-close look as to what shape the Chinese fleet is in.... The Chinese can't be this blatant in making a headlong charge. They have spent their assets in this first go around; how in the hell are they going to get troops landed and supplied. This obviously was only round one in this fight. General, we'll reconvene when we establish a link with my team."

—

"Okay, gentlemen, this is it. What have you got for us?"

Dennis began. "Here's what I have, General: We arrived on scene and found that the entire Chinese fleet was dead in the water. You've got downed fighter wreckage everywhere for miles. It is the eeriest sight to see these lifeless hulks adrift."

"What about troop ships. Where are the troop ships?"

"Well, sir, that seems to be the missing piece in this. We can't find much for troop carriers. It's almost like they threw these assets away."

I nodded my head as I assessed Paul's observation.

"You're right. General O'Brien and I concur, something isn't right. Why would they stop short of invasion?"

"Excuse me, men," said General O'Brien, "but we have an old spy satellite video feed coming in from the Pacific. You're not going to believe your eyes."

As the live video feed came in we began to murmur.

"What the hell is this! It looks like an armada of flying saucers. Are these aircraft or are they ships? Look at the size of these damn things. Cripe! They look like they could carry half of the Chinese army! General, how fast are these vessels traveling?"

General O'Brien shook her head. "Gentlemen, it appears that these are sea-going vessels. We estimate that they are traveling at speeds in excess of five hundred miles per hour. Given there speed and present location they'll be on our shores within hours."

We all were nearly spellbound by the spectacle we were watching. I pulled myself out of my awed state and instantly got back on my game. "Okay, General O'Brien, this is what we prepared for let's put our plan into action. Team, get into your fisherman routine. Look out for these guys, they may just decide to run you over, and ease in on them. General O'Brien, after our briefing with the president I'll meet you at Cornelius Air Field. It's time to set this dance into motion."

As we were closing our meeting I smiled and said, "Okay, guys, fifty years ago we had to part ways to meet our mission. Who would have ever thought we'd be doing it fifty years later. Stay safe, brothers till the end."

Shortly after the team signed off General O'Brien and I conferenced into the president's emergency cabinet meeting. As I entered the briefing, several of the joint chiefs were having a discussion.

"Hello, General D'Angelo. How are preparations coming along?"

I gave a slight grin. "In spite of our circumstances we are ready to execute our plan."

Just then the president joined in. "Ladies and gentlemen, the battle assessments that I have received are grim. The Chinese have neutralized our air and ground defenses and are on the move to take key West Coast ports, major airports, and cities. They have decimated our pacific fleet and are in all likelihood days away from taking our key Midwest agricultural centers. We are in total disarray!"

The president turned to his Secretary of Defense. "Darius, have I left anything out?"

"No, sir."

There was a slight pause then the president asked General O'Brien and me, "When will the Chinese hit the West Coast?"

General O'Brien answered. "Our satellite Intel shows that the second wave of naval vessels will be on our western doorstep in a few hours."

"You're kidding, right? Didn't we just obliterate their entire navy? How in the hell are they going to get an invasion fleet across the Pacific in a few hours?"

General O'Brien turned to her computer terminal and opened a live satellite video link. As the video feed came into focus the president became agitated. As the president, his cabinet, and the joint chiefs watched in near horror the president turned to his cabinet.

"Shaw! Dillon! What the hell is this? I thought the Chinese were years away from achieving this technology…For cripe sakes. Beam weapons, naval vessels that travel as fast as a jet…What else do they have!"

The president then asked the group, "Can we stop them at sea with our subs?"

Secretary Dillon replied. "First, sir, they hit our Pacific assets…We'd never get what's left of our Atlantic fleet there in time. And secondly, at this stage only a missile strike would get their quick enough to stop them, but, like us, they've developed strong defenses against missile strikes."

The president turned to me and General O'Brien. "It looks like your contingency plan is in play. For all intents we have to assume the Chinese will successfully invade us. Let's review our plans as to how we will evict this plague from our shores with all prejudice. What I want to hear now is our tactics for getting the job done."

General O'Brien looked to me to take the lead.

"Well, sir, as you know we have our forces strategically

placed throughout the Midwest and along the west coast mountain foot hills…all under MAGS cover. We know that as soon as we reveal these assets the Chinese will hit us with all they've got from above. We just can't give them the cover they'll need. It would be a wholesale slaughter to mobilize them now. General O'Brien and I have prepared a reception for the Chinese.

"In phase one of our operation we would ask that you keep up your efforts to sue for peace, keep pushing for some form of an agreement to cease hostilities. Hopefully, your dialogue with the Chinese will keep them off guard. Keep them talking but agree to nothing. In this phase of our operation we will have a contingent of our forces put up resistance as the Chinese get ashore, small bands of insurgents. If nothing else we want to slow them down from moving into the Midwest, keep them guessing and cautious. Our forces will use MAGS cover and hit-and-run tactics. The bulk of General O'Brien's forces are to remain under MAGS cover until we have executed phase two of our plan.

"Sir, this is our most critical phase. We all agree that General Tzu Sun Khan will lead his Special Forces into the Midwest. As he does we ask that you make an appeal to the Chinese that their commanding general meet your commanding general—me—for a parlay to discuss terms of a truce. We will have leaked my background as an old traditional Special Forces warhorse. I'm sure it will pique Khan's interest. Sir, if all goes according to our plan we will lead Khan into a death trap and in one swoop annihilate Khan's forces and destroy all of the Chinese's air and naval assets. General O'Brien's forces will finish the battle."

Encouraged by what he had heard, the president smiled. "Dear Lord I pray you're right. Please continue."

"Sir, as it stands the Chinese command believes that we are militarily blind and inept. They are convinced that we have no way to gather intelligence, that our weapon systems are destroyed and what remains has zero targeting ability. Most importantly, they believe that we've lost our holographic weapons capability.

"The Chinese are convinced that we cannot stop them with conventional weapons and tactics. They believe they can invade us with impunity. What they did not plan for was 'Overlord.'"

Hearing this, the president and the joint chiefs began to sidebar with their aids and advisors. They had no idea what or who Overlord was.

The president spoke up first. "Okay, Sam, what is or who is Overlord?"

"Well sir, some fifty plus years ago a brilliant scientist, Doctor Franz Detrich, designed the SCRAM-1 system. Franz knew that SCRAM-1 would not remain a viable system forever. He created a double redundant system for SCRAM-1. As you know SCRAM-1 was capable of self repair, small attending drones that serviced the main satellites, like worker bees tending and maintaining the hive. So, when a SCRAM-1 component broke down the other components would take over its function until the drones repaired it. What was known to only a few in the Department of Defense, and eventually forgotten, was that a constellation of SCRAM-1 backup satellites where hidden in high earth orbit. This constellation was named Overlord.

"Doctor Detrich ingeniously disguised this system as space debris. The system was hidden inside booster rocket casings and old payload containers just tumbling freely in space above the planet. For the past half century 'Overlord' has been asleep. The Overlord system is programmed so that as soon as SCRAM-1 experiences a catastrophic failure it will activate and deploy to its coordinates. Overlord will loiter and remain quiet until it receives the go command from us. Sir, in short order my team and I will reestablish communications with Overlord."

"Ladies and gentlemen, this is it! Generals D'Angelo and O'Brien, let's prepare to execute your plan. We will keep channels open twenty-four hours a day."

There was a slight pause as the joint chiefs got their brains around what they had just heard. The president began to speak.

"Okay, now it is time for us to discuss our plans as to how we will evict this plague from our shores with all prejudice."

The president paused for a moment to collect his thoughts. "General D'Angelo I know this is late, but this nation owes you a sincere apology. Your writings and speeches over the years were nearly prophetic. You warned us this day would come. And so it has. History will show that this was the darkest hour that our nation had faced. Let history also show that we persevered to a total victory. Now I ask you, in the name of God, will your plan work?"

I paused and then cleared my throat to speak. "Mr. President, only God knows the answer to that question. However I firmly believe that the element of surprise is on our side. This, sir, I submit will be the Chinese's down fall."

The president smiled. "Let's see if the Chinese take the bait. Godspeed...We will brief at the same time tomorrow."

I closed my holo-link and was deep in thought. As I exited my private study Alex was anxiously waiting for me.

"What's our plan, Sam?"

I smiled as I gently touched Alex's cheek. "Our plan is you, the girls, and their families will hunker down here. I'm heading down to Nebraska to meet up with General O'Brien. We've got a real mess on our hands. Hopefully we stop the Chinese in their tracks."

Alex winced with concern. "Sam, stay with us. I just don't want you to go."

I took Alex's hands into mine and looked into her eyes.

"I love you, Alex. I have to do this. Please understand, I have to do this."

Later that morning I got a call from General O'Brien. "Sam! They're hitting our beaches as we speak. My teams are in place harassing the hell out of them. This is it! Good luck, Sam!"

"Marlene, keep your head down. No matter what happens out on the plains, be patient. Let this play out. I'll be traveling tomorrow. I'll catch up to you and my team then."

The Trap is Set

Over the next two weeks the Chinese poured their forces ashore and with all brutality and total disregard for life began their occupation. General O'Brien's teams harassed and raised havoc with the Chinese troops. They managed to achieve their goal of keeping the Chinese off balance and guarded in their moves. The president pressed forward with his dialogue and successfully convinced the Chinese president to call a cease fire and to have Khan meet with me to discuss the terms of cessation of hostilities.

General Khan's forces made their way to the Midwest plains. However, every step of the way his troops were dogged and harassed by General O'Brien's Special Forces. They performed their mission brilliantly. Without Khan realizing it their tactics led Khan's forces on a chase right on to the plains of Nebraska.

—

I joined a holo conference with General O'Brien, the president, his cabinet and the joint chiefs.

"Ah, Hello, Sam," said the president. "Are you ready for your meeting with Khan?"

"Yes, sir. I just hope the cease fire will hold out long enough for us to meet. Khan's troops are just itching to get at us."

"Don't worry, Sam. I convinced the Chinese president that this meeting was a formality for us to understand the terms and conditions of ceasing hostilities. I'm confident that I convinced him of that. General O'Brien you'll have your teams stand down during the cease fire, correct?"

"Yes, sir, that's correct."

"We will reconvene after General D'Angelo's meeting with General Khan. Godspeed, D'Angelo."

The End

I stood gazing out the window of my office deep in thought. A voice calling to me seemed to pull me back to reality.

"General. General. Sir, I hate to interrupt your thoughts, but it's nearing 'D' hour sir. We are ready."

"Thank you, Sergeant. I'll be with you straight away."

As I walked to the outside of the command center a large gathering of troops were in formation waiting for me. The officer in charge, Major Thomas Lightfoot, called the troop formation to attention.

"Ten Hut!"

"At ease," I said.

As I stood looking over the troop formation I choked up with pride. These young men and women were the future. Tomorrow's leaders, indeed.

Major Lightfoot was a strong leader. His troops respected his ability to lead and faithfully followed him. Lightfoot was a proud Native American. His Sioux heritage was full of warrior history. His Sioux name was "Stalking Wolf." His hit-and-run tactics against the Black Dragons had been very affective. His teams performed brilliantly. Their ambushes and night attacks kept Khan and his forces off balance. Khan and his troops, with disdain, called Lightfoot's teams "The Mosquitoes."

As I approached the formation to speak I collected myself. I cleared my throat and prepared to address the troops. As I stepped forward to speak I noticed that Major Lightfoot was holding a four foot long spear, a battle lancer.

Major Lightfoot smiled and said, "Permission to address the general, sir!"

"Please do, Major."

The Major approached me in a slower ceremonial step, with the spear lying across his out stretched hands.

"Sir, we would be honored if you would carry this symbol of courage into battle."

My heart swelled with honor and pride as I took the hand-forged, hand-made spear. It had colorful streamers representing our nation's heroic past, the minuteman militia to our present day. What struck my emotions the hardest was the five eagle feathers streaming from the spear...a feather for each of the brothers.

"Not so many years ago our young nation was faced with a near impossible battle. Yet, a band of determined citizen soldiers met the challenges they faced. These heroes' saw beyond the battles that they had to face. They saw the future—victory, freedom, and self-determination for their nation. Out manned, out gunned, and against the odds they fought and defeated tyranny. The reward for their determination and sacrifice was the birth of our great nation. Today, we are faced with such a task and mission. Let history show that we answered the call of our ancestors. Liberty and freedom for all!"

I raised the spear with my right hand and called out, "I will carry this symbol of courage proudly into battle!"

"Ooh Rah! Ooh Rah! Ooh Rah!"

Major Lightfoot saluted me and said "Your transportation is ready, sir. Godspeed."

"Thank you, Major. No matter what happens tomorrow stay focused on the mission."

The major saluted me. "You can count on us, sir."

As my vehicle drove off to the staging area for my meeting with Khan the next day I couldn't help but to recall the evening the team spent with General Theo Cornelius. I recalled vividly the general's story and depiction of "The Brothers of The Spear." Fitting that I would carry the spear to the meeting with Khan.

My vehicle drove the better part of an hour straight out into the open plains. My convoy was heading to an encampment that was about one mile from the advancing Chinese troops' encampment. I was to meet with Khan at sunrise the next morning in the center of the valley to discuss terms of surrender or death. It was Khan's belief that opposing generals should meet face to face to discuss the terms of battle. For this very reason Khan agreed to a twenty-four hour cease fire and personally guaranteed my safe passage to and from the meeting.

As I approached the encampment I smiled as I saw a familiar sight. It was my horse Buddy. The troops attending him had set up a small corral area for Bud to graze.

As I stepped out of the vehicle I called to Buddy.

His ears perked up and he greeted me with a whinny. Bud was a highly intelligent horse. He could untie himself, open gates and he had a great sense of humor. He'd steal your hat off your head or take the gloves out of your pocket and run with them.

"Hey, Bud! How's it going today? Are you ready for the big day tomorrow? We ride at dawn, big fellar."

Bud reacted to my voice as if he understood what I had said.

Suddenly a soft voice spoke from behind me. “Are you gonna kiss that horse, cowboy?”

“Only if he doesn’t tell on me,” I replied.

Alex approached smiling widely. Our love for each other extended from our very souls and spirits. We walked right into each others embrace and kissed. “Surprised to see me?”

“Well, young lady, I thought we discussed this earlier this week. I’d be home after I took care of this business with Khan.”

“Well, Sammy my boy, about fifty years ago you went off to ‘take care of some business’ as you put it and I didn’t get a chance to see you off. Well, this time I’m gonna make sure my hero is sent off proper.”

We talked for a while and watched the sunset. Alex pointed to the valley in front of us and asked, “Are you going to meet General Khan out there tomorrow?”

I smiled and said, “Ya. Bud and I will jog out at sunrise to meet him.”

“Do you have to go?” Alex asked.

I looked into Alex’s teary eyes. “Alex, I believe with all my heart that I was called forward in life for this very purpose.”

As we looked across the valley to the opposite ridge we could see the dimly lit encampments of the Chinese. Given that we were in a twenty-four-hour cease fire both sides were cautiously at ease. The truce didn’t matter much to us. Despite how honorable a warrior Khan thought himself to be, the Chinese were nothing more than dishonorable murderers and invaders. I posted my sentries and remained on high alert.

Alex and I turned and walked toward our quarters, in lockstep and bumping hips.

—

As I buttoned my BDU shirt my eyes caught my left breast pocket. There was a newly sewn-on campaign patch. It was a spear with five eagle feathers. Written within the patch was the logo "Brothers Till The End." I placed my right hand on the patch and whispered the words. "Brothers Till The End."

As the morning broke the sun was just high enough in the east that we could make out the image of the ridge across the valley. My forward observers radioed back that it appeared General Khan was preparing to ride out to meet me. My troops brought Buddy forward. His saddle blanket bore the U.S. Cavalry insignia.

I mounted Buddy and squared myself up in the saddle. One of the troops asked, "Would you like your cap, sir?"

"No thank you, son. Bud and I are going casual this morning."

Major Lightfoot handed me the ceremonial spear. As I placed it into the saddle's scabbard I smiled at Major Lightfoot and said, "Remember, Major, no matter what happens today our plans must be executed to perfection."

I turned and winked at Alex.

"Be back in a jiff," I said.

As Buddy and I started across the valley floor I gave him the cue to pick up the pace. He broke into a comfortable lope. As we progressed across the valley I could sense the entire Chinese army was observing my every move. The sun was rising behind me. The full moon hung low in the sky as it was setting in the west.

I could see Khan begin his decent into the valley.

I arrived at the center of the valley and held the spear upright. The eagle feathers and streamers gently waved in the early morning breeze.

Khan stopped his horse. His eyes scanned me top to bottom.

"General D'Angelo, it is good for warriors like us to meet to discuss the terms of life or death. Your reputation as a true warrior precedes you."

My expression did not change. "General Khan, you have invaded the sovereign territory of the United States of America. Withdraw your forces at once or face the consequences."

Khan laughed. "Consequences, you say. And what might those consequences be, dear General?"

"Swift annihilation of you and your forces."

"General, General, General, you are in no position to demand anything from me. Be realistic. We have cut through your forces and defenses like a sword through water. Your continued resistance is futile. It is obvious that your forces are outmatched. We have defeated your technology, but most importantly we have defeated your forces' spirits. They have no more will to continue this fight. I implore you, General, choose life for you and your brave but foolish troops. Surrender to us. After our total victory over you and your forces we will assimilate your culture into ours. In a few generations your people will be fully indoctrinated to our ways. Lay down your arms and choose life for you and your army."

The morning calm was broken by a high-pitched hissing

sound. I heard a deep thump and found myself ripped backwards from my saddle. Buddy nervously stepped sideways to avoid stepping on me.

Khan leapt off his horse and knelt beside Sam's lifeless body and began to somberly apologize. "General, this was not my plan. We were to meet in battle as warriors. I assure you whoever did this despicable act, I will wipe him and his family from the face of this planet. Goodbye, General. This war is over for you."

My eyelids began to twitch and then opened. "General Khan, help me to my feet."

And so Khan did.

I quickly collected my wits, drew a few deep breaths, and gingerly mounted Buddy. Holding my left side I turned to ride off. "Your assassins are poor shots. Withdraw your forces or die!"

As I reached the U.S. encampment there was a scramble. Alex charged forward to meet me. "Whoa, Buddy! Sam! Are you okay?"

"Easy, Alex, I'm okay! They got me in the side. It looks worse than it is."

As I dismounted Buddy, I was swarmed by the medics.

"You should have seen Khan's face when I came to. He looked like he had seen a ghost. He thought I was dead!"

"So did we!"

I looked up at Major Lightfoot and said, "Major, I have one thing to say to you—outstanding restraint! You performed your duties brilliantly, son."

I stood to my feet and with vigor and energy addressed the

troops. "Okay, troops back to the command center. Leave all non-essential equipment behind."

At that the team headed back to the command center.

At the command center I was greeted by Colonel Sandra Delback. "General, are you okay, sir?"

"Fine, Colonel. Are my fire teams in position?"

"Yes, sir. Venegas, Clark, Cato, and Thomas teams are in place and are ready. Our mobile and infantry forces are deployed as planned."

"Excellent! Get me a holographic link up with General O'Brien, the president and the joint chiefs. We need to brief them and the president as to our progress. Knowing Khan this battle will start at any moment."

"Yes, sir! We will have your holographic feed within the next half hour."

I turned to Alex and said, "It's time to go."

Alex began to cry. "Oh Sam, please come with me."

"Now young lady, you have a mission. No matter what happens here tomorrow don't let them forget what happened."

I turned to Alex's driver. "Sergeant, take good care of her, son."

The sergeant saluted and replied, "Yes, sir! I will get Doctor King home safely."

I stood and watched as the staff vehicle drove away. With a lump in my throat and forcing a smile, I waved to Alex. As the staff vehicle drove off Alex was turned looking back at me and waving from the rear window. I swallowed hard to fight back my tears. I gazed at Alex as she drove off. I smiled as I recalled how Alex stole my heart so many years ago. How her overpowering smile and captivating blue eyes pierced my very soul. I stood watching and waving until Alex's vehicle was out of sight.

As I turned to head back inside of the command center Colonel Delback met me at the door. "Sir, your holographic conference with the president and the joint chiefs is on in five minutes."

"Thank you, Colonel. I'll be there straight away."

As I entered the holographic conference I could hear voices. General O'Brien and the joint chiefs were in sidebar discussions as they waited for the meeting to begin. As I took a seat General O'Brien greeted me.

"Ah, hello, Sam. How are things progressing?"

I forced a smile and replied.

"We're ready, General. Everything is in place."

With a tired and stressed look about him the president looked to his advisors.

"I want to make sure that we do the right thing for the American people. If we fail I dread to think of what will happen to this nation. General D'Angelo, will your plan work?"

With confidence I replied, "Sir, as your emissary I met with Khan and looked deep within the man's soul. I am convinced that his arrogance and impetuous nature is his weakness. His forward observers have kept a close eye on our troop mobilization at the front. My teams have allowed his recon teams in for a close look. Khan is convinced that we will meet him in a head on battle, a 'glorious battle.' What Khan is unaware of is that as we hurriedly rushed our troops and equipment forward to the front we were at the same time withdrawing them and replacing them with a holographic army. At this moment Khan appears to be convinced that we are doubling our troop strength to take him on. Knowing Khan this should further entice him into our trap."

"General D'Angelo, how can we be sure that the last phase of your plan will work?"

"As you know we have lured Khan toward the very prize that he hopes to win. My team has reconfigured the harmless agricultural MAGS into high-intensity military MAGS. Once Khan and his army enter the critical zone we will detonate the MAGS. Khan and his army will be destroyed. As for the Chinese Navy, for a few months now my team has been deployed on fishing trawlers that have been tending nets in the vicinity of the Chinese fleet. Over the past several weeks these fishing trawlers have been boarded, searched and watched by Chinese patrol boats. My team reported that they have been boarded so many times that they are on a first name basis with the Chinese boat commanders. They are confident that they can smuggle the MAGS on board for deployment. It is our intent that we will deploy the MAGS on these vessels and in a coordinated attack detonate them when we detonate our land based MAGS.

"The last leg of our strategy is the annihilation of the Chinese Aero-Space plane fleet. Overlord will take care of that for us. As the battle unfolds and the space planes move into attack position Overlord will quietly plot their position and direct our MAG Cannons hidden in our abandoned Midwest missile silos to fire. In a coordinated attack we will simultaneously obliterate the Chinese's land, air, and sea forces. After that, sir, the rest is up to you in how you negotiate a peace treaty. I believe that if we are successful the Chinese won't have the stomach to continue prosecuting this war."

The room remained quiet for a few long seconds then the president spoke.

"General D'Angelo, may God be with you and your team. Now we must discuss the difficult issue of what happens if General D'Angelo's plan fails. General O'Brien, let's discuss your insurgency plan."

"Well, sir, as you are aware our insurgency plan has been in play since this invasion began. We took a page right out of the insurgency handbook. Sir, our small fire teams have dogged and harassed Khan's forces since he has landed on our shores. Our teams have wreaked havoc with Khan's troops."

"General O'Brien, my question is if General D'Angelo's plan fails do we continue the struggle or do we surrender? When this battle moves into our population centers think about the civilian casualties."

"Sir, look at the wholesale slaughter the Chinese have unleashed in the initial stages of this invasion. We have no choice but to fight to the end!"

The president somberly responded, "It has been fifty years since our last shooting war. Our forces are outmanned, outgunned and have no wartime experience. Do you honestly believe that the Chinese will sit still while we take pot shots at them? Once they cross the Great Plains into our population centers they will begin a pacification process none like the world has ever seen! Our intelligence estimates that they have a one million-man occupation army ready to deploy to occupy us. To complicate the matter they know that we can't and won't use nuclear weapons on our own soil. As my advisors are you suggesting that we fight to the bitter end?"

"Sir, we submit to you today that we stop them in their tracks!"

The president turned to me and said, "General D'Angelo, let July 27, 2060, be forever known as Victory America Day. Good luck and Godspeed."

As the conference ended General O'Brien asked me to remain for a moment. As the others left the link up the general asked, "Why didn't you tell the president that the MAGS detonation had to be done manually?"

"Marlene, that's not really important. What is important is that this mission is completed one hundred percent."

"Sam! Just who is going to detonate the MAGS?"

"A wise old man, my dad, once taught me to never ask your team to do what you yourself wouldn't do. Take care of yourself, Marlene. Don't let this battle be in vain. Accept nothing short of total victory."

General O'Brien fought back the tears and then saluted. "I will never forget you, Sam. I will never let those I lead forget what you stood for."

I left the holographic chamber and headed to the command center control room.

"Colonel! Get me a cryptic holographic link up to my fire teams—Venegas, Clark, Cato and Thomas!"

As I entered the chamber I could hear the team jostling and laughing amongst themselves. For a moment I flashed back to 2010 when the team was in their prime.

"Okay let's go through our final check. Dennis, have we established a secure link with Overlord?"

"Overlord is a go!"

"Excellent! Have the MAG System modifications been completed?"

"Check boss, we've completed the program modifications as well as we've got some interesting programs that will run."

"Will Overlord control the firing of the land-based MAG cannons?"

Dennis replied, "Check, boss. You'll get a signature tone at your terminal when the space planes have been painted by Overlord. All you have to do is confirm the signal to fire the cannons. We've rigged it to fire when we detonate the MAGS."

I nodded my head and asked, "What's our status on the sea MAG System deployment?"

Paul answered. "We've put the sleeper hold on the patrol ships, boss. They have boarded us and inspected us so many times that they just wave us through to our fishing nets. On the way back to unload our catch we give the patrol boat commanders some fresh fish. They just wave us back through."

Looking down as Paul was speaking I paused for a moment then looked up.

"Well, I guess this is it. Let's keep a cryptic channel open just in case we hit a snag. Remember, you are free to carry out your portion of the plan if the other actions fail. However, my team has good intelligence that Khan has moved his troops forward and has his space planes loitering over the Midwest. We are confident that he'll attack sometime in the early morning tomorrow. At 'D' hour I will broadcast a signal to set the plan in motion."

As the five men stood in a circle they solemnly raised their right fists in a final salute to each other.

I looked around the circle at each man and said, "It has been an honor and privilege to have served, fought, and shared lives with you. Brothers till the end!"

The team replied in unison, "Brothers till the end!"

—

On the morning of July 27, 2060, the sky was clear and blue. A gentle westerly breeze blew across the open plain. The plains teamed with life. Birds sang and busily moved about feeding their young. Honey bees were busy collecting pollen as the wildflowers swayed in the breeze.

The early-morning calm was slowly interrupted by a rumbling sound that grew louder as it source moved in from the west. Out on the pacific, twenty miles off the California coast, dawn was breaking. As in days past, several fishing trawlers were making their way to their nets to collect their daily catch. As the trawlers slowly sailed to their fishing locations patrol boats moved in to intercept them. The trawler crews coolly and calmly prepared to greet and receive the boarding parties. As the Chinese patrols approached each fishing vessel the ships' captains, Paul, Dennis, Kym, and Neal, stepped forward to be identified. The patrol boat commanders recognized the crews and allowed them to pass. One patrol boat commander called to Dennis.

"On your way back we would like some fresh fish!"

Dennis smiled and waved to the commander in acknowledgement of the request. As Dennis's boat moved off Dennis smiled and murmured to himself, "Do I have a tuna for you!"

Back on shore in the Midwest General Khan's forces were

on the move. As Khan's forces drew near to the American front lines Colonel Min commented, "General, sir, it appears that the mosquitoes are not biting today."

Both men laughed.

"Min, today I honor my ancestry with this glorious victory!"

As Khan's forces moved closer he assessed the opposing forces' troop placement. He lifted his field glasses to scan the battlefield. To his surprise he saw Sam in full battle dress, battle spear in hand, on his horse parading back and forth in front of his main column of troops. The horse was prancing and rearing while the troops behind Sam where cheering. The sight of this infuriated Khan.

He turned to his aids. "Bring me my horse! Such insolence! We will crush these fools! Leave no one alive!"

Khan's aids brought him his horse and assisted him in mounting the steed.

"My ancestral sword! Bring it now!"

As Khan paced his horse in front of his troops he raises his sword and yelled a command to his troops. "Their general is mine! Follow me!"

He briskly headed forward not taking his eyes off of Sam. As Khan and his forces drew closer to Sam and his forces an eerie sound that grew louder by the second could be heard in the distance.

High in the sky an undistinguishable object approached from behind Sam's forces. It grew in size with every second. As the object grew and took shape the eerie sound grew louder. Then in a blink of an eye Sam and his army disappeared. Khan and his advancing army hesitated in disbelief. As Khan's army slowed a deafening screeching sound came from the sky above them. In an instant a giant screeching American Bald Eagle with fully stretched wings came into view. Clutched in the eagles' talons was a dead black dragon. Looking up in horror Khan gasped and yelled.

"No!"

The trap was sprung.

Khan's forces were engulfed by fear and confusion. Troops dropped their weapons and began running in all directions. Troops ran into troops, vehicles ran over troops as well as into each other.

An instant after the holographic eagle disappeared the MAGS hit critical mass. A massive pulse of energy was released by each MAG System. Like heat rising from the desert floor a massive wave of shimmering energy rushed in from all sides of Khan's forces.

Khan and his Black Dragons lay dead. Their equipment was rendered useless.

In the Pacific the Chinese fleet became silent. The huge vessels loitered in their positions like ghost ships. In fact they became floating graveyards.

Precisely at the moment of the MAGS detonations, in obscure farmland in the northern Midwest, the cement bunker doors to abandoned missile silos blasted wide open. Instantly MAG cannons repeatedly discharged their energy into the sky.

Moments later space planes came falling back to earth in a spectacular fiery crash. Their demise provided onlookers for many miles away a fireworks display none which had ever been seen before. Debris showered the earth for hundreds of miles.

News of the battle traveled through the entire nation at the speed of light. The news of the Chinese's defeat on land, air, and sea turned an entire nation's despair and hopelessness into renewed strength and courage.

General O'Brien wasted little time unleashing her forces on the remaining Chinese troops. They captured two hundred fifty thousand Chinese troops occupying the West Coast.

Throughout the country bells rang, sirens blared, and people celebrated in the streets. The president made a tearful speech to the nation declaring victory.

As troops moved back into the battle zones, land and sea, they had one mission in mind—to bring the five brothers home. General O'Brien led the troops into the Midwest battle front.

As she entered the command center she paused. "Do not disturb one thing. This area will become a national monument. Let history always remember the sacrifice that was made here."

The room was in a complete shut down. As she shined her spotlight around the room she stopped at the main control terminal. There in a slumped position was the lifeless body of Sam D'Angelo. Beside him was the spear of courage and in his lap was an envelope, a very old and yellowed envelope addressed to Alex King.

General O'Brien's troops carefully removed Sam's body from the center. General O'Brien posted guards around the center with this command: "This is our nation's most revered monument. You are its first honor guard. Stand tall, stand proud! Never forget the sacrifice that was made here!"

General O'Brien escorted Sam's body home. The bodies of

the remaining four brothers were escorted home by the joint chiefs.

On July 30, 2060, Sam's body was flown to an air strip close to his home. As the small jet landed Alex and members of the D'Angelo and King family were there to receive Sam home.

As the jet came to a stop Alex fought back her tears. She knew that this time her cowboy wouldn't be deplaning with his smile and wink. As the jet engines wound down to a stop the aircraft door opened and the steps rolled into place. General O'Brien emerged from the aircraft first. She carried the spear of courage with her. As the general approached Alex, eight honor guard members carefully carried Sam's flag draped casket to the vehicle awaiting him.

The General looked into Alex's eyes and with deep remorse and empathy. "Doctor King, our nation weeps at the passing of your husband. Words cannot express the debt of gratitude we as a nation owe you and General D'Angelo. May God bless you, your family, and our nation."

She handed Alex the spear of courage and the yellowed envelope.

As the family headed off for a quiet burial service, Alex reminisced the years her and Sam had shared. As the motorcade drove to the private burial site, Alex recalled how she and Sam enjoyed horseback riding through these same rolling hills. How they laughed and loved over the years.

She slowly broke the seal as to preserve the envelope's integrity. She slowly slipped the letter out and carefully unfolded it. The letter was dated May 29, 2010.

My Dearest Alex,

If you are reading this letter it means I didn't make it home. I want you to know that the love I have for you knows no bounds. For me, you were the reason I drew breath…my very reason for living. I'm sorry if my passing has made you cry. It pains me to think of you being sad. Please don't let them forget our sacrifice. Let them know that from the depths of our spirits we fought and died for the greater good of our nation. Let them know that "We stood watch as the children slept."

With All My Love Forever,
Sam

PS: Give Tucker a kiss for me.

October 30, 2061, was a beautiful fall day on the Great Plains. The early morning air was crisp yet the sun still gave its warmth. The rolling hills and meadows teemed with life. Wildlife hurriedly prepared for winter. In the near distance the rhythm of footsteps could be heard as a voice called cadence. It was a group of Special Forces candidates heading to "Courage Hill" to take their special services oath, "Never Again!"

As the young candidates headed up Courage Hill a statue began to come into view. At the hill's summit was a life-size statue of the five brothers with their arms around each other as if helping each other up the hill. There, standing on either side of the statue, were family and guests of the candidates. Among the guests stood Alex, Sami, Jonni, and family members of the other four brothers. At the bottom of the statue was the inscription:

No Greater Love Does a Man Have Than He Lay His Life Down for Those He Loves. We Stood Watch As the Children Slept.